THE BLADE MAN

Debra Purdy Kong

GYPSY MOON PRESS
Port Moody, British Columbia
2020

THE BLADE MAN
(Casey Holland Mysteries #6)

Copyright © 2020 by Debra Purdy Kong

Gypsy Moon Press
www.debrapurdykong.com
ISBN: 978-0-9699211-9-6

Editor: Joyce Gram
www.gramediting.com

Jacket Design: Deranged Doctor Design
www.derangeddoctordesign.com

This book is a work of fiction. Names, characters, places, and incidents are either products of the author's imagination or are used factiously. Any resemblance to actual events or specific locations, or persons, living or deceased, is entirely coincidental.

PRAISE FOR

CASEY HOLLAND MYSTERIES

"A traditional mystery complicated by the characters' desires to keep secrets and the self-serving manipulations of others . . . A good read with urban grit and a spicy climax." —*The Hamilton Spectator*

"A mystery that fits the bill." – *National Post*

"The novel's short, punchy chapters whisk the story along to a thrilling climax, while the characters' relationships and rivalries provide a strong emotional anchor." – *Quill & Quire*

"This is truly a fast-moving, action-packed thriller . . . Great story with strong plot!" – *Nightreader*

"The modest but resourceful Casey is a perfect heroine for our times, a combination of thought and action." – *Lou Allin, Crime Writers of Canada*

AUTHOR'S NOTES

A huge thank you to former transit operator Veronica Laurel Greer, whose experiences and insights taught me a great deal about the difficult encounters bus drivers often face. The bus company and situations in this book are my own creation, but Veronica's thoughts provided plenty of inspiration.

Also, many thanks to writing colleagues and members of Port Moody Recreation's Creative Writing Program, whose input and support have helped me become a better writer.

Thank you again to editor Joyce Gram who is always a pleasure to work with. The same is true for the talented book jacket designers at Deranged Doctor Design.

Of course, heartfelt thanks to my husband who never complains about the amount of time I spend at the keyboard, and who joins me at many bookselling events. It means the world to me.

ONE

"**W**esley, look out!" Casey Holland ducked behind the bus driver's seat and glanced over her shoulder. "Everyone down, *now!*"

A Molotov cocktail bounced off the driver's window next to Wesley Axelson's head, but Wesley merely revved the idling bus engine and blasted the horn. "Candy-ass punks!"

Casey didn't know why Wesley bothered with the yelling or the horn. Minutes ago, a mob of teens and young adults had overtaken the road, ignoring his earlier blasts. Why would they listen now?

The Molotov cocktail exploded on the road, rocking the bus slightly. Somewhere outside, a woman screamed. Casey peeked out the window to see a woman running from the flames flaring up just a few feet from the bus. If they had to evacuate, she'd make damn sure that the half dozen passengers who'd decided to stay on board got out of here safely. A decade of security work had taught her to stay calm in tense situations. She'd be deceiving herself if she wasn't worried, though. A drunken mob was a new experience she'd rather live without.

"That was too damn close!" A middle-aged passenger glared at Casey. "I thought you called the cops."

"I did."

"Then where the hell are they? The RCMP detachment's just two blocks from here."

"Manpower shortage, most likely. From what I hear there's trouble at the rally in the park."

"Then they should have called for reinforcement by now," the passenger grumbled as she opened a window. "It's too hot in here. Don't you have air conditioning on this stupid bus?"

Casey admitted it was unusually warm for mid-May. "Sorry, no. This is an older model."

"Stupid company," the woman muttered. "This is the last time I'll ride an MPT bus."

Casey hoped so. She stood and used her phone to record the broken glass and burning rag on the road. She zeroed in on the five culprits in ball caps, hoodies, and bandana-covered faces who were laughing and high-fiving one another. The stench of gasoline and smoke made her cough. She'd closed all the windows when the trouble started, but she wasn't going to make anyone close them again in this heat, at least not right away.

"Is the ambulance here yet?" a tentative voice asked.

Casey turned to the injured teenaged girl slouched in the seat across from her. She was holding a bloodied gauze pad above her right eye. "Soon."

The girl had waved them down just after they turned onto Glen Drive. She said she'd fallen on the sidewalk and cut her forehead on broken glass. Casey could still smell beer on the girl's breath.

God, how had things unraveled so quickly? Based on what she'd heard from passengers, a union rally at the stadium in Town Center Park had somehow turned into an angry protest, thanks to a bunch of punks who started a bonfire and began throwing things at the crowd.

Wesley had cruised into the area just as families began running from the park, ignoring traffic lights in the rush to reach safety. The panic had created a major traffic snarl, forcing Wesley to take another route. Many of the families were parked at the mall four or five blocks away. News reports said there were so many attendees at the rally that the park's lots had filled quickly. Besides, parking was free at the mall. Most of the families were now safely away, which left a younger, bolder, and tougher crowd anticipating—even wanting—mayhem.

Wesley turned off the engine.

"This bus needs to move!" the middle-aged woman shouted. "We've been stuck here for fifteen minutes! The M28 bus shouldn't even be on this street. You bloody well should have stayed on Pinetree Way."

Casey struggled to keep her annoyance in check. "Ma'am, I'm sure you saw the police officer gesturing for us to turn away."

"You can see how well *that's* working." The woman ran her hand through graying hair brightened with red streaks. "You said you're security for this stupid bus company, so can't you do something? Mainland Public Transport should be taking better care of its customers!" She pointed to the teenager. "That poor girl could bleed to death!"

"Head wounds bleed a lot, but the cut isn't large or deep. I'm sure she'll be okay."

The woman scowled. "So you're a doctor now? Are you even qualified to touch her?"

Casey told herself to remain calm. "I have enhanced first-aid training."

And what did the woman expect her to do about the mob? Make a citizen's arrest one punk at a time?

4 Debra Purdy Kong

"Tell your driver to nudge the idiots with the bus!" the woman barked. "That'll get them moving. They have no right to treat us this way! It's *disgusting*."

Casey understood that some people reacted to fear with rage, but this passenger was going too far. None of the others were acting out and all were just as inconvenienced. Trapped midway between High Street behind them and Pacific Avenue in front, the bus had nowhere to go on this narrow block. With only one lane each way, they were hemmed in by the cars parallel-parked in front of retail shops and condos.

Wesley made his second call to MPT's dispatchers. "We've gotta get out of here. Some moron just tried to throw a Molotov cocktail into the bus," he said. "Situation's gettin' ugly and it's about to turn into a freakin' riot."

As far as Casey was concerned, ugly had already swooshed by and calamity was setting in. She couldn't hear dispatch's response, but Wesley looked even unhappier than he had before. She worried about her fiancé Lou, who'd been attending the rally with coworkers and might still be there. As an MPT bus driver, Lou still resented the company's president for squashing his and coworkers' efforts to unionize employees eighteen months ago. It had cost Lou a promotion. Today, he'd hoped to connect with people who could help them find a more effective way to achieve their goal.

"It was a stupid idea to host a rally in Coquitlam," the complaining woman said. "Those gatherings belong in Vancouver. They're used to this crap."

It would be pointless to argue that thugs, crime, and violence surfaced in every municipality in Metro Vancouver, and beyond. After the riot debacle in June 2011, following the Vancouver Canucks's loss in the final Stanley Cup hockey game, Vancouver officials seemed to fear any emotionally charged, large-scale gathering. Given that Coquitlam was only a half hour east of Vancouver, it had seemed a good alternative, until now.

"If your driver moved the bus just a few more yards," the woman went on, "he could turn onto Pacific and get us out of here."

Casey sighed. Pacific Avenue was more than a few yards away. "We don't want to hit anyone."

"So you'll keep law-abiding paying customers who aren't causing trouble in danger? Well, that's just great. Who's in charge of MPT? I'm sending an email."

"Gwyn Maddox is the president." After reciting his email address, Casey turned away to hide the smile. *Good luck, lady.*

Gwyn used to go out of his way to accommodate customers, sometimes at the expense of employees, but that had changed as MPT grew deeper into debt. These days he wasn't overly friendly or accommodating to anyone. Complaints from the public wouldn't improve his perpetual irritability.

Wesley stood and crossed his beefy arms. "I can open the door for ya anytime, ma'am. You're not a hostage here. Lots of riders have already left."

"But this bus runs right by my house, or it's supposed to."

"Door-to-door service ain't happening tonight," he replied. "Sorry."

Not that Casey blamed Wesley, but she wished he'd keep quiet. Known as Rude Wesley Axelson, people skills weren't his strong suit.

The sound of shattering glass made Casey flinch. Laughter and joyful shouts clashed with cries of dismay. Three doors down, a goliath in shorts and a muscle shirt swung a sledgehammer through a boutique's plate glass window. Oh dear lord, how many thugs had brought tools and weapons? Too bad that none of the shop windows around here had bars. In the frenzy to loot the store, two young women were knocked down. Assholes trampled right over them.

"Damn," Casey murmured and began recording the scene.

Since it was just after 7:00 PM on a Saturday night, most of the shops were closed.

"What's happening?" the injured girl asked as she sat up and peered out the window.

"They broke into a store."

"I feel kind of sick."

Casey reached into the first-aid kit by the girl's feet. Drunks and motion-sick people had taught her to keep barf bags handy.

"Use this if you need it."

The girl took the bag from Casey. "I still don't get it. One minute we're listening to speeches and the next people are throwing shit and losing their minds. What's wrong with standing up for workers' rights?"

"Nothin'," Wesley answered. "The problem is the idiots who only came to stir things up."

More glass shattered, this time from a coffee shop beside the boutique. Casey gasped as a fifty-something man with a broom frantically tried to keep looters from coming in. Three guys dragged the poor man from the entrance. The crowd roared. Beer bottles flew through the air.

Wesley stood and opened the bus door. "That guy's gonna get killed. I gotta stop him."

"Don't, Wes!" Casey hurried up to him.

She should have known that Wesley would want to jump into the fray. The man was also an amateur wrestler who spent his free time either working out or competing in matches.

"If the Bandana Boys see you leave, they could commandeer the bus," Casey whispered. "I can't take them all on." She turned back to the commotion in front of the coffee shop. "Look, the victim's getting help."

A group of guys were taking on the three bullies while others assisted the coffee shop owner back inside. Shouts escalated. Fists flew as more people dived into the melee.

"Call Stan again," Wesley said. "See what he wants us to do."

"He'll say the same thing he did ten minutes ago. As long as passengers are on this bus, their safety comes first, so we stay with them."

Wesley glared at the brawlers. "Your supervisor doesn't know how violent it's getting."

"I know him, Wes. Stan won't change his mind."

"Easy for management to sit in their comfy chairs miles away and tell us what to do." Wesley scanned the sidewalk. "Hell, they're going after another store."

"This is insane," one of the passengers said.

The injured girl moaned.

Wes glanced at the girl. "This crowd ain't movin' and the ambulance is takin' too long. If we're gonna keep these people safe, then we gotta leave the area."

Although Wesley had a point, his plan made Casey nervous. If the mob tried to stop them, there could be more injuries. People were still wandering all over the road. Some were so wasted that they were staggering. Others had stopped to record whatever action caught their attention. Wesley closed the door, sat down, and started the engine.

"About time," the angry woman said with a huff.

Wesley blasted the horn. A handful of people hurried out of the way, but most didn't. Inch by inch, he eased the bus forward and honked again. Those forced to move gave him the finger. A few slammed the palms of their hands against the bus.

"For crying out loud!" the angry woman yelled. "Those delinquents are coming back!"

As the Bandana Boys rushed toward the bus, Casey spotted the baseball bat one of them now carried. Where on earth had that come from? He raised the bat.

"Everyone get down and cover your heads!" she shouted.

The M28 wasn't moving nearly fast enough to escape the jarring thwack against the window right behind Wesley. In short order, the window gave way. Breathing heavily, her face burning with anger, Casey crawled to the first-aid kit where she kept a can of mace. Not legal, but sometimes necessary.

The injured girl threw up in the paper bag. A Bandana Boy kicked the front entrance.

"I've got mace." Casey spotted the strobing lights of an RCMP cruiser turning onto Glen Drive a block ahead of them. "Might not need it, though."

"Wanna bet? We're inside and protected. The cops'll be way more interested in the looters than getting us out of here."

Another blow rattled the door. The Bandana Boys whooped and urged their buddy to kick it in. A second bus window shattered next to the back entrance. The only passenger who hadn't taken cover was the angry woman. Gripping the seat in front of her, she glowered at the boys.

"Screw this!" Wesley jumped to his feet. "If they want in that badly, then fine."

"Not a good idea, Wes."

Wesley clenched his fists and didn't look at her. At six-foot four and built like a refrigerator, Wesley Axelson could spar with the best of them. Known as the Bear in the wrestling circuit, he was fond of emitting a menacing growl before going after opponents. Casey had seen a couple of his matches, which were both amazing and horrifying. If sufficiently provoked, he could break bones or damage a spinal cord.

"Wes, no!"

Wesley opened the door. The noise level ramped up, as did the stench of smoke.

Damn it, why wouldn't he listen? A Bandana Boy leapt onto the platform. Before he could take another step, Wesley yanked down the blue bandana, knocked off his ball cap, and spun him around, pinning the guy's arms behind his back.

"Take a photo of this loser."

"Fuck you!" the guy yelled.

Casey snapped a headshot of the scraggly black hair and acne on a kid of about twenty. She stepped back and took a full-length shot. "Done." Figuring Stan would expect a full account of events, she began recording the action.

As Wesley pointed Bandana Boy toward the exit, he lifted his size-fourteen, steel-toe boot and slammed it against the kid's butt. The kid flew off the platform and into his buddies who were either too stupid or too stoned to get out of the way. They went down like bowling pins.

The punk in the red bandana jumped to his feet and charged onto the platform. In remarkably short order, Wesley had the punk upside down and was banging his head against the floor. She'd seen Wesley perform a version of this dangerous move in his matches.

She turned off the video. "Stop it, Wes!" He could lose his job or face a lawsuit over this, or both. "I need a snapshot."

Wesley uprighted the punk, whose gaunt cheekbones and sparse goatee suggested malnourishment or perhaps drug addiction. The glittery eyes dimmed into confused grogginess. Casey took a headshot and full-length photo, right down to his bright green shoelaces.

"Okay," she said. "Got it."

Wesley tossed the guy out the door, causing him to hit the road in a spectacular face plant. The guy with the baseball bat charged forward. He might have done some damage if the dumbass hadn't tried to enter with the bat raised. The bat smacked against the doorframe, jarring the Bandana Boy backward. Wesley wrenched the bat from him and tossed it on the bus floor. Casey kicked the weapon under the nearest seat, but Dumbass was undeterred. He leapt onto the platform, only to have Wesley kick his shin. The guy yelped. His black bandana slipped down to reveal a boy who looked about sixteen. The kid stumbled backward, fell off the platform, and landed on his ass.

"Anyone else?" Wesley demanded, scowling at their obscenities and threats. "Didn't think so." He stepped back and closed the door.

Casey snapped more pictures of the punks until the rude woman shouted, "Don't you dare!"

Oh lord, she was smacking a Bandana Boy with her purse as he tried to climb through the broken window. The punk's cap fell off, revealing light blond hair. The woman yanked the green bandana down to reveal a kid who appeared even younger than the others. Casey marched down the aisle.

"MPT Security." She flashed her ID, then took his picture. "What do you think you're doing, smart guy?"

"What's it look like, bitch?"

"That you're cutting your hands up pretty good there." She nodded to the blood oozing between his fingers. "Just how messed up are you, Junior?"

"Fuck!" Junior released his grip and dropped to the ground. He stayed there, gaping at his wound. "There's glass in my hand! Call an ambulance!"

Shouts and screams several yards beyond the bus drowned

him out. Three shirtless guys were jumping on the roof and hood of a sedan parked in front of a computer repair shop. One of them lost his balance. His arms pinwheeled and he fell off the car. Cheers rang out. Raised phones recorded the incident.

An ambulance turned onto Glen Drive and eased up behind the stopped police cruiser. Horn honking and siren blaring, the ambulance driver attempted to veer around the cruiser without hitting pedestrians apparently oblivious to their arrival.

Two officers stood near the vehicle, attempting to move people off the road, but it was slow going. Casey shook her head. No one seemed to care that they were trying to get to an emergency. Mob mentality had turned these folks into deranged nut jobs.

"Casey, look behind you," Wesley said.

She turned and gasped at the riot squad moving with militaristic precision toward the crowd milling about behind the bus. The formidable uniforms, batons, protective gear, and raised shields sent some people scurrying away. Too many others, though, decided to taunt the squad, as if daring them to attack. Adrenalin shot through her. A couple of morons began throwing objects. The riot squad pressed on, maintaining the same methodical pace. It was hard to tell if things were about to improve or become much worse.

"See what they're carrying?" Wesley mumbled. "Tear gas, pepper spray, flash-bangs. This could turn into one hell of a shit storm."

Casey swallowed hard. She turned away, fearful of the brutality that could come from both sides. Paramedics emerged from the ambulance and threaded their way through the crowd. As they edged closer to the bus, Junior intercepted them.

"I'm bleedin'! I need help!"

Wesley opened the door and leaned out. "That asshole busted bus windows and his buddies tried to take over the damn bus! He can wait! We got a girl with a head injury in here."

"Screw you!" Junior shouted, holding out his dripping hand.

"Shut up or I'll really give you something to whine about!" Wesley bellowed.

"He's a lunatic!" the kid yelled to the wary paramedics.

One paramedic stayed with Junior while his partner stepped onto the bus. Casey provided an update on the girl's condition until cheers, shouts, and screams from behind the bus sent her and Wes rushing down the aisle. Flames and smoke rose high.

"The punks just torched a car half a block down," Wesley said. "Maybe to distract the riot squad."

The squad was pushing back the crowd and now marching past both sides of the bus. More cops appeared from side streets. Judging from the variance in uniforms, officers from different jurisdictions were now assisting the Coquitlam RCMP. No surprise there. A multi-level command structure existed for all kinds of situations and disasters. Why hadn't they arrived sooner? Or had they been busy with the mayhem in the park? The altercations had skewed Casey's sense of time. She actually had no idea how long they'd been stuck here.

Yelling erupted from all directions. Casey's heart pounded as cops clashed with the crowd around the flaming car behind them while the riot squad made their move on the crowd in front. Tempers were unleashed in a tangle of beating, kicking, and bashing. Blood poured down a woman's arm as she ran. Rioters shouted obscenities and threw beer bottles and placards at the surging squad. Batons struck arms, legs, backs, and shoulders. A few people managed to dash for cover. Others seemed frozen in place. Some people were simply dragged away.

"It's all goin' to shit," Wesley muttered.

One heck of an understatement. Flames and strobing lights from arriving emergency response vehicles cast an ominous light. Casey caught sight of a helicopter hovering above. Probably the media, observing and reporting the debacle. A reminder that she should be doing the same.

Casey fetched the backpack she kept under a seat and removed her notebook. As she wrote, she worried about Lou. Was he still at the stadium? Casey rang his cell. Sweat made her T-shirt cling to her skin. Why wasn't he answering? She left a message, asking him to call. "I really need to know you're okay."

The second paramedic appeared and helped his partner assist the injured teenage girl off the bus. Wesley started the engine and opened the driver's window.

"What are you doing?" Casey asked.

"Getting us out of here. Riot squad's moved the crowd far enough away to make turning onto Pacific easier."

"But there's still people on the road."

"Not as many."

"Then at least close your window till we're out of the danger zone."

Ignoring her, Wesley eased the bus forward. Casey spotted a Bandana Boy darting out from a cluster of people, his arm raised.

"Wes, watch out!"

A beer bottle soared through the window and struck Wesley on the side of his head. He recoiled, slamming the brake. "Goddamnit!"

"Gotcha, dickhead!" Bandana Boy shouted.

Stepping forward, he swore at Wesley. Casey recorded the guy's behavior until Wesley reached out the window and grabbed his hand. He yanked the guy so hard that his body thudded against the bus. He pulled down the black bandana and rammed his fist into the guy's face. Bandana Boy yelped and collapsed onto the ground.

"Wesley!"

"He had it comin'."

Two more Bandana Boys pounded on the windows and shouted, "You're dead!"

"Back at ya, losers!"

Casey gripped the pole by Wes's chair and gulped down air. Her stomach roiled so fast she thought she'd be sick.

Wes blasted the horn and eased the bus forward. "We're out of here, folks!"

A couple of passengers clapped.

"About bloody time!" the angry woman shouted.

She'd been on her phone the past few minutes, complaining about MPT's "incompetence."

Wesley started a left turn onto Pacific Avenue. He hadn't completed his turn when a crash erupted behind them on Glen Drive.

Wesley again hit the brakes. "What was that?"

Casey hurried to the back. "A Smart car's been turned upside down."

"It's on fire!" a passenger yelled.

Rioters who'd managed to avoid the officers up to this point tossed whatever they could find onto the conflagration. The Bandana Boys dashed toward the commotion. Soon, the car was completely engulfed in flames. The riot squad swarmed them.

"Whoa," Casey said. "That sure went up in a hurry."

"Somebody probably poured gasoline on it," Wesley replied, edging the bus forward once again.

A firetruck blasted its horn. Sirens wailed as the truck

crawled toward the fire. Once more, people were slow to move out of the way. An older man in a white dress shirt and black pants ran toward the Smart car. Arms flailing, he screamed at the crowd. One idiot shoved him toward the flames. His arm caught fire.

"Oh my god!" the angry woman shouted. "Can't we do something?"

Anxious passengers glanced at her before turning back to the horror before them.

"Maybe." Casey marched up to the supplies kept behind Wesley's chair and grabbed the fire extinguisher. By the time she reached the door, firefighters had reached the screaming man.

"Stay," Wesley said to her. "They've got this. Like you said, it's safer for everyone if we're inside."

She had to admit that mob behavior had deteriorated from belligerent to unhinged at a startling rate. A few morons were now attacking the firetruck with sticks, hands, and feet. Law enforcement swarmed them and the melee escalated into frenzied fighting, cussing, and screaming.

Defiant thugs threw anything they could get their hands on, but they were no match for the pepper spray. Anguished cries filled the air as injured people stumbled into one another like out-of-control bumper cars. Some collapsed to their knees. Others were already on their butts, kicking at officers who were swinging batons with frightening speed.

Casey's breath caught in her throat. Arrests were made. Both law enforcement and spectators were recording everything, as was she.

Wesley eased the bus forward, braking every few seconds to avoid hitting someone. In slow motion, he completed his turn onto Pacific Avenue while Casey headed down the aisle, recording as much as she could of the mayhem. Looters poured through more busted windows with the eagerness of starving rats who'd just whiffed a huge buffet.

"Thank god we're out of there," the angry woman remarked.

At the corner of Casey's screen, a man fell among the pushing and shoving crowd on the sidewalk. In the fray, no one paid attention to him and Casey lost sight of the guy. She stopped recording.

A right turn took them toward Johnson Street, a normally busy four-lane street that was now empty. As they reached Johnson, a traffic cop waved Wesley through. Casey looked up and down the road, not surprised to see the police had barricaded the road. She slumped into a seat and looked at her phone just as the battery died. Why hadn't Lou returned her call?

"Hey, Wes, can I borrow your phone? I need to call Lou, see if he's still at the stadium."

"He'd better not be," Wesley replied. "Heard everyone's gone bat-shit crazy there too."

Casey sighed. Adrenalin was fading away, exhaustion settling in. "At least the worst is over."

Wesley snorted as he handed her his phone. "Ya think? There's gonna be major blowback from all this, and we'll be stuck in the middle of it."

TWO

Seated on the comfy cushion in the bay window of her third-floor apartment, Casey let her fingertips dance over the laptop's keyboard perched on her thighs. Her thoughts were working faster than her hands, thus all the typos. She was too tired to care. They were only notes for the incident reports she'd have to write tomorrow.

She'd never experienced so many altercations and events in a single night. Molotov cocktails, broken bus windows, physical confrontations, an injured passenger, and an irate passenger would require a lengthy, accurate report. She'd been home for over two hours and it still wasn't easy to process everything that had happened. She needed sleep, but she was too wound up.

As soon as she returned to MPT's administration building tonight, she'd spoken with Stan who'd been monitoring the situation in the communications room all evening, as were supervisors and a couple of executives. She felt a little guilty for not telling her supervisor everything, but she didn't know how much to reveal about Wesley's actions. Casey hated the idea of creating trouble for a coworker, but neither could she lie or omit incidents that could cause legal problems later on. Stan wanted her report by 4:00 PM tomorrow. She'd figure out what to do after she had some sleep.

Casey rubbed her eyes and tried not to be overly concerned about her growing headache. She hadn't had a migraine in a long time, but tonight's disaster had catapulted her stress level, and stress was a major trigger. That it was two-thirty in the morning didn't help. Maybe she should give up waiting for Lou and go to bed. Even her guinea pig, Ralphie, nocturnal critter that he was, had gone to sleep. She gazed at his cage on the bottom shelf of her bookcase. The cage needed a good cleaning. Another thing to add to the to-do list.

Casey turned to the window and peered down at the front yard of this big old Victorian home. Three hours had passed since Lou finally returned her call. He'd taken his coworker Mitch and Mitch's wife to the hospital, after the wife was struck in the eye with a rock. Lou was reluctant to elaborate, but promised to fill her in when he got home.

Casey had gotten ready for bed and watched a news report showing the huge brawl and conflagration that had taken place at the stadium in the park. She'd squinted at the images, looking for Lou, but hadn't seen him among the throng of confused, frightened, and agitated people. When the footage turned to the action on Glen Drive, she switched the TV off. No need to relive that debacle.

Casey closed the laptop and was drinking the last of her chamomile tea when Lou opened the door and trudged inside. Sliding the laptop off her legs, she got to her feet. Relief swept through her and she grinned at the way his thick brown hair stuck out in all directions, as if gelled without the benefit of a mirror. The beer stench on his damp-looking hoodie caught her up short.

"Good lord." She crinkled her nose. "How many beer were dumped on you?"

"Dunno. A few, I guess." He lifted the hoodie over his head. "You didn't have to wait up."

"I wanted to." The circles under his gray eyes were expected.

The dark red mark on his right cheek was not. "Did somebody hit you?"

"There was a fair bit of punching going on."

"Why didn't you tell me on the phone?"

"You already sounded anxious." Lou groaned as he sat on the sofa. "Didn't want to make it worse."

Hmm. How much had he kept from her? "Is Mitch's wife okay?"

"Yeah, there's no major damage to her eye. Glad I had my truck. They took the bus to the rally and an ambulance would have taken too long." He sighed. "Emergency room was so packed that people were sitting on the floor."

Casey sat next to him. "What exactly happened out there?"

"Some jerks started a bonfire next to the bleachers," Lou said. "When the cops showed up, the jerks threw alcohol on the flames and that's when things really went off the rails." Shifting his weight, Lou grimaced. "By the time the firefighters arrived, there were fistfights and people getting hurt. Different groups of guys seemed to have issues with one another. Some assholes were just out to create chaos for fun. It was gross."

Lou slowly sat forward, resting his elbows on his knees. As his T-shirt rose up, Casey spotted a large red welt on the right side of his lower back.

"You were struck on your back too?"

"Probably. Gave as good as I got, though." He kept his head lowered. "I'll be fine."

An uneasy feeling wriggled through Casey. At five-foot nine, Lou wasn't a large man, but regular gym workouts had made him lean and strong. He also knew how to fight. Something told her that tonight's brawl was nastier than he wanted to admit.

"Did a doctor take a look at you?"

"No. Plenty of people were worse off than me."

"You should go tomorrow."

"Tomorrow's Sunday. We'll see how I feel on Monday."

Casey didn't like it. She saw how pale he was beneath the spray of freckles. "Lou, are you sure—"

"Did you see the guy who was stabbed to death on Glen Drive?" He turned to her. "Must have happened right near you. Heard it on the news while driving home."

"What stabbing? Nothing was said on the eleven o'clock news. I turned the TV off after that."

"It happened around seven. Suspect's not been caught."

Images flashed through Casey's brain. "I saw a man being beaten for trying to stop people from looting his store, but I didn't notice anyone with a knife." She picked up her now fully charged phone and scrolled through the videos she'd taken.

"Witnesses described someone in a black hoodie and ball cap who'd been behind the victim."

"Tons of guys were wearing that. Wesley tussled with a few of them." She had no doubt the Bandana Boys would have brandished a knife if they'd had one.

"Wes doesn't tussle, he pulverizes," Lou remarked. "What happened?"

Too exhausted to provide a detailed account, she gave him the abridged version.

"What the hell was he thinking?" Lou responded. "Someone was killed tonight and Wes was daring strangers onto the bloody bus?"

"I'm not sure anyone had died at that point, and you know Wes can't be calmed down when he's riled up."

"He's freakin' lucky nobody came at him with a knife."

Casey continued reviewing her videos until she reached the final one she took as they were leaving the area.

"Oh." In the top right corner of her screen, she saw the man fall. For one second, she glimpsed a figure in dark clothing right behind him. She remembered losing sight of him when Wes made the turn onto Pacific. Had she recorded a murder?

"What is it?" Lou asked.

"Take a look at this." Casey handed him the phone. "Keep your eye on the top right corner."

Lou squinted at the tiny image. "Can't see much except for a guy falling. It could be him, or not." As Lou got to his feet, he grunted.

"You okay?"

"Yeah. Just need a shower and some sleep."

"If you start peeing blood, we're going to the hospital."

Lou shuffled toward the bedroom and shut the door, something he rarely did. Did he not want her to see the extent of his injuries? Sooner or later, she'd find out. For the moment, backing off seemed smarter. Lou was a patient man, but even he had his limits.

Sighing, Casey rose and turned out the lights. She entered their bedroom, her body aching from the long night. She climbed into bed and reached over to switch on the red lava lamp on Lou's night table. It didn't provide much illumination, but he loved his lava lamp collection that was sprinkled throughout their apartment. Casey switched off her own light and closed her eyes. By the time Lou emerged from the bathroom, she was drowsy.

He grunted as he slid into bed.

"All right?" she mumbled.

"Yeah. Have you seen Summer tonight?"

"She's staying over at Stacy's. Why?"

"Thought I saw her at the rally late this afternoon." He

paused. "She was too far away to be sure, though."

Union rallies wouldn't hold much appeal for her teenaged ward. After quitting the swim team a while back, Summer was more interested in cooking, fashion, and friends.

"Doubt she knows anyone from Coquitlam," Casey mumbled.

"We've hardly seen her lately."

True. It was easy to miss someone in a house with three floors and a basement, especially when Summer's room was one floor below theirs. Casey didn't often see the two university students who rented bedrooms at the back of the house either. Although she passed by Summer's door every day, their schedules often didn't mesh. She'd make a point of catching up with her tomorrow.

Lou shifted his weight and again grunted.

"I'm worried about you," she said.

"It's just a few bruises," he murmured. "I'll be in good shape for our wedding next month. Don't worry."

Easier said than done. Their late June wedding was six weeks away. She hadn't forgotten that it was supposed to have taken place last August, but she'd been hospitalized after a maniac attacked her. Their subsequent October date hadn't panned out either when Lou came down with the worst flu of his life. As far as Casey was concerned, this third attempt would happen no matter what.

THREE

$\mathbf{M}$onday morning meetings with Stan were usually relaxed. This one would be an exception.

Casey stepped out of her Tercel and gazed at MPT's two-story, white-plastered administration building. Stan's office was on the upper floor in the right corner, his window overlooking the parking lot and yard. Taking a calming breath, she strode toward the entrance.

It had taken six hours to write and revise her report about events at the riot. Less than an hour after she emailed it to Stan late yesterday afternoon, he had called for clarification on a couple of points, then told her he wanted to meet a half hour earlier than usual.

Casey was about to enter the building when driver Dimitri Klitou, sporting a wide bandage on his forehead, barged outside. Black wavy hair draped over the bandage. His olive skin looked pale.

"Dimitri? What happened to you?"

"Some shithead tried to slice my face with a busted beer bottle Saturday night." His dark eyes flashed. "Freak threw up on the platform, splashing my shoes and pants." He muttered something in Greek.

"Were you working near the riot?"

"Heading out to Maple Ridge, but he boarded in Port Coquitlam."

The municipality was just east of Coquitlam and not far from Town Center Park.

"Was the guy wearing a bandana, by any chance?"

"Yeah, he wiped his face with it." Dimitri squinted in the sunlight. "How'd you know?"

"We had trouble at the riot with some guys sporting bandanas. What color was his?"

Dimitri rolled his eyes. "Does it matter?"

"It'll help me identify him."

"Don't remember. Check the camera."

Dimitri was fortunate to have driven a bus equipped with cameras. MPT's older models didn't have them. The dramatic rise in attacks on Metro Vancouver bus drivers had prompted MPT drivers to request protective barriers. Gwyn had rejected their request, insisting that alarms, radios, and cellphones were sufficient. His stance understandably infuriated most of the drivers, including Lou. If Gwyn had to deal with the number of drunk, high, or mentally ill people that drivers and security staff did, he'd change his mind in a hurry.

Dimitri was heading toward the buses when he stopped and spun around. "Big mistake working that shift. I shouldn't even be here today. Feel like shit."

With two kids, a wife, and parents to support, Dimitri couldn't afford to turn down extra work. MPT employees weren't paid for sick days, which is why Casey cut him some slack for the lousy attitude.

"Do you remember anything else about him?" she called out.

"His eyes," Dimitri replied. "They looked crazy, and he wore a stupid beard."

"Sounds like one of the guys that Wesley tangled with. Did he have a goatee?"

"Think so," Dimitri grumbled. "Wes should have put the freak in the hospital. I would have had less trouble, and there should have been security personnel on board. Anoop got there way too late to be of any help. What's the point of having a guard driving around if he can't show up fast enough to help out?"

"You know a lot of crap happened that night. Anoop couldn't be everywhere."

Although Casey supported this fairly new initiative to have guards patrol troublesome zones in the security vehicle, clearly there were limitations.

"Sorry I wasn't there to help," she added. "We were spread pretty thin Saturday night."

Dimitri rolled his eyes. "A woman couldn't have handled that bastard. He was out of his mind."

Casey sighed. The macho attitude hadn't earned him a lot of respect from female staff.

"Gwyn Maddox should be forking out bucks for better protection instead of buying fancy new cars and taking a damn cruise every year," he ranted on.

In other words, hire big, burly guys who didn't mind getting physical with passengers. Casey bit back a nasty retort.

"Tell Stan that we're tired of being spat on, threatened, and punched every damn week! Someone's gonna get killed if he doesn't do more!" Dimitri stormed off.

"Doubt it'll make a difference," a quiet voice said behind her.

Casey turned to find one of their newer drivers, Ethan Carruthers, sauntering up to her. An energetic twenty-four-year-old, Ethan also happened to be an incredible vocalist for a rock band. Every time she and Lou went to see him, the venues were packed. She sometimes found it hard to reconcile the quiet, long-haired bus driver with the glitzy performer who wore makeup and facial jewelry in front of screaming fans.

"Hi, Ethan," she said. "How's it going?"

"Okay." He watched Dimitri enter a bus. "Dimitri's right about the violence. It's getting worse out there, so is Gwyn too cheap to do something about it, or too broke?"

"Broke?"

"I've heard rumors."

No surprise there. Cutbacks and frozen wages had happened before and new rumors about MPT's financial problems had started up over recent months. She'd asked Stan about it, and he confirmed, confidentially, that the company's debts were growing. Casey hadn't told anyone, including Lou.

"Stay safe," Ethan said, and continued on.

"You too."

On one level, Dimitri wasn't wrong about the security team's inadequacies. There were only five of them, which wasn't nearly enough lately, but Gwyn refused to spend money on expansion. She and Marie were the only full-time employees. Part-time guard Anoop Verma was experienced, but busy with school and his young family. The other two part-timers were rookies.

Casey jogged upstairs and entered the rectangular room that security shared with accounting and human resources. The four desks allotted to security were empty for the moment, and Stan's secretary was on a month-long vacation. Casey glanced between the row of dracaenas and palms that separated security from HR and accounting personnel.

"Casey!" One of the HR staff waved to her. "Everyone's talking about the riot. Are you okay? What went down out there?"

"Lots. I'll tell you over coffee later."

"You bet."

As far as Casey was concerned, MPT's greatest asset was the staff, most of whom helped and supported one another, personally and professionally. These days, the company employed a terrific roster of administrative personnel who got along well.

Casey entered Stan's office to find him typing as quickly as his awkward, two-finger style could manage. Beneath the gray brush cut, three furrowed lines stretched across his brow, his usual sign of concentration while composing an email.

"Dimitri Klitou wants you to know that MPT needs more security staff. Men only."

"Noted." After a few mouse clicks, Stan swiveled his chair and turned the screen toward her.

"Wow." Casey gaped at the zebra-striped tie and salmon-and-white short-sleeved shirt. Stan's reputation for mismatched ties and shirts was legendary. "New tie?"

"Yeah. Grandson bought it for my birthday."

"Ah."

"Take a look at the footage of his altercation," he said. "The audio's fairly useless. Too much yelling and background noise."

She figured as much. The tiny microphones embedded in the bus walls weren't great. Dispatch could only hear what was happening after the driver pressed the alarm button. Tinny-sounding words were often missed or inaudible. Worse, the stupid things automatically shut off after thirty seconds.

"I know it's a long shot, but does the suspect look familiar?" Stan asked, freezing the footage.

The bright green shoelaces and red bandana confirmed her suspicion. "He's one of the Bandana Boys who went after Wesley." In her report, she'd only briefly mentioned the dustups with the Boys. Didn't write that Wes had turned him upside down and rammed the guy's head into the floor. So, the guy had turned his anger on Dimitri. Just great.

"Here's his photo." She showed Stan her image of the thug.

Stan nodded and continued playing the footage. Casey winced as Bandana Boy slashed Dimitri's forehead with a broken beer bottle. Dimitri recoiled and raised his arms. Bandana Boy went after him, but this time Dimitri kicked him in the knee. A second kick caught Bandana Boy's shin. He doubled over, yanked his bandana down, and vomited. Dimitri kicked the guy in the head.

Casey gasped. "For god's sake!"

Bandana Boy collapsed onto his side. Dimitri then shoved him off the platform and onto the sidewalk.

"Nice, huh?" Stan froze the image. "Lawsuit's probably in the works."

Casey didn't know what to say. Dimitri's actions were as appalling as Bandana Boy's.

"Your report says you have recordings of those punks," Stan said. "I need to see all of it."

Casey pulled up the first recording and handed him the phone. Stan's face gave nothing away as he watched the Bandana Boys high-fiving one another after the Molotov cocktail exploded. Next came Wesley's unceremonious dispatch of the Boys trying to board the bus, followed by more clips of their behavior.

Stan plunked the phone down. "Well, shit. Why didn't you write about Wesley's crazy pile-driver move?"

"Didn't think it was necessary," she answered. "The report's long enough."

"Since this is the same thug who tangled with Dimitri, it sure as hell is now."

Stan stood and began pacing the room. His office wasn't large. Hands on hips, he stopped in front of the windows.

"I thought about deleting everything to do with Wesley," she added. "I mean, we're supposed to protect employees as well as passengers, but what happens when their integrity and behavior is wrong?"

Stan turned around. "Keeping the videos was the right call. Any of the passengers could have recorded the same incidents or your actions. If we tried to hide it and their footage became public, we'd look even worse than we do." Stan plodded across the green linoleum floor and dropped back into his tattered Naugahyde chair. "The whole riot thing's a bloody mess."

No kidding. If the police learned of Dimitri's and Wesley's behavior, MPT's reputation would suffer. Stan had worked hard to build a rapport with officers from all jurisdictions. He wanted his security team to be regarded as helpful, reliable professionals who were more than capable of providing assistance when asked. Drivers were expected to uphold the same standard, and now two of them had blown it.

"Does Gwyn know about the altercations yet?" she asked.

"I'm meeting with him in an hour." Stan shook his head. "Won't be pretty. Those two could get canned."

"Lou says there's a driver shortage, and an argument could be made that they if they hadn't fought back hard, they could have been badly beaten," Casey answered. "By the way, Dimitri said that Anoop arrived too late to be of much use. What was his location when Dimitri pressed the alarm?"

"Stuck in traffic near the riot." Stan leaned back in the chair. "He took Dimitri to the hospital, but I need to rethink the whole vehicle patrol thing. It would've been better if he'd been on the bus."

"Despite his conflict resolution training, Anoop's no fighter and the passenger was out of control," Casey replied. "Anoop could have been cut with that broken beer bottle."

Stan gazed at the dwarf jade bonsai plant on the corner of his desk. It was a habit he'd picked up whenever he was mulling over a problem, a habit Casey had learned not to interrupt.

"Our PR person says there've been online threats about hurting MPT drivers," he murmured.

"Really?" She didn't bother much with social media, but thoughts of Lou out there on the road made her anxious. "I wouldn't be surprised if the Bandana Boys are behind that."

"Maybe, but some of the drivers are now refusing to work the Coquitlam routes."

"Can't blame them. Have the cops been told about the threats?"

"Yeah, they're searching for the sources." Stan leaned forward. "Gwyn wants a stronger security presence in Coquitlam. He also thinks that troublemakers will be deterred if you and the team wear your uniforms."

Casey's stomach clenched. "With all the hostility lately, it's more likely to attract trouble. Gwyn knows this has happened before, which is why we're in street clothes in the first place."

"I reminded him of that. Also pointed out you're my second-in-command because of your judgment and skill, which entitles you to wear whatever you want."

"Thank you. Did Gwyn back down?"

"He's agreed to let you wear street clothes under your uniform jacket. You decide when to lose the jacket." Stan handed her a sheet of paper. "Here's the new schedule. You, Marie, and Anoop will work from 7:00 PM to 1:00 AM near the riot area, and as far east as Maple Ridge."

Marie was a single parent and Anoop's wife often worked evenings, which meant they would need to hire a babysitter. This wouldn't go over well.

"Have you told them?" she asked.

"I will." He paused. "You should also know that Gwyn wants experienced drivers on those routes, which means Lou, Wesley, and Benny will be carrying the load."

Crap, Lou hadn't yet told her about the extent of his injuries. He had been up and dressed before she got out of bed both yesterday and today, which was totally out of character for him. As she pondered this, her fingertip traced a deep scratch in Stan's old mahogany desk.

"I know you're concerned about Lou," Stan said, "but he can handle himself better than most employees. He'll be okay."

Casey nodded, but said nothing. It was always unsettling when Stan read her thoughts like that. She didn't have to read his mind to know that he wouldn't let her ride with Lou. From day one, Stan feared that she'd put Lou's safety before the passengers in dangerous situations. His stance had always bothered her, but considering the escalating violence everywhere maybe he was right.

"I want you to ride with Adrianna Friday night," Stan said. "She's been assigned to Coquitlam because something came up with Wesley and he can't work that shift."

Casey liked Adrianna. She'd been with MPT for a few years, but she was easily rattled when things didn't run smoothly.

"She's the best they could do?"

"Yep. Five other drivers turned down the work, even with the offer of overtime pay. She said she'd only do it if you were with her," Stan added. "Benny's got the M28 route."

"I hate to say this, but what about Lou?"

"His supervisor wants him to take a couple of days off."

"Why?"

Stan put on his new black-framed reading glasses. He already looked distinguished with the trim beard and moustache, but the glasses made him look like an executive.

"I think he's afraid Lou will quit if he's pushed too hard." Stan gathered sheets of paper together. "There's been stories that he's thinking about it." He peered at her. "That true?"

"Not that I'm aware of."

After the bid for unionization failed, Lou had talked about quitting. Was he discussing it with coworkers again and, if so, how had Stan heard about it before she had?

"Lou's a huge asset," Stan went on. "Nobody wants him to leave. How's he doing anyway? Heard he got into a serious scrap at the rally."

Casey sat up straighter. "What exactly did you hear?"

As Stan removed his glasses, the lines between his eyebrows became more evident. "What did he tell you?"

"Stan! *Please.*"

He sat back, raising his hands defensively. "Seems that some guys pinned him down and kicked the shit out of him before others came to help."

Casey's body stiffened. "What else?"

Stan shifted in his chair, looking pretty damn uncomfortable.

"One of the kicks was to Lou's head. He was out of it for a bit."

Casey jumped up, then sank back down again. She was about ready to carve a brand new gash in the damn desk. Did Lou honestly think she wouldn't find out? Tempted as she was to call him this minute, she needed to cool off.

"Moving on," Stan said, tapping the sheet of paper in front of her. "You'll see that you're now off Tuesday and Wednesday.

You'll ride with Wesley on Thursday, Adrianna is Friday, and Benny the rest of the weekend. Better catch up on paperwork today."

Casey folded the sheet in half and tried not to stew over Lou. "Did the cops say anything about the man who was murdered Saturday night?"

"Why would they? It doesn't have anything to do with us." Observing her, his expression darkened. "I'm right, aren't I? Didn't read anything about it in your report."

"I might have seen something, but it's hard to tell." She picked up her phone. "Look at the last video, upper right corner. The image is tiny."

"I see a man falling," Stan squinted and his nose nearly touched the screen. "He's the victim?"

"Don't know. Maybe."

"Share it with the cops. I'll give you the investigating officer's number. Meanwhile, we have our own problems to deal with. If MPT's sued, the lawyers will expect more details in your incident report." He handed Casey's report to her. "I've marked where you'll need to elaborate."

"Fine." She didn't feel great about what could happen to Wesley, or Dimitri for that matter. But denying, lying, or covering it up wouldn't work. Stan had far too much integrity.

Casey slowly got to her feet. "I need a coffee. Want any?"

"No thanks. Any more caffeine and I'll be jumping out of my seat."

Casey left, softly shutting the door behind her. She didn't need caffeine as much as she needed a few minutes alone to decide how to confront Lou about his injuries. The man wasn't a complainer, but silent suffering wasn't going to cut it this time. He needed to see a doctor if she had to drag him there.

Downstairs, Casey nearly bumped into Benny Lee on his way out of the lunchroom. He looked a little more tired than usual.

"Glad you weren't hurt Saturday night," Benny said. "How's Lou doing? Heard he got into quite a brawl."

"Yeah, and he's refusing to see a doctor. Will you talk to him, Benny? He listens to you."

"Sure, but he can be stubborn, that one."

"Tell me about it. The idiot won't even tell me how badly hurt he is."

"Don't worry, I've got your back."

"Thanks, Benny." Casey gave him a hug. "Oh, and I received your RSVP to the wedding."

"Can't wait for your big day. This wedding will happen, sweetie. You two deserve all the happiness in the world." Benny squeezed her hand. "If I get emotional at the ceremony, just ignore me. I was a mess at my daughter's wedding. Since you and Lou are practically family, it could happen. Thought I'd give you a heads-up."

Casey laughed. "You won't be alone. A few of us will be crying happy tears. How's Yvette doing? Still substitute teaching?"

"She finally got a full-time position, but with two little kids and a husband working two jobs, she's exhausted all the time. I'm trying to help out with babysitting, but my shifts don't make it easy."

"I bet. Do your boys still live at home?"

"Yep, and I blame them for my hair loss and the lines on my face." He swept his hand over the few strands left on his scalp. "You'd think a nineteen- and twenty-two-year-old would want to be out living their own lives, but I guess they have it too good. Neither of them can afford to move out anyway."

Benny always was a soft touch, but since his wife's death a decade ago, Casey thought he'd grown even softer. The man had a hard time saying no to anyone. When his boys were teen-agers, he'd been known to show up for work super stressed be-cause of some mess they'd gotten into.

"Your eldest boy Max apprenticed here as a mechanic for a while, right?"

"Yeah. He works at a garage now, but can't save a dime."

"What's Reese up to these days?"

"Trying to figure out what to do with his life, which means doing a whole lot of nothing. I want him to work here until he comes up with a better plan, but he thinks the pay's too low." Benny shook his head. "Like he can afford to be choosy. The spoiled brat doesn't appreciate that MPT has fed, housed, and clothed him for years."

Given the frustration in Benny's voice, Casey changed the subject. "I hear we're working together this weekend, after Fri-day night's shift with Adrianna."

Benny glanced up and down the corridor. "You might have your hands full. She's already freaked out by the online threats."

"Which is why I'll be with her."

"You'll keep her safe." Benny patted her arm. "That's what you do."

FOUR

Casey sat by the bus's front entrance in a seat reserved for seniors and the physically challenged. Since it was nearly 11:00 PM on a Friday night, she was the only person at the front of the nearly empty bus.

Adrianna had been gripping the steering wheel all evening as if afraid to let go or let her guard down. Every young man who'd boarded had been treated to an intimidating *don't you dare cause trouble* glance. Adrianna's dark eyes seemed almost too large for her face, a stark contrast to the brown hair and light blond highlights that stopped at her jawline. She'd told Casey that she'd been working out, trying to get her body back to what it was before the birth of her son eighteen months ago. Tonight, Adrianna was both nervous and defiant, a demeanor that made Casey uneasy. If trouble arose, Adrianna's attitude could make things worse.

Compounding the unpleasant ride was another chorus of "Wheels on the Bus" being sung a few rows down. The singer, an immature seventeen-year-old named Felicity Akenhead, and her pals, Del and Lawrence, were part of a small group of high school outcasts who began riding MPT buses about ten months ago. They'd caught the bus a couple of stops back and hadn't settled down yet tonight.

Calling themselves "MPT Friends," these three always rode together and apparently had been friends since elementary school. For some reason, they'd developed a particular interest in everything to do with Mainland Public Transport, including its routes, bus models, and fleet maintenance. What they loved most, though, was riding different routes. It was a weird hobby, but better than drinking and drugs, Casey supposed. The kids were always respectful and endlessly curious about MPT's operation.

Late last August, Felicity's parents met with Stan to tell him that bus riding was one of the few drug-free remedies that helped their ADHD daughter relax enough to sleep better at night. As long as Felicity was with Del and Lawrence, the parents permitted these evening excursions.

Felicity was bouncier than usual tonight, seemingly oblivious to the smirks and snorts from a couple of guys at the back of the bus. A bemused elderly rider also watched her. Del waved at Casey. Felicity also waved and stopped singing. Before Casey knew it, all three were moving toward her. Oh joy.

"Hi, Casey." Del sat next to her. The two took the nearest seat facing the front. "Quiet night, huh? We've never seen you on a Coquitlam route before."

"And I've only ever seen you catch a bus in Vancouver. What brings you out this way?"

"Travis lives nearby," he replied. "After his family moved out here, we started riding the Coquitlam routes."

Travis was an anomaly Casey didn't understand. The kid suffered from motion sickness, so he rarely rode buses, yet he loved everything to do with them. He used to live within walking distance of MPT and often visited the garage to chat with the mechanics. She'd heard him say that he wanted to work for MPT one day.

"I take it this isn't grad party weekend for you?" she asked, knowing that all three of them were about to graduate from the same high school.

"Next week," Lawrence replied without enthusiasm.

Tall and lanky and sporting black-framed glasses, Lawrence Tam was the quietest of the trio. His MPT passion was photographing the buses, inside and out, with the Nikon he always had on him. Apparently, his photos had already won awards.

"We heard you got trapped at the riot," Felicity said.

"Oh?" Casey's eyebrows rose. "Who told you that?"

Del gave her a weak smile. "Word gets around."

Although Del Darzi would never admit it, Casey suspected that this kid's particular MPT interest was more surreptitious than that of his cohorts. She was pretty sure he hacked into MPT's databases. Del knew too much about the company and often showed up wherever she was working, which creeped her out at times.

"How come you brought your security jacket?" Felicity nodded toward the jacket folded beside Casey.

"It's a better raincoat than anything else I own." Given the heavy clouds threatening to spill, she just might need it.

Adrianna eased the bus up to the next stop. Two people left through the back entrance. No one else boarded. So far, this shift had gone smoothly.

"Did you see the man who was stabbed at the riot?" Del asked.

Casey had no intention of sharing information about that night. "No."

"I heard that your bus got caught in a mob."

"Did you now?" She met his gaze and held on.

Del was short for a seventeen-year-old. His facial features were delicate and his tawny beige skin unblemished. If his black hair was longer, he could be mistaken for a girl. His androgynous appearance caused riders to stare occasionally, but Del's charm and empathy also made him popular with most of the drivers. He was a sweet kid who once told Casey that he thought her and the drivers' choice of work was heroic.

"Travis and Hedley were at the rally until the fighting started." Felicity fidgeted in her seat. "They took off after that. Saw your bus stopped on Glen Drive."

Casey nodded, surprised to hear that Craig Hedley had been with Travis. Hedley was the Friends' founder. Since he started college last September, she'd heard that his interest in the group had faded.

"How's Hedley doing? I haven't seen him in a while."

"He's been busy with school, but semester's over now," she replied.

"Why would they go to a union rally?" Casey asked.

"Something to do, I guess," Felicity answered. "Travis has been homeschooled since he moved away. Any excuse to get out of the house works for him."

Casey noticed Lawrence pointing his Nikon at Adrianna.

"Remember, you can't take pictures of anyone without their permission, and never of security personnel, okay?"

"Yep." Lawrence opened the bus window and began snapping pictures of buildings.

"You didn't get hurt Saturday night, did you?" Felicity asked her. Under the bus's lousy lighting, her porcelain skin and dark red hair adopted a greenish tinge. "We know your driver had some trouble. It's been posted everywhere."

Casey nodded. They didn't need to know that Stan had already told her this. "I don't spend much time on the net." Nor did she want to.

"You should." Del's expression became solemn. "Someone's threatening to hurt drivers."

Casey glanced at Adrianna, who kept her gaze on the road. "Let's sit further back." After they'd settled into seats, she said, "What exactly do the posts say?"

Del exchanged pensive glances with his cohorts. "That he wants to bash the drivers' heads in. Someone else posted that they should be burned alive."

Casey's neck and shoulders became prickly. Despite the anger swirling in her gut, she kept her expression impassive.

"Any specific drivers or routes mentioned?"

"No," Del answered, "but I might be able to find out who posted the remarks."

"The cops can do that."

"Doubt they'd be as fast as me."

Her phone rang. She wasn't surprised to see Stan's name. He was driving the security vehicle in this area.

"What's up?" she asked.

"Benny triggered his alarm on the M28. Dispatch could hear two people shouting at him. What's your twenty?"

As she thought about the posts, Casey's adrenalin raced. She glanced at the street, then moved out of earshot of the Friends and Adrianna.

"We're heading north on Johnson Street, just about to reach Guildford Way. Why didn't dispatch use the radio to notify me?"

"They don't want to upset other drivers," he answered. "Benny's at the stop just past Town Center Boulevard and Pine-tree Way. I'm about ten minutes from there. I'm hoping you can reach him faster than me."

"The RCMP detachment's only a couple of blocks from Benny's location," she murmured. "Can't they help?"

"Dispatch called them, and were told that officers are dealing with major incidents right now. Benny doesn't think the drunks are carrying weapons, which means the cops will probably treat it as a low priority call."

Casey's hand clenched. Given the public threats, Benny could have a major problem on his hands.

A passenger pulled the bell cord. The traffic light turned red.

"We're nearing the next stop. Adrianna'll be too distressed if I pull her off her route, and I'm less than ten minutes away on foot." Casey put on her jacket and marched to the front exit. "I have Benny's cell number. Should I call him?"

"Worth a try, but don't panic if he doesn't answer. Sounds like he has his hands full. See you shortly."

If anyone could stay cool in a tense situation, it was Benny Lee. He'd dealt with plenty of unruly drunks and junkies over the years, which was why Stan hadn't placed security personnel on the M28.

"What are you doing?" Adrianna asked, her tone anxious.

Casey kept the explanation brief, playing down the danger to Benny. The light changed to green.

Easing the bus forward, Adrianna mumbled, "I knew there'd be trouble."

Casey glanced at the Friends, who appeared anxious. They'd either eavesdropped or were adept at reading body language.

Casey dialed Benny's number and was relieved by his quick response. "What's happening there? Stan and I are on our way."

"Just a misunderstanding," he murmured. "No worries."

His flat monotone concerned her. In the background, Casey heard, "Who are you talking to, old man? Gimme that phone!"

The line went dead. Casey gripped the pole by Adrianna's chair, every muscle in her body tightening. Adrianna moved at a snail's pace through the intersection. God, was she deliberately going slowly? Casey bit back the urge to yell at her to move faster. Her shoulders twitched.

Finally, Adrianna stopped the bus and opened the door.

"You'll be back, won't you?"

"That's the plan." Casey leapt off the platform and bolted down Guildford Way.

FIVE

Casey was already breathing heavily, not just from racing down the sidewalk but out of fear for Benny. Rational thinking was losing ground to panic. Glancing at the sky, she welcomed the sprinkling rain. It cooled her skin and in a strange way helped her focus on ways to protect Benny once she reached the M28.

Several yards ahead, a man ambled down the sidewalk with his poodle.

"Coming through!" she shouted. "Emergency!"

Beneath the streetlight, a wrinkled, wary face turned to her. The senior picked up his dog as she darted past him.

"Thanks!" Bright yellow security jackets had their uses.

Casey tried to see beyond this block, toward Pinetree Way, but the curving road made it impossible. This part of Guildford was wide. A grassy boulevard ran down the center of the road. Leaves rustled from branches dangling over the sidewalk.

A firetruck siren ripped through the silence, somewhere too far ahead to see. Her scalp prickled and her shoulders rose. Were they heading for Benny? . . . No. Don't go there.

"Hurry up, Lawrence!" Felicity yelled behind Casey. "You're too slow."

Crap! Casey glanced over her shoulder to find Felicity leading the charge. "What are you three doing here? Go home!"

"We can help!" Del yelled out. "Take photos, or keep the crowds back."

Why would there be a crowd this late at night? Shoving that and thoughts of the Friends aside, Casey focused on getting to Benny. Sweat trickled down her sides as she kept running. Spotting the intersection ahead, Casey glanced at the RCMP detachment across the street, at the corner. No one appeared to be around.

As she reached the side road called Town Center Boulevard, a man darted from behind the closed aquatic center to her left. He crossed the road and raced into a condo/townhouse complex. The dark ball cap and hoodie reminded her of the Bandana Boys. Why was he running?

Suspicion sent Casey charging down the road to see where he went, but by the time she reached the complex's entrance the man had vanished. Trees and bushes along the winding road created too many hiding spots to search. Besides, she needed to get to Benny.

Continuing on, she passed the aquatic center and adjoining parking lot and soon found herself on Pinetree Way. The M28 bus was stopped across the road a block further north, along with a firetruck. Her heart sank. A dozen people stood on the sidewalk, gazing at what looked like an empty bus.

Forced to wait for an opening in traffic, Casey bent over and put her hands on her thighs to catch her breath. She looked up. Raindrops spritzed her. The traffic moved on. Casey bolted across the multi-lane street. Drawing closer to the cluster of bystanders, she raised her ID.

"MPT security. What's going on?"

"Someone stabbed the driver and took off," a woman answered.

"What?" Casey's head and ears pounded. "Stabbed? Are you sure?"

"Afraid so." The woman shuddered. "It was just awful."

Skirting the bystanders, Casey leapt onto the bus via the open back exit. An ambulance and RCMP cruiser arrived. She stampeded down the aisle, toward the firefighters tending to Benny. One of them had his hands on his abdomen.

"How bad is he?"

The paramedic looked up. "Who are you?"

"His coworker." She flashed her ID.

"He sustained a single knife wound."

Casey stood frozen in place, unable to see much of Benny at all, thanks to firefighters. She waited, desperate for more information, for confirmation that he would be okay.

"Ma'am, step off the bus, please" a voice ordered behind her.

Casey turned around. The large RCMP officer looked like he meant business.

"He's a colleague." Casey's voice cracked as she again showed her ID.

"I appreciate that, but we don't want the crime scene contaminated."

Crime scene? Yeah. She supposed it was. Lightheaded and queasy, Casey made her way down the aisle, touching the backs of seats for support against her weakening limbs. She'd seen injuries and violence, even dead bodies, before. But this was Benny. He had to survive. No other option was acceptable. Stepping onto the sidewalk, she stumbled. Lawrence and Del grabbed her before she hit the ground.

"I'm okay," she mumbled. "You guys should head home."

"We'll go back with you," Felicity replied. "Safety in numbers, right?"

Casey had no idea how to respond to that. She looked around, vaguely aware again of the rain on her face. Where was

Stan? He should be here by now. The constable who'd escorted her off the bus stood close by but said nothing. She felt useless just standing here. Surely she could do something.

"Hey! I'm with MPT security!" she blurted to the spectators, displaying her ID. "Anyone see the attack on our driver?"

Some people shook their heads. Others just gawked at her.

"I was sitting near the front when two young men started harassing the driver." This came from the woman who'd told her about the stabbing. "He stopped the bus and tried to talk to them, but another man jumped onto the platform. I thought he was going to help the driver, but . . . I didn't even see the knife at first. It all happened so fast."

Moving closer, the constable said, "Did you see which way the man went?"

"I think he crossed the road, toward the aquatic center."

Oh hell. Was this the guy who disappeared in the townhouse complex?

"Did you see his face?" Casey asked.

"He wasn't a kid." Raindrops made her auburn hair sparkle under the streetlight. "Maybe late thirties or older, and dressed in black, head to toe."

Casey turned to the constable. "I saw a man dressed in dark clothes less than ten minutes ago. He was racing into the town-house complex on the other side of the aquatic center. It felt wrong, so I tried to see where he went, but I lost him."

"Any idea of his height and weight?"

"Not really. Just average, I guess. He wore a ball cap with a hoodie pulled over it."

"Yes," the woman said. "I remember that too."

The constable pressed his radio mic button and stepped away from her.

"Were the guys who were yelling at the driver covering their faces with bandanas, by any chance?" Casey asked the woman.

"No."

"Would you mind if I showed you a couple of photos of people we've been looking for? They've been harassing drivers."

"Sure, go ahead."

While the woman removed a pair of glasses from her purse, Casey scrolled through the photos. She was showing headshots of each Bandana Boy when two more RCMP cruisers pulled up. The constable who'd been near her returned.

"That's him, with the long black hair and acne," the woman murmured.

Casey glanced at the shot of the Bandana Boy with the blue scarf. "Thanks."

A young man who'd been standing nearby said, "Can I see the photos?"

She held the phone in front of him. "She's right. That's him."

"See if you recognize anyone else." She scanned through the images until the young man said, "That's the other one. Skinny guy, with the wild eyes in the red bandana."

Damn. He was the punk Wesley had turned upside down and who'd battled with Dimitri.

"Did either of you see which way they went?" the constable asked.

"South. When they saw the blood, they ran off," the woman replied. "I think they were as shocked as I was. My impression was that they didn't know the third man."

A familiar voice yelled, "Would somebody *please* tell me what is going on!"

"Stan!" Casey waved her arms. "Over here!"

As he charged toward her, spectators jumped out of the big guy's path.

"Two of the Bandana Boys beat up Benny," she blurted. "Then a third guy boarded the bus and stabbed him. No connection to the first two suspects, though."

"Holy shit. Will he be okay?" Stan looked at the bus.

"I think so. Firefighters got here first. Looks like paramedics are with him now."

"Bandana Boys?" The constable stared at Casey. "You know them?"

"Another bus driver and I had a run-in with them at the riot. I took photos of all of them that night." She turned to Stan. "Looks like the Bandana Boys wanted some payback."

The constable turned to the witnesses. "What exactly did they do to the driver?"

"They'd been calling him names, trying to start a fight, I think," the woman replied. "When the driver answered his cellphone, the acne-faced guy grabbed it from him and smashed it with his foot. He and his buddy then started pummeling the driver until the third guy boarded. The other two jumped back, probably because they saw the blade before anyone else."

"Like this lady said, it happened quick," the young man said.

Casey hugged herself. The damp night and the horror of what had happened to Benny chilled her bones.

"Did you see his face?" the constable asked.

"Not much," the young man answered. "Just dark stubble, like he hadn't shaved in three or four days. Hoodie was pulled low over his forehead."

"What color was the hoodie?" the cop asked.

"Black. He was all in black."

"Sounds like the guy we saw running," Del stated from behind Casey.

Glancing over her shoulder, she saw the worried-looking Friends who were clearly incapable of following instructions. Casey shook her head and sighed.

While the cop again radioed his colleagues, Casey and Stan exchanged grim stares. The lines on Stan's face looked deeper, his expression resigned to realities beyond his control. Knowing Stan, he'd feel guilty for not being closer to the M28 in the first place. Lord knows she wished she'd been riding with Benny.

"This isn't a designated stop," Stan said, glancing around. "How did the suspect manage to board here?"

"Good question." Casey looked up and down the street.

"When those two punks started yelling at the driver," the young man said, "he pulled over right away and opened the door."

Did the suspect simply seize an opportunity to hurt someone or had he targeted an MPT driver? Casey was dwelling on this, barely listening to the cop speak with the witnesses, when she realized she was being dismissed.

"Thanks for all your help, everyone," the constable was saying. "There might be more questions, so I'll need your names and contact information."

As witnesses provided the info, Casey scribbled everything down, should she need it for her own report.

"I'll drive you to Adrianna," Stan said to her. "There's nothing more we can do here."

"Thanks, but it's not necessary. The streets are already filling with cops. Besides, three of our MPT Friends followed me off the M30." She nodded toward the trio. "I'll escort them back."

"Benny wasn't alone," he replied. "I'll take them too."

The paramedics were carrying Benny off the bus and onto a gurney. Stan charged toward them. Casey hurried to keep up.

"I'm in charge of Mainland Public Transport security," Stan said to them. "What's the driver's condition?"

"There's one stab wound but it could be deep," a paramedic answered. "He might need surgery."

"Oh god," she murmured.

Stan looked over his shoulder. "Take the kids to the car and wait there."

Casey nodded, afraid that if she spoke she'd burst into tears. Her head spun. She pressed her hand against her stomach to try and control the nausea that made her insides frothy. She turned to the Friends. Lawrence was snapping photos of the bus while Del and Felicity texted.

"You three," she ordered. "Come with me."

Leading the way, she marched toward the security vehicle, determined to maintain a steady pace despite her weakening legs. Above Casey, an incoming SkyTrain broke the silence. She looked up. Its two cars were illuminated inside, but she saw no passengers, just emptiness. Of course there was nothing to see up there. The drama was all here on the street. God, who would tell Benny's family what had happened? And what about coworkers? Benny was a popular employee. A lot of them would be devastated.

"Will Mr. Lee be okay?" Lawrence asked.

"Absolutely." She stared straight ahead. "He's one of the strongest people I know."

A raindrop splashed directly into her eye, merging with the pooling tears. She wiped her eyes as the ambulance took off, lights and siren sabotaging her hope that Benny would be fine and back at work soon. She glanced over her shoulder to see Del and Felicity still texting.

"Who are you texting?"

"Travis," Del answered.

"Hedley," Felicity added.

Casey didn't know how to interpret the strange glance Del gave Felicity. It was almost as if her answer annoyed him. She opened the back door and waited as the trio climbed into the vehicle.

"Let me be clear," Casey said, sliding onto the front seat. "I don't want you posting details about tonight on social media. Keep what you saw and heard to yourselves, and that applies to the two you're texting, understand? We can't risk compromising the police investigation."

"No problem," Del said, while the other two nodded.

Stan slid behind the wheel. Without saying a word, he started the engine and pulled away. Casey studied the small forested area in front of the aquatic center on the north side of Town Center Boulevard. Her gaze swept from tree to tree. No sign of movement. Just shadows and far too many hiding places. A breeze swooshed through the lighter branches. Leaves fluttered.

Casey thought she saw something, or someone, move behind the trees. Peering into the darkness, she held her breath as Stan cruised past the trees. Nothing. Maybe she was being paranoid.

"It's weird that two guys were stabbed just a few days apart in the same area," Felicity said.

"Could be a coincidence," Del replied.

"Or not," Lawrence said. "Lots of people carry knives, but not many go around stabbing people in the same area of a city."

Stan and Casey exchanged glances. Two police cruisers were parked at the entrance to the townhouse complex. Beneath the streetlights, Casey spotted officers walking through the complex, flashing bright lights on gardens, hedges, and driveways.

"Is there a full moon tonight?" Felicity asked.

"No," Casey answered. "Why?"

"Things always go crazy on full moons. That's why there's more security people on duty, right?"

Casey glanced over her shoulder. "And how do you know that, Miss Felicity?"

"Um." She tossed a furtive glance at Del. "A driver probably told us."

"Uh-huh." Casey looked at Stan. "Should we call Benny's family?"

"I'll do it when we get back," he mumbled. "Word's out among the drivers. Call Adrianna and find out where she is."

Casey did so, not surprised that Adrianna answered on the second ring.

"Please tell me it's not true about Benny," she pleaded.

"He'll be okay. I'll fill you in shortly." She then arranged to meet Adrianna at the Guildford and Johnson bus stop.

As tempted as Casey was to call Lou, it'd be better to tell him in person. Lou wasn't working tonight and probably hadn't heard the news. Benny was his good friend and mentor. He'd take it hard.

"Look at that guy hurrying down the sidewalk," Felicity said. "I think he's in black clothes! Is that the man with the knife? The blade man?"

Casey's breath caught in her throat. She noted that his hands were in his pockets and the hoodie pulled low over his forehead. Stan slowed the vehicle. As they drew nearer, she saw enough of the man's full beard to know he wasn't one of the Bandana Boys or the assailant. Aside from all the facial hair, this guy wore dark brown pants rather than black jeans.

"Not the suspect," she said.

The man stared at them as they drove past. At that moment, Casey was glad they weren't walking. Given all the hostility drivers had experienced lately, maybe there was no such thing as overly cautious.

"We should plan our next rides," Felicity said to Del.

"Stay away from Coquitlam," Casey said. "You'll be busy with grad celebrations next weekend anyway, right?" Their silence didn't surprise her. "You should go. The dinner-dance might not be your thing, but After Grad parties are fun."

"Did you go to yours?" Felicity asked.

"Sure." More than fifteen years had flown by, but memories of dancing, karaoke, games, and making out were still clear. "It's one of my best memories of grad year."

"It'd be fun to ride the buses after midnight on grad weekend," Lawrence said.

"Totally," Felicity replied.

Casey stifled a groan. Their single-minded focus was kind of depressing. "Not really, guys. Things can get rowdy."

Past experience had proven that there were always a few graduating morons who decided to become bad-ass wannabes on grad night. Drinking, fighting, and dumb acts of vandalism on buses weren't unusual.

"There's tons of photo ops at grad parties, Lawrence," Casey remarked. "Take advantage of them."

As Stan reached Johnson Street, Adrianna's bus approached.

"Can we have your business card?" Felicity asked. "In case we see someone suspicious?"

"Since you won't be coming out here for a while, I don't think it's necessary."

Felicity hesitated. "Travis might see something. It'd help if we all had a way to contact you."

"And we might need to come out this way for Travis," Del added. "He doesn't like being alone much."

Casey had a feeling she wouldn't be able to deter them. Admittedly, this bunch was more observant than most riders. If one of them spotted someone suspicious, a phone call might help.

Casey handed her card to Del. "Since I don't have many, share this between you."

"Awesome!" Felicity said.

As the trio examined the card, Casey wondered if she'd just made a big mistake. "Only call if there's real trouble, is that clear? Even then, you should call 9-1-1 first."

"Your cell number's not on here?" Del asked.

A smile brightened Stan's face as he pulled up behind Adrianna's bus.

"No, and don't make me regret this."

"We'll guard it with our lives," Felicity said.

Casey didn't find this especially reassuring.

SIX

Three days had passed since Benny's surgery and Casey was worried. She'd spoken with his daughter Yvette, who said that although Benny's condition was stable, he needed to remain in the hospital.

Lou hardly spoke all weekend, preferring to keep busy by washing his truck and doing yardwork. Physical labor was how he coped with anguish and fear. Pounding and pulling his way through emotions was much more comfortable than conversation.

It didn't help that she'd confronted him about his injuries. Lou was annoyed that she'd found out about the extent of the beating. Worse, he still refused to see a doctor. They'd argued about it but he wouldn't back down. The riot happened just over a week ago. Lou moved more easily now and didn't groan as much. Yet anger had settled in his eyes. He wore tension like a badly fitted suit, as if afraid his thoughts would burst through in a tirade.

After the intense discussion about his injuries, Casey hadn't brought up the rumor about Lou quitting his job. The last time he wanted to quit, Benny was the one who'd persuaded him to stay.

As they drove to the mandatory staff meeting, Casey could almost feel resentment oozing from his pores. Lou kept the volume up on the radio, switching from a rock 'n' roll station to the news. Staring at the heavy eastbound traffic, he sighed.

"Leave it to bloody Gwyn to demand that everyone show up first thing in the morning. What about the guys who didn't finish work until after midnight? He's such an ass."

Gwyn Maddox rarely gathered all personnel together. He hadn't done so after the riot debacle or the attack on Benny. But when Gwyn heard that someone had spray-painted *MPT SUCKS* all over the admin building last night, he demanded a meeting.

Lou turned into Mainland's parking lot, where the repeated phrase was sprawled across the first-floor windows and glass door.

"Stan says no one saw anything," Casey remarked. "The vandal must have struck between 2:00 and 5:00 AM. It's the only time when no one's here."

"Serves Gwyn right for being too damn cheap to install cameras."

As they got out of the truck, she caught Lou glaring at Gwyn's shiny new Mercedes in his reserved spot by the entrance. He marched past the vehicle, yanked the entrance door open, and charged inside. In the hallway, Lou stopped to talk with a handful of mechanics and drivers.

The new mechanic, a thin, middle-aged man named Maurice Wallace, cast a nervous glance in her direction. Maurice spent his breaks either smoking or reading the Bible. Today, the guy looked especially haggard. Was it because of Gwyn's summons or something else?

Marie Crenshaw came up to her. "Stan just assigned me to work with Lou in the hot zone this weekend." She tossed back her thick red hair. "Don't worry, sweetie. I'll keep him safe."

Three years ago, her smug expression and tone would have annoyed the crap out of Casey. Marie had serious feelings for Lou back then, which had caused trouble. But all that had passed. She had a new man in her life now and seemed happy.

"I'm sure you will."

"You don't sound overly confident," Marie remarked. "I can protect him as well as you."

Casey sighed. Too bad that her colleague's professional rivalry dragged on. "I know you can." The woman was fearless.

Marie studied her. "You still think Stan should let you ride with Lou, right?"

Denying it would be useless—Marie knew her too well. "My main worry is that he'll have too many shifts in the hot zone."

"Wesley's doing more than his share as well, which isn't fair to either of them, but since when does fairness matter to management?"

Casey couldn't argue the point. "Is Stan in his office?"

"Yeah."

Casey bounded up the steps and into the security department. She knocked on Stan's partially open door and stepped inside without waiting for a response.

"Any more news on Benny?"

"No, but an RCMP contact of mine provided a bit of info about the man who was stabbed at the riot." Stan picked up a sheet of paper. "He was a thirty-eight-year-old grocery store manager, no enemies or criminal activity. Looks like a random act, a case of wrong place, wrong time."

"Think the assault on Benny was random too?"

"Good question." Stan paused. "My contact isn't willing to say publicly that both crimes were committed by the same man."

Casey frowned. "Even though both wore dark clothing and stabbed their victims in the abdomen?"

"They want more details before announcing that a serial killer could be on the loose." Stan picked up another sheet. "What they do know is that the suspect doesn't have glasses, tattoos, or piercings, and he's in his late thirties, average height and weight. Not enough info to come up with a decent composite sketch."

"That sucks." She sat down. "The punks who taunted Benny might have gotten a better look at the man. Do you know if they've been found?"

"Not that I've heard." Stan rubbed his beard and frowned. "I've been in touch with TransLink's security people."

"Really?" Stan didn't often contact the competition. "What'd they say?"

"Their drivers managed to stay out of the riot fray and none have had violent encounters this week."

Casey sat up straighter. "Are we being targeted?"

Stan drummed his fingers on the desk. "It's a theory that the police and Gwyn are tossing around, but keep it quiet, okay? Gwyn doesn't want to upset staff more than they are."

"The drivers'll figure it out, Stan." She paused. "Think the graffiti's linked to the attacks?"

"No idea, but it's pretty clear that MPT has enemies." Removing his glasses, Stan added, "If we're lucky, the police will find answers soon."

Casey didn't have the heart to reply that good luck and MPT seemed miles apart right now.

SEVEN

Casey watched Lou step out of the bedroom. "I've put a sandwich and a couple of protein bars in your lunch box. Coffee's ready."

"Thanks." He adjusted the cuff on his uniform jacket.

His thick hair, washed and blown dry, shone like copper. He looked refreshed from his nap, ready as he could be for an eight-hour shift. But she wasn't ready. The bruises on Lou's lower back had turned into an unsavory rainbow of ochre and greenish shades, which told her he wasn't yet a hundred percent better. At least Marie would be there to handle dicey situations.

Although there'd been no further incidents since Benny's assault six nights ago, this was Thursday, the start of what could be another dangerous weekend. Lou would be taking Benny's place indefinitely.

As she feared, it hadn't taken drivers long to believe that they were being targeted. A couple of them had called in sick for tonight's shift. She wished that Stan hadn't removed her from the roster. She'd much rather be working than waiting to see if some maniac would go after the love of her life.

Lou poured coffee into a thermos. "What are your plans for the evening?"

"Well, I'll see if Summer wants to share a pizza."

"Good idea. Is she home? I haven't seen her all day."

"She should be."

He placed the lid on the thermos. "Sometimes it feels like she's drifting away from us."

"I know, but it's good to see her hanging with a nice friend for a change."

Friendships had been tricky for Summer since her mother's incarceration three years ago. The snubbing and cruel remarks from former friends and classmates had created a wound not easily healed. Over recent months Summer had developed a couple of solid friendships, and Casey had allowed her to hang out with the girls a lot.

"I'll go talk to her now."

Casey jogged downstairs to the second floor, pausing outside Summer's bedroom door. All she could hear were TVs and running water from the tenants' studio suites at the back of the house. Casey's knock prompted the familiar clicking of Cheyenne's nails on the floor. Summer had to be inside. Her golden retriever followed her everywhere.

Casey knocked again and opened the door a crack. "Summer? It's Casey. Can I come in?"

"Hi," she called out. "I'm in the bathroom."

"Wanna split a pizza?" Casey peeked inside. Good lord, clothes and shoes covered most of the floor. Books and her backpack had been dumped on the unmade bed. "I was hoping we could catch up." She scratched Cheyenne's head.

"Can't, sorry. I have to go to Stacy's. She has a big project that's due and needs help. I could make us a pizza tomorrow, if you want."

"That'd be great, but can we eat early? I'll have to leave for work at six."

"Sure."

Summer's passion for cooking had prompted Casey to let her prepare meals in the kitchen on the main floor. This meant that they didn't eat together as often as she would like, and the kitchen was always a mess. Casey missed her company. She decided to head downstairs and see what needed to be restocked in Summer's fridge.

Casey was reading the expiry date on a carton of milk when she heard footsteps jogging downstairs. Seconds later, Summer entered the room, followed by Cheyenne.

Casey's mouth dropped open. "Wow!" And what the hell?

Summer glanced up from her phone, her expression startled. "I didn't know you'd come down here."

Yeah well, surprise worked both ways. The sophisticated hair and makeup had transformed Summer into a young woman ready for a fancy club instead of a fourteen-year-old about to help a friend with homework. Summer's bright blue eyes sported three shades of eye shadow and false eyelashes. The sequined tank top didn't quite match the jeans and running shoes, but she was probably carrying more clothes in that big tote bag.

"That's a pretty glamorous look for a school project."

"I'm a model for Stacy's photography course. Tonight's theme is glam."

"Sounds interesting. Have there been other themes?"

"Sports, business, formal." She shrugged. "It's a lot of work, but it's also kinda cool. Maybe I'll try modeling professionally."

"You'd be great at it," Casey replied. "Where'd you learn to apply makeup so well?"

"Stacy. She wants to be a beautician after high school."

"Did she teach you to do your hair like that too? It's gorgeous." Summer's raven hair had transformed into a cascade of loose curls pulled back from her face with crystal clips.

"Her sister did it." Summer headed for the back door.

"Think she could do something with mine for the wedding?"

"I'll ask." Summer scrutinized Casey's loose, shoulder-length perm. "I like that light shade of brown on you, but highlights would be awesome." Summer paused. "Which reminds me, Grandma phoned and asked if I could stay with her for a few days in July. I told her about your wedding and it almost sounded like she was hoping for an invitation."

"But Winifred doesn't like me."

She didn't get along with her own daughter either. It was partly why Rhonda made Casey Summer's legal guardian instead of Winifred. The old woman probably still resented that Casey paid little rent here in exchange for looking after Rhonda's house. Resentment, however, worked both ways.

Casey hadn't quite forgiven Winifred for moving in uninvited shortly after Rhonda went to prison. Winifred's constant criticisms of her and Summer had forced a confrontation and Winifred's permanent departure from the house. Since then, Casey had rarely spoken to her.

"Maybe she just wants something to do and free food," Summer said. "Her life's totally boring."

"Do you want her at the wedding?"

Summer shrugged. "She won't know anyone, which means I'd feel obligated to spend a lot of time with her. But it's your wedding, so invite who you want."

"Okay. No invitation." Casey glanced at the dirty plates on the countertop. "I thought you were going to clean all that up a couple of days ago."

Casey could almost see the cloud darkening Summer's cheeriness. Chores were an ongoing issue between them. Casey didn't want to nag, but Summer had become quite the procrastinator.

"Sorry, but I've been busy with school. They're giving us tons of homework before final exams." She opened the door. "I'll do it on the weekend. Gotta go."

"Need a ride? Looks like it's about to rain and the news said a thunderstorm's coming."

"No thanks. Stacy's only four blocks away."

Casey knew this. Still, it seemed silly not to accept her offer, unless her ward had an ulterior motive. The normally chatty Summer hadn't spoken about her social life lately. The last time she was evasive and uncommunicative was over a nasty boy-friend who encouraged her to keep things from Casey. Happily, that relationship was short-lived, but had she found someone new?

"I can give you a ride home," Casey offered.

"Thanks, but Stacy's brother'll drive me."

Ah. Stacy had two older brothers. Probably cute, given how much time Summer was spending over there and the care she'd taken with her appearance. Was the school project thing completely bogus?

"Can't wait to catch up tomorrow," Casey said. "You've been rushing about so much, it feels like ages since we've talked."

"You've been busy too." Her tone was cool. "We'll have plenty of time once exams are over."

Cheyenne started to head outside, but Summer stopped her. "Not this time, sweetie."

"Did she get out for a walk today?"

"I let her out for a pee in the backyard." A flicker of guilt flashed behind that perfectly made-up face. "I'll take her for a long walk after school tomorrow."

As Summer quickly shut the door, Casey shook her head. She'd known Summer all her life, but these last three years hadn't taught Casey nearly enough about raising a strong-willed teen forced to deal with a major family trauma. So, how far should she go to learn what Summer was keeping from her? A search of her bedroom didn't seem ethical, but was it necessary?

Lou entered the kitchen, lunch pail in hand. Casey's stomach knotted.

"Where's Summer?" he asked.

"Just left for Stacy's."

Lou's gray eyes peered at her. "What's wrong?"

Casey shrugged. This wasn't a good time to discuss her ward's secretive behavior. "Just anxious about you working the hot zone tonight."

Lou gently lifted her chin with his fingertips and kissed her. Lord, she loved his mouth.

"I'll be fine. Try not to worry, even though you do it so well." He opened the door. "See you tonight."

"I'll wait up."

He smiled. "I'd rather you keep the bed warm."

"I bet you would." She chuckled until the door closed and he was gone. Worry was an insatiable beast. It took only one second for things to go wrong, for lives to change forever.

As she listened to Lou drive away, Casey took a deep breath. She needed to keep busy, do something productive. Too bad she wasn't taking another criminology course. What with the wedding and honeymoon, she'd skipped the summer semester. The problem with one or two courses per semester was that she'd earned only thirty credits in four years. The hundred and twenty needed to graduate felt a long way off, not that she knew what she'd do with a degree. Casey sighed. It was pathetic to be thirty-three years old and still undecided about a career choice.

She looked at Cheyenne. "Would you like a treat?"

The golden retriever wagged her tail while Casey retrieved a biscuit and the dog brush. Five full brushes later, she decided to tackle the crusted, dirty dishes. Summer could wash the floor and clean the fridge on the weekend.

Casey filled the sink, wondering how she'd pass the time once this chore was completed. Wedding preparations were pretty much done. Lou's mom Barb wasn't involved like she had been last year, which made things simpler. Her best friend Kendal was arranging a bachelorette spa day. All Casey had to do was show up.

Taking a closer look at dried food on the plates, it was clear that the dishes needed a good soaking first. Casey sighed and looked at the dog. "Shall we go for a walk, Cheyenne?"

The dog scrambled for the leash dangling over the basement door. She brought it to Casey and practically vibrated with excitement as Casey clipped it on. Outside, the early evening air was warm and humid. Dark, heavy clouds threatened to soak the city, but at least it would clear the haze and freshen the air. Cheyenne strained on her leash so hard that Casey needed both hands to control this seventy-pound bundle of energy.

By the time they'd ventured three blocks from home, Casey figured there was no harm in walking one more block to Stacy's street. If Summer spotted her, she wouldn't be pleased, but so what? If she'd taken the time to walk Cheyenne earlier, Casey wouldn't be here now. Besides, she needed to make sure her ward wasn't engaging in reckless, dangerous behavior. Rhonda would expect nothing less from her daughter's legal guardian.

Casey kept Rhonda updated because this was what she wanted. Rhonda called weekly but the conversations weren't always easy. Unresolved issues and resentments triggered arguments. Real-life distractions and Rhonda's inaccessibility often created an emotional distance between mother and daughter. The best solution was a prison visit, although this sometimes made things worse.

Stacy's place was three doors down on the right. There were two cars in the driveway, but no lights on in the living room. Strange. She supposed they could be at the back of the house or in the basement. On the other hand, what if they weren't there at all?

Casey stared at the windows until she thought she saw a curtain ripple slightly in one of the bedrooms. Damn, had someone seen her? Summer maybe? But what would she be doing in a darkened bedroom? Oh god. Casey's body grew rigid as she tried to figure out what to do. Should she head down the back lane and view the house from another angle? Should she charge up to the front door and start pounding?

A raindrop plopped on her forehead, then another. An ominous rumble filled the sky, followed by lightning. Cheyenne whimpered and pulled on the leash. The dog wasn't going to put up with a recon mission in wet, thunderous weather.

"Okay, girl. Let's go home." An impulsive act wouldn't help anyway. She needed to think through a strategy to find the truth about Summer's activities.

Picking up the pace, Casey barely made it to the end of the block before the deluge started. She and Cheyenne began to run. The only good thing about the weather was that fewer people would be out tonight, which could mean fewer problems for Lou.

Another lightning bolt made Cheyenne bark. Cheyenne couldn't get home fast enough. She raced up the back steps, whining and fidgeting until Casey opened the kitchen door. Fetching Cheyenne's towel, she soaked up the worst of the raindrops before they headed upstairs.

Inside her apartment, she peeled off the wet clothes, then checked her phone. A text message from Summer sent less than ten minutes ago said, *Change of plans. Gone to Theresa's. Bigger space.*

Interesting timing. Casey didn't know where Theresa lived, but since Summer's friends went to the same high school, it likely wouldn't be far from here. Not that this put Casey's mind at ease. Still needing a solid plan, she texted *OK*. Texting made lying far too easy.

. . .

Casey had dozed off in front of the TV when her phone rang. Calls at one-thirty in the morning were never good. At least Summer had come home just before her curfew and was safely in bed. Casey jolted upright and grabbed the phone. It was Lou.

"Are you all right?" she blurted.

"Yeah, fine. Thought you should know that Gwyn's office has been torched. I had to park the bus a block from the property. Fire department and cops won't let us in."

"Holy crap. Are the dispatchers okay?"

"They were evacuated before the smoke got too bad."

"Any idea how it started?"

"Looks like someone smashed his window and threw a Molotov cocktail inside. Cops found a ladder on the ground. Gwyn's here and he's pissed. Asshole's busy sharing suspicions about staff to the cops."

"Just great." Yet, Casey couldn't ignore the possibility that Gwyn might be right. Did an employee hate him enough to send a dangerous message?

EIGHT

"There's nothing in the budget for surveillance cameras, *period*, so get that out of your head." Gwyn Maddox glared at Stan and the rest of the security team seated around the conference table. "You people will have to patrol the premises from eleven till six in the morning, 24-7, understand?"

Casey shifted in her chair. The extra shifts didn't irritate her as much as Gwyn's condescension toward Stan. Her boss was too good at his job and too highly regarded by his team to be treated this way. Stan's stoic expression told Casey that he hated the idea of babysitting the building. She also knew he wouldn't argue about it in front of his team. The two newer part-time guards, Wayne and Zoltan, shifted uncomfortably in their chairs. Anoop Verma gazed at the table while Marie returned Gwyn's glare.

"There aren't enough of us to work graveyard shifts and the hot zone," Marie told Gwyn. "Isn't it cheaper to hire temporary guards than pay us overtime?"

Casey hid her smile. Bringing up the budget was poking the bear. Surely Marie could see that Gwyn's shiny bald head had already grown as pink as his round face; always a warning sign.

"That's an issue for me and Stan, thank you very much. And I expect a guard here tonight."

"What's your endgame?" Stan asked. "If you want prevention, then graveyard patrols might work, but if you want the suspect caught, then a guard's presence will only put him off."

"Catching him *is* prevention." Gwyn turned to the group. "Observing from darkened rooms in this building or sitting in one of the buses or your own cars should work. Call the cops when you spot someone behaving suspiciously. How hard can that be?"

Stan's mouth disappeared between his beard and mustache. Casey had lost track of the times she'd seen him press his lips together to keep from saying something he'd regret.

"Maybe the suspect won't be back," Marie remarked. "The point's been made, hasn't it?"

An even darker shade flooded Gwyn's face. "And what point is that, *Mizz* Crenshaw?"

Marie tucked strands of dark red hair behind her ear. "That someone doesn't like Mainland Public Transport very much."

Casey cringed. She could practically read the little bubble caption above Marie's head saying, "And You." Now would be a good time for her to shut up.

"Any idea who that someone might be?" Gwyn's blue-green eyes glittered.

"No."

"Are you sure?"

The only sound in the room was traffic noise on the other side of the window. Casey could almost feel the old grudges surface between those two. After learning of Marie's role in the unionization bid, Gwyn had suspended her for a short period. She doubted that Marie had forgiven him for it.

Leaning back in the chair, Marie crossed her arms under her ample boobs. "Quite sure."

"Gwyn and I discussed the possibility that the culprit might be the same guy who went after Benny," Stan said. "Maybe one of those punks from the riot."

Casey's eyebrows rose. Did they really think that a maniac with a knife came to Burnaby to toss a Molotov cocktail through the president's window? As much as she hated to admit it, a disgruntled employee—or ex-employee—was the likeliest candidate. It was no accident that Gwyn's was the only office set ablaze. If a current employee was responsible, no one would turn him in, not with the strong camaraderie among staff, and the *us versus him* mentality.

"I didn't get a chance to talk to Wesley and Ethan when they pulled in last night," Gwyn said to Casey. "Ask them if they saw anything. Ethan's working again this afternoon, so he should be here shortly." He stood. "I'm late for a meeting with the damn insurance adjuster."

Gwyn marched out of the room, slamming the door shut.

"Gee, I can't imagine why anyone would want to torch Gwyn's office," Marie remarked.

The part-timers snickered. Anoop barely smiled.

Stan didn't smile at all. "I need a volunteer for tonight, or should I just assign one of you? You'll be paid above the usual rate."

"I'll do it," Anoop offered.

"Thank you."

At six-foot-two and a little on the stocky side, Anoop Verma would be an imposing figure were it not for the glasses and self-deprecating manner. Anoop was a sweet man who had a wife and child to support, and a post-secondary education to finish. He rarely turned down a chance to earn extra cash.

"I'll come up with a schedule shortly," Stan said.

He left the room, leaving the others to wonder who would be stuck with the graveyard shift after Anoop. Zoltan and Wayne didn't look happy. Wayne was a retired custodian who simply wanted to earn a little extra cash. Nineteen-year-old

Zoltan had worked at a gas station before he got this job, and had no clear career aspirations that she knew of. Given his overall apathy and laziness, Casey figured he wouldn't last here much longer.

Following the group out of the conference room, she inhaled the lingering stench from last night's conflagration. The conference room was midway between the security department at one end and Gwyn's office at the other. Near Gwyn's office, a stranger jotted notes on a clipboard while Gwyn stood nearby. Casey headed downstairs and strolled beside Marie toward the lunchroom.

"Think a coworker started the fire?" Marie murmured.

"Don't know."

"I'd be careful about questioning people." Marie glanced up and down the corridor. "What with the attacks and the fire, some of them are paranoid."

"I'll go through the motions to keep Gwyn off my back, but I don't expect or want anyone to tell me a thing."

Marie moved closer to her. "What would you do if they did?"

"Don't want to think about it." And why was she asking?

"Best not to think about staff involvement at all. Remember what happened before." Without waiting for a response, Marie headed inside the locker room.

Right. Like she needed that warning. After a security team member was murdered nearly three years ago, Gwyn had ordered Casey to question coworkers. The tension she'd created among colleagues took a long time to dissipate. She'd worked hard to regain their trust.

Peering into the lunchroom, Casey noticed that every window was open, presumably to clear out the smoky odor that had found its way down here. She glanced at glum faces but didn't see Ethan among them. Casey continued down the corridor to view drivers' schedules posted on a board near the dispatchers' room.

She was studying Ethan's schedule when she spotted him stepping out of the men's locker room. Today his hair was tied in a single ponytail that trailed down his back and swung slightly as he marched to the exit.

"Ethan!" Casey jogged up to him. "How's it going?"

"Shitty."

Casey followed him outside. "What's wrong?"

"I've got two gigs this weekend, which I booked off weeks ago, but my stupid supervisor's making me work Saturday night."

"I'd ask Lou to cover for you, but he's already scheduled to drive."

"I know, but thanks." Ethan put on his sunglasses. "Why can't they respect our schedules?"

"After what happened to Benny, there's been a shortage of drivers. Too many sick calls."

"Don't blame 'em for calling in sick. Any idea how Benny's doing?"

"I got in touch with his daughter Yvette this morning. He's out of intensive care and in a regular ward now."

"Benny's cool," Ethan said. "He trained me, you know."

"Me too. I used to be a driver."

"No shit?"

Casey smiled. "I had my security license before I joined MPT to drive."

"You drove? Why?"

"It was a break from security work, and my first husband was a driver here, so he encouraged me to give it a try."

"Didn't know you were married before."

"Practically out of high school, which was way too young. It ended over five years ago." She shrugged. "Anyway, I was working one night when a passenger came at me with a knife. Luckily, the defense training I'd taken kicked in, but the incident scared the hell out of me. I decided that drivers needed better protection, so I joined Stan's team and taught the drivers some self-defense techniques. Unfortunately, the program died when Gwyn decided that drivers would have to take it on their own time, without pay."

"That jerk has a lot to answer for."

"No argument here."

Ethan began strolling through staff parking. Casey walked with him, observing the far end of the admin building, where Gwyn's office was located. Other than the tape cordoning off that side of the building, she couldn't see any damage from this angle.

"Weird about last night, huh?" she said.

Ethan looked away, his jaw tightening. "Lots of weirdness happening lately."

"Did you arrive at the yard before or after the fire started?"

"About five minutes before it went up."

So he would have parked in the yard. "Notice anything strange?"

Ethan slowed his pace. "Now that you mention it, when I was getting off the bus I thought I saw someone over by the fence." He nodded toward the eight-foot-high wooden fence on the west side of the yard, separating MPT from a flooring warehouse.

Casey studied the trees and overgrown bushes shielding most of the fence. "Lots of hiding spots there."

She turned to the east side of the property, where a chain link fence paralleled the street. The sparse foliage offered few hiding spots.

"It was probably a moving branch," Ethan added. "There was some wind."

"Did you tell the police what you saw?" she asked.

"No. Like I said, I wasn't sure." He peered at her. "Gwyn thinks one of us torched his office, right? Who else would know where it is, or the best time to spray-paint the building without being seen?"

"Gwyn doesn't know any more than the rest of us. He's only guessing."

Ethan frowned. "The bad blood between him and drivers was obvious my second week here." He stepped onto the bus platform. "Time to roll. Try to make the gig, if you can, because I'll be there no matter what."

"Wish I could. Stay safe."

The adjuster, accompanied by Gwyn, stepped outside. Both men made their way toward the cordoned-off area. Casey was on her way inside when she caught sight of someone crouching down between the cars. What the hell? She glanced around. No one else was nearby. Taking cautious steps, she moved closer as a familiar face popped up.

"Lawrence?" She hadn't seen the Friends since that horrible night with Benny a week ago. "What are you doing here?"

He lowered his Nikon and adjusted his glasses. "We heard about the fire. I was hoping to take a photo."

"Shouldn't you be at school?"

"Dentist appointment. I'm going back after lunch."

"You aren't going to post those pictures on social media, are you?"

"Only on our private Facebook group. No one else can see them."

"Are you sure?"

"Hedley started the group and keeps it protected." Lawrence pointed to the pale blue van parked on the side street. "He gave me a ride."

Craig Hedley leaned against the van and waved at Casey, who returned the gesture. She had no idea why the guy preferred to go by his last name, but she did know why he stayed by the van. The kid was once caught wandering through the admin building. After that incident, Gwyn banned all Friends from the property. At least Hedley respected the rules.

"The arsonist could be one of the haters on Facebook," Lawrence said. "Have the police identified them yet?"

"No idea." Casey watched Gwyn and the adjuster turn the corner and head down the side of the building, out of sight. "You know you're not supposed to be on the premises, especially when the president's here."

"Sorry," Lawrence mumbled. "But this is an unusual moment in MPT's story that's worth capturing."

"I didn't realize we had a story."

"You do. It'll be legendary one day."

"If you say so. Come on." She escorted him to the sidewalk.

"Hi," she said to Hedley. "Heard you're in college now. What are you studying?"

"Kinesiology."

"Cool. Are you working this summer?"

He nodded. "Teaching fitness programs at kids' camps and a couple of adult spin classes."

"So, you're getting paid for working out. Lucky you."

He grinned. "It has its perks."

Hedley's closely cropped hair was much shorter than she remembered. Those green eyes were as vivid as ever, and the athletic build hadn't changed.

"Brutal about the fire." Hedley peered at the building. "Any idea who did it?"

"Not yet." Even if she knew, she wouldn't tell the Friends.

"You'll figure it out before the cops," he replied. "Word is you're a good investigator."

Whose word, she wondered, then decided she didn't want to know. "Thanks, but I don't think the cops want me doing their job. All we're supposed to do is patrol this building at night from now until the culprit's caught."

Hedley grinned. "Good luck with that."

"We could help keep an eye on things," Lawrence said. "All of us, except Travis, only live a few minutes away, and school's nearly done for the year."

Hell no. She wished she hadn't said anything. It'd be safer if these kids weren't anywhere near the area.

"I appreciate that, but we've got it covered. Besides, your grad celebration's this weekend. Have fun and forget about all this for a couple of days."

Seeing Lawrence's hesitant nod, Casey wondered if he'd take her advice.

NINE

Casey shivered on the M28 bus. The wind and rain had created an unusually low temperature this last Saturday in May. In fact, it seemed to have dropped a little more every hour. Poor Anoop was working the graveyard shift at MPT again. No one could fault him for wanting to stay inside as much as possible.

"Wesley, can you turn the heat on?"

"Come on, Casey. It's not that bad in here."

Enormous guys like Rude Wesley Axelson didn't feel the cold that normal human beings did. Nor did he care if security personnel froze their butts off. Rubbing her arms, Casey strolled closer to Wesley.

It was after eleven and most of the passengers were high school students on their way to After Grad parties. Although the overwhelming majority of kids were driven to and from events and a tiny number rented limos, some teens rode the bus. Tonight, a couple of girls were still in their fancy dresses and sporting backpacks that probably contained casual clothes for the After Grad party.

"Got a question for ya," she said to Wesley. "You were coming back around the time Gwyn's office was torched, right?"

"Yeah. Why?"

"See anything interesting?"

"A friggin' zoo. Firetrucks, cops, gawkers."

"Did you happen to notice if any of the gawkers seemed a little too interested or happy about the chaos?"

Wesley glanced at her. "Gwyn wants you questioning staff, huh?"

She'd learned not to underestimate him, so his response wasn't a surprise. "Not my idea, but if I don't Gwyn'll give me grief. He wants to know if you and Ethan saw anything."

"Tell the moron I didn't see nothin', which is true."

Wesley stopped to pick up a man wearing the typical jeans, dark hoodie, and ball cap worn by guys of all ages in Metro Vancouver. Keeping his head lowered, the passenger started down the aisle. It took Casey two seconds to recognize Hedley. What on earth was he doing here? Wesley turned in his chair and frowned.

"Problem?" Casey asked, half expecting him to ask Hedley to leave. Wesley didn't like the Friends, so they tried to avoid him.

"Thought I recognized that guy," Wesley mumbled. "Don't know from where, though."

While Wesley merged into traffic, Casey strolled down the aisle until she reached Hedley midway down, across from the exit.

She slid in beside him. "Didn't expect to see you two days in a row, and definitely not on an MPT bus."

"My van broke down after I saw you yesterday, but I'd already committed to helping Travis and his dad fix their deck."

"Sounds like it was a long day," she remarked.

He shrugged. "They bought a lot of beer and pizza, so not all bad."

Casey nodded. "You know that this driver's not a fan of the Friends, right?"

"That's why I pulled my hood up as soon as I saw him. Not my lucky night, nor yours, having to work on a Saturday," he said.

"It happens."

"With three security officers on duty and your supervisor driving the security vehicle tonight, MPT resources must be maxed out."

Casey studied him. "How do you know how many of us are working?"

"Felicity."

If she knew, then Del had probably hacked into their database to look at schedules. Gwyn would go ballistic if he found out.

"Have a good night," Casey said, and headed toward the back of the bus.

Wesley reached the next stop. The five teenage girls now boarding made Casey think of Summer. She'd not only finished all of her chores today but had been cheerful about it. Over a shared pizza, she'd babbled about Stacy's photoshoots and complained about her perfectionism. Summer had promised to help out Stacy again tonight, or so she said. Something about Summer's animated banter had been off, like she was working too hard to make Casey think everything was perfectly normal. What was normal, though? Casey removed her phone from her pocket and called her.

When she got voice mail, hope began to sink. Casey asked Summer to call her back. Ten minutes went by, then twenty. Casey tried again. Another voice mail. Damn it. Summer had an annoying habit of letting her phone battery die. It was the reason Casey had persuaded her to share Stacy's number in case of emergency. This might not be an emergency but it was close enough.

Hedley was now moving toward the back of the bus. He chose a seat across the aisle and only one row up from her.

It took four rings before Stacy finally answered.

"I've been trying to reach Summer," Casey said, "but her phone keeps going to voice mail. Could I speak to her please?"

"Um, she's in the bathroom."

Hardly convincing, but saying so wouldn't help. "Could you have her call me as soon as possible?"

"Sure." Stacy paused. "Is there a problem?"

Casey glanced at Hedley, aware that he was within earshot. "I'm not sure. Gotta go."

Man, she was getting tired of secrets, of not knowing nearly enough to keep her family and colleagues safe. Casey found herself staring at Hedley. The Friends were secretive about the way they monitored MPT and weren't forthcoming about what they did with the information they gathered. Maybe it was time to learn a little more about them.

Once again, Casey sat next to Hedley, noting the way his eyes widened. "How long have you been hosting the private Facebook group?"

He looked out the window. "A little over a year."

"What do you discuss?"

"Just the rides we've taken." He turned to her. "Why?"

"I've never minded the Friends' interest in us, but if MPT executives found out that you've been discussing details about the company's operation even on a private chat group, they'd be ticked."

The corners of Hedley's mouth twitched. She couldn't tell if he was suppressing a smile or a grimace.

"We won't." His smile broadened. "No worries."

But had they discussed MPT's operating procedures in the past? She'd heard that Stan and the VPs had recently met with IT experts to discuss upgrading encryption software, among other things. If they discovered that Del had been snooping through databases, the Friends could be in legal trouble.

"Given the nasty comments on MPT's page, it wouldn't surprise me if the police were already red-flagging all activity about the company," she said.

"They should," Hedley replied. "Lots of nastiness out there. God knows what could happen if some nut followed through on his threats."

Which worried her more than she wanted to say out loud. Casey stood and found a seat at the back, where she spent the next few minutes watching cheerful, animated high school students come and go. Despite the celebratory mood on board, Casey began to fume over Summer's lack of response to her call. What the hell was she up to? Casey called again. Still no answer. She rang Stacy's number. It went to voice mail. Avoidance wasn't going to cut it. She left a message.

"Do I need to contact your parents to find out what's going on, Stacy? Have Summer call me right now or I'll be at your door after my shift ends at 1:00 AM."

Thirty seconds later, Stacy's frantic voice was saying, "Don't talk to my parents! Summer's not here."

Big surprise. "Where is she?"

"I don't know, I swear."

She sounded too panicky to be lying. Casey covered her ear with her hand to drown out the exuberant high school chatter.

"Who's she with, Stacy?" No response. Casey's patience withered. "I don't want to send the cops to your house, but if you won't talk to me, then what choice do I have?"

"She's *fine*. She's with her boyfriend."

A quick intake of breath trapped the swear word in Casey's throat. "*What* boyfriend?"

"Summer'll kill me if I tell you, but please don't worry. He's a good guy who'll take care of her."

That made her feel so much better. "Is her boyfriend one of your brothers?"

"No! Listen, I've been trying to get her to tell you, but she's afraid you'll be mad. Please don't come to my house." Stacy hung up.

Holy crap. Bringing a boy home had never been a problem for Summer before. Granted, Casey despised last year's loser, Devon Price. So, what was wrong with this one? Was he a lot older? Some dope-head high school dropout? Was it actually possible that she'd hooked up with someone worse than Devon Price? Unless . . . Uh-oh. What if she'd given Devon a second chance? Summer couldn't possibly be that dumb, could she?

Anger coiled in Casey. She forced herself to calm down. This was not the time to lose her mind. Stacy had probably given Summer a heads-up by now, so why hadn't she called? Was she too busy with the boy? Oh lord, she didn't dare think about what they were doing right now.

Wesley stopped in front of a high school. The teens exited while adults wearing reflective vests and carrying flashlights stood on the sidewalk and at the drop-off area.

Casey's phone rang. Summer? Disappointment rippled through her. It was Stan.

"Adrianna's bus stalled near the Westwood and Lougheed intersection and she can't get it started. She's freaking out because a group of guys insist on boarding."

Casey glanced at Hedley, who was focused on his phone.

"Are they threatening her?" she murmured.

"Not sure. She pressed the alarm button and dispatch called the cops. Since no weapons are involved, I doubt they'll tear over there."

"After what happened to Benny, they'd damn well better."

"I'm on my way," Stan said, "but backup would be good if those guys get out of hand. What's your twenty?"

After Casey told him, he said, "Get off at the next stop. I'll pick you up."

"Has the mechanic been contacted?"

"Yeah, he's on his way."

MPT had one mechanic on call at night. Sometimes it wasn't enough.

Casey approached Wesley. "Let me off at the next stop."

After she explained why, Wesley said, "Adrianna shouldn't be driving out here in the first place, and you should be with her. Whose stupid decision was it to put you with me and not her?"

"First of all, there was another sick call and she was the only available driver. Second, Stan thought she'd feel better if he stayed nearby in the patrol car. She was fine with that."

"Doubt she is now," he muttered.

Casey sighed. "Yeah."

Within sixty seconds, she was sliding into Stan's vehicle. Rain had started to fall and was coming down harder than it had the night Benny was stabbed. She didn't think of herself as a superstitious person, yet this downpour felt like a bad omen. Tension overwhelmed any desire for conversation. Casey could feel her entire body clenching in anticipation of yet another bloody confrontation.

Adrianna's bus came into view. She was in the driver's seat but otherwise the bus appeared to be empty. Stan pulled up in front of the bus. On the sidewalk, a half dozen guys stood by the front entrance.

One of them was banging on the door. "Come on, lady! It's wet out here!"

The digital *Out of Service* sign glowed above the windshield. Adrianna, still as a statue, didn't look at the boys.

"Here we go," Stan mumbled, his face grim.

Casey stepped out of the car and slammed the door. She and Stan flashed their IDs as Stan identified himself. None of the boys were familiar.

"Sorry, guys. The bus broke down," Stan said. "Next one won't be here for forty minutes."

The kid who'd been pounding on the door scowled. "All we want is someplace dry till the next one gets here. Is that too much to ask? What's the big deal anyway?"

"Drivers don't have to admit anyone who makes them uncomfortable, and pounding on the door like that makes her plenty nervous. There's been a lot of violence against drivers lately."

"Well, it's not us," the kid shot back. "She's being paranoid."

"She's being careful." Stan glared at the kid. "The cops are on their way."

The kid sneered. "We're minors. They can't do nothin'."

Casey had had enough of smartass punks lately. "But we can."

"Like what?" The kid smirked. "Beat me up?"

"Take your photo." Casey raised her phone. "As soon as we post this, every MPT driver will refuse you access."

"Bullshit."

"Try TransLink," Stan remarked. "The park 'n ride isn't far from here."

"Screw you!" The kid sought his buddies for support, but they kept quiet. "Let's go," he ordered them.

The group tramped down the sidewalk. Adrianna opened the door for Casey who saw that she was shivering uncontrollably. With the bus not working, there'd be no heat at all.

Stan joined Casey on the bus. "They're leaving."

"Thanks."

"I've got an extra security jacket in the car," Stan said, "and I'll update dispatch. Back in a couple of minutes."

As he headed for the vehicle, Adrianna said, "Why is everyone so hostile these days?"

"Don't know, but I sure wish it would stop."

Adrianna's skittish demeanor wasn't helping things. Casey watched the boys continue west down the sidewalk. By the time she turned around, Stan was sitting behind the wheel of his car and a man was approaching him. Probably a passenger who wanted to know what was happening with the bus.

"I can't take this anymore," Adrianna mumbled. "One day some nut's going to kill one of us. Look how close Benny came. I should quit this stupid job."

"Please don't. We need you."

The tears in Adrianna's eyes weren't a surprise, but they were worrisome. She was in no shape to be driving this route, especially at night.

"If I hand in my resignation, maybe supervisors will finally respect my requests for safer routes," Adrianna said, staring out the window. She leaned forward and squinted through the rain-splattered windshield. "What's up with Stan?"

Through the blur of the downpour, Casey studied his car. The dome light was on and the car door open, but Stan was just sitting there. The man was gone.

Tucking wayward strands of hair behind her ears, Adrianna said, "Does Stan look slouched over to you?"

A chill washed over Casey. "Open the door!" She jumped off the platform and darted to the car. "Stan!" Blood was seeping through his shirt. "No!"

Stan groaned. "Didn't see . . ." He closed his eyes.

TEN

Sweat coated Casey's body as she applied pressure to Stan's wound. Oh god, could she keep him alive? Where was the damn ambulance? Short raspy breaths were all she could manage when she'd called 9-1-1. Even now, she inhaled and exhaled in stingy bursts, afraid of breathing too deeply, taking too much air from him.

"Help's coming," she murmured. "Keep fighting." Stan opened his eyes. His eyelids fluttered and closed as if exhausted by the effort.

Blood oozed between her fingers, dark and menacing in the vehicle's dim light. Adrenalin surged through her in a swell of anxiety. Nothing felt safe, or sane, or right. The sound of approaching sirens offered only some relief. She maintained the pressure on Stan's stomach, focusing on him completely until persistent taps on her shoulder and the word "Ma'am" caught her attention.

"We'll take it from here," the paramedic said.

Reluctantly, Casey let the woman take over. Cooling blood coated her hands, a droplet dripped from her fingertips onto the road. Someone handed her a wet wipe. She didn't have the energy to even look up and thank this person.

"Ma'am?" another voice asked. "Let's go onto the sidewalk."

She found herself gaping into the concerned face of an RCMP constable.

"Just like Benny," she mumbled.

His browed creased. "Can we start with you telling me who you are?" the constable asked, escorting her to the sidewalk.

"Casey Holland. I work for Stan Cordaseto, the man in the car." She glanced at the vehicle, where Stan was now hidden from view. "He's lost a lot of blood." She gaped at the bloodied wipe. "Seems I have it." She dropped the wipe on the ground.

"Can you tell me what happened?"

Although traffic was fairly light this late at night, the light had changed and the few vehicles passing by forced her to raise her voice. It wasn't easy. She felt woozy and was pretty sure her babbling wasn't making much sense.

"Perhaps we could speak inside the bus," he said.

Casey followed him onto the platform, aware that the rain had let up. Adrianna, seated in her chair, appeared almost green. She'd joined Casey at the car, but then screamed and ran off.

Adrianna wiped her nose with a tissue. "Is he alive?"

"Yes," Casey answered.

"Will he be all right?"

The million-dollar question. "Dunno." She slumped into a seat and turned to the constable. "I didn't see it happen." Casey told the cop everything she had observed, making her words clearer this time. "I can't even give a description of the suspect. All I saw was his back as he headed east."

"You said that it was just like Benny," the constable stated. "What does that mean?"

While Casey described the attack on Benny, the officer's eyes widened. "I was there that night, searching the area."

"I think it's the same suspect." She shook her head. "But why Stan? He's not a bus driver."

"We'll find out." The officer surveyed the area.

Casey hated that Lou was driving right now. Was he okay? Was the maniac on a tear, determined to hurt someone else tonight? The thought of this happening to him made her queasy.

"Casey?" Roberto de Luca stepped on the platform. "You okay?"

She shrugged. Roberto was a friend and MPT's best mechanic. "They've got you working on a Saturday night?"

"Yeah, I'm training Maurice."

The short and wiry Maurice stood outside the door, shuffling his feet and sucking on a cigarette. His jacket hood was pulled low over his forehead to escape the rain.

"Hell of a night for training," she murmured.

Roberto sat down and wrapped his arms around her.

"Can you tell me what you saw?" the constable asked, moving closer to Adrianna. "Any detail might help."

As Adrianna mumbled words too quiet to hear, Casey gazed out the windows, where blurred emergency lights flashed and strobed with the gaudiness of a fairground arcade.

"Stan's a strong guy," Roberto said, his tone calm and gentle. "He'll be fine."

"I'll hold you to that."

Images bounced around her head. Shock, she supposed, and the disturbing realization that someone was crazy or angry enough to stab MPT personnel in public. She peered out a window to see Stan being lifted into the ambulance. A sprinkling of people had gathered on the sidewalk. One of them was all too familiar. Why was Hedley here and how had he located them? The guy snapped a picture.

Casey sprang out of her seat and jumped off the platform.

"Hedley! Stop taking pictures!"

He turned. "It's just for Travis."

Casey's phone rang. Lou. "Are you okay?" she blurted.

"I was about to ask you the same thing," he replied. "Heard there's trouble. What's going on?"

She told him while watching the ambulance speed away. For a brief moment, it occurred to her that she should be riding with him, but she was too late. Roberto and Maurice were both outside now, searching for the cause of the mechanical issue.

"Shit, Casey. I'm so sorry. This is bad," Lou said. "Are you heading back to Wesley?"

"Probably." Stepping back inside the bus, she wiped the rain from her face.

"I don't want you walking alone. That knife-wielding freak's still out there."

"I'll ask one of the cops here to give me a lift."

"We'll talk when I get home. Stay safe, hon."

"You too." Casey slumped onto a seat next to the constable, who was again writing notes. "I should call Stan's wife."

"Mr. Cordaseto's wife is being contacted," he answered. "He gave the paramedics his number."

Casey looked up. "If he was still conscious, then that's a good sign, right?"

The constable hesitated a fraction too long. "I'm sure it is."

"I still don't understand how this happened," Casey said. "Stan's always alert. The suspect must have struck incredibly fast. He sure did with Benny."

"The area's being searched right now," the constable replied.

Casey sighed. She had a feeling they wouldn't find him. "I need to get back to the bus I was working on. Is it possible for someone to drive me?"

"I can do that. Just give me one more minute."

She checked her watch. "Adrianna, do you want to come with me?"

Sad dark eyes turned to her. "I'd better. Looks like Roberto will be a while."

Casey's phone rang again. This time it was Marie, who was riding with Lou.

"How bad is Stan?" she asked.

Marie's abruptness didn't surprise or bother Casey. She cared about him too. "He's conscious. Paramedics got to him fast."

"What the hell happened?"

Casey heard recrimination in her tone. Marie was wondering how an experienced security officer could let their supervisor be ambushed right in front of her. She'd been wondering the same thing, and probably would for a long time.

"I'll tell you everything later." Her voice cracked. "Can't right now."

"I get it, but it looks like you're now in charge of the team. A lot will be expected of you, and make sure the cops keep you in the loop."

In charge? Crap. Her phone beeped. "I've got another call coming in. We'll talk tomorrow."

"Count on it."

She winced at Rude Wesley Axelson's unnecessarily loud, "What the hell went on there?"

Despite his gruffness, Casey knew that he liked and respected Stan. After she supplied a quick update, she arranged to meet him at a specific bus stop in ten minutes.

The cop escorted her and Adrianna to the police cruiser. Adrianna climbed in the backseat and leaned her head against the window, closing her eyes. Casey wanted to do the same, but resting wasn't an option and wouldn't be for who knew how long? Working both her and Stan's job would be overwhelming, but she'd have to find a way.

Glancing down, Casey cringed at the sight of small splotches and speckles of blood on her bright yellow jacket. She took a deep breath, but it didn't ease the sick feeling inside. She needed to clear her head, calm down and think. She should call Stan's wife, Nora. If something terrible ever happened to Lou, she'd want a firsthand account. Only how could she tell Nora that she'd been only yards away and still hadn't protected him?

The officer let them wait in the vehicle until Wesley pulled up to the stop. Once settled inside the bus, Casey dialed Stan's home landline.

When Nora answered, Casey's mouth grew dry. "It's Casey. Sorry to call so late."

"It's okay, sweetie. I'm about to leave for the hospital. Tell me what you know."

Casey was amazed at how calm she sounded, but then Nora was a retired ER nurse. Forty years of experience wouldn't completely vanish, even for her husband.

After Casey provided the highlights, she mumbled an apology. "I should have paid closer attention. Maybe I could have stopped him."

"Or maybe you could have been killed. Now listen to me. It's better that you weren't too close, and you know how strong Stan is. He'll pull through and we'll both be at your wedding. It'll take a lot more than this for him to miss such a special day."

Casey choked out a thank-you as tears began to spill.

ELEVEN

From her third-floor suite, Casey peered out the bay window overlooking the front yard. The willow tree's draping branches obstructed much of her view of Napier Street, a view she'd scarcely stopped scanning for over an hour. Summer was ninety minutes past curfew and she'd just trashed the last of Casey's trust. Her anger was accompanied by the revelation that she wasn't particularly shocked about the missed curfew.

The attack on Stan had upset Casey so much that she'd come home just after eleven instead of her usual time of 1:30 to 2:00 AM. On Saturdays, Summer was supposed to be home by midnight. No doubt she'd show up in a few minutes, and then what? Casey's emotions were running too high and she wasn't sure she could rein them in. Her latest call to Summer minutes ago had ended in yet another voice mail.

"I want you to call me right now," Casey ordered. "I'm home and you're way past curfew."

Casey listened to her guinea pig Ralphie munch on a small piece of carrot. Aside from Lou's voice, it was the only comforting sound she'd heard all night. Cheyenne had fallen asleep by Ralphie's cage, and Lou would be home shortly. If Summer wasn't back by then there'd be hell to pay.

Lou had phoned her again a half hour ago to ask if she was feeling okay, to tell her how certain he was that Stan would pull through. But Lou hadn't seen the blood on her hands. He hadn't been there. She wanted to believe him, but . . . Stretching out on the window seat, Casey propped her back against the wall, dialed Summer, and left another message.

"If you don't call me back, I'll phone the cops." A lame threat. They couldn't do anything, but she wanted to say it anyway.

What if Summer wanted to call back but couldn't? No. That kind of thinking wasn't helpful. Anger and strategizing were better. If she could figure out who the boyfriend was, then it would at least answer one question. His name and number would be in Summer's phone. All she had to do was take a peek somehow.

Casey closed her eyes. Had it really come to this? She thought Summer had learned something after hanging with that petty criminal Devon Price. Maybe she had. Maybe she was making brand new mistakes.

A vehicle stopped out front. Casey opened her eyes and jumped to her feet to see a small black car idling in front of the house. The passenger door opened. A fairly tall, skinny guy hurried around the front and helped Summer out of the car. She couldn't see his face, just his short dark hair. Wait. Devon Price had a similar build, didn't he? She couldn't quite remember.

Casey bounded out of her apartment. Not wanting to wake the tenants, she left the hall light off and jogged down the carpeted steps, with Cheyenne scampering past her.

The deadbolt turned and Summer stepped inside. Cheyenne whimpered and did her happy dance, nudging Summer's hand with her nose.

"Shush," Summer whispered to Cheyenne, and closed the door.

"Hello, Summer."

Summer gasped, smacked into the wall and fell. Casey flipped on the light to find her on the floor, her raven hair in her face, a beer stench wafting around her.

Casey crossed her arms. "Why didn't you return my calls, and where the hell have you been?"

"My phone died. I was at a party and didn't know."

Casey fought to keep her voice hushed. "You're over two hours late for curfew."

"I am?" Summer swept her hair off her face to reveal smudged eyeliner and red lipstick. She struggled to her feet, reaching for the railing, and started upstairs.

"How much beer did you drink?"

"What?"

"I can smell it from here, Summer."

Her ward managed two more steps before she swayed and gripped the railing. "Whoa." The bags under her blue eyes gave her a haunted appearance. She groaned and climbed each step slowly.

Casey stayed close behind to make sure the kid didn't break her neck. "Stacy said you were out with your *boyfriend*. Who is he?"

Summer put her hand on her stomach. "I don't feel good."

"Don't care. You broke house rules and at least one law that I know of. Give me a name."

"He's just a friend. Not a boyfriend."

Casey's patience unraveled a little further. "What is the *friend's* name?"

Summer groaned again and continued up the stairs. Casey's neck and shoulders tightened. "You're grounded for three weeks."

"Not fair!"

"Show me your phone."

"No! Oh god. I'm gonna puke."

"Then get upstairs."

Summer picked up the pace and rushed into her bedroom. Within seconds, came the sound of well-deserved retching.

Casey sat on the bed and waited. Lou appeared in the doorway, lunch pail in hand, his jacket tossed over his shoulder.

Heavy-lidded eyes peered at her. "What happened?"

The more Casey explained, the more annoyed he looked.

"You think grounding her for three weeks will help?" The weary lines on his brow lengthened.

"It was all I could think of." What else was she supposed to do, and why debate this right now? "We've both had a long night. Let's figure it out tomorrow. I'll be up shortly."

Casey heard his footsteps pound the staircase while more retching noises came from the bathroom. Should she have dealt with Summer differently? How? What could she possibly do to fix this?

Summer finally emerged, her head lowered, her eyes partially closed as she shuffled to her bed and collapsed.

"Drink lots of water and take a couple of Aspirin," Casey said, glancing at the clothes littering the floor. "I expect you to clean this messy room tomorrow and do your laundry."

"Why are you being so mean?"

"Because you put your health and safety at risk, and you hid your *friend* from me."

Summer draped her arm over her forehead and eyes. "You'll hate him before you get to know him."

"You're not giving me a damn chance!" Casey shot back. She waited for Summer's response, but none came. "Tomorrow's Sunday, which means your mom will call. One of us will have to tell her about this."

"Who's she to judge me?" Summer propped herself up on her elbow, her face twisted with disdain. "What she did was a lot worse than anything I've ever done!"

Where on earth did that come from? "You never used to think that way."

"I was eleven when she went to prison. I'll be fifteen in two months." Summer scowled. "You expect me to think the same?"

Casey had no answer for that. Summer's attitude toward her mother had been an emotional pendulum. Sometimes she missed Rhonda terribly. Other times anger and resentment took hold, but usually not to this degree. What if the animosity became permanent? Did Summer hope to lessen the pain of missing her by staying angry? Casey shook her head. She lacked the energy or desire to start a lengthy discussion about Ronda.

"We'll talk about this tomorrow."

"Whatever."

Casey left the room. Summer's issues wouldn't be resolved in one conversation. But before this weekend was over, she would learn this so-called friend's name one way or another.

TWELVE

Casey trudged upstairs to the security department. For the first time in ages, there'd be no Monday morning meeting with Stan. Ordinarily, the department's administrative assistant Amy would prioritize the week's tasks, but she was still away.

Catching up on work here yesterday afternoon had seemed like a good idea, given that no admin personnel worked Sundays, but there'd been a bombardment of emails and voice mails asking about Stan. She'd responded only to the security team, telling them that Nora was certain Stan would be okay. Better not to reveal the rest of their conversation.

"I don't want to worry you," Nora had said, "but Stan could start thinking about retiring after this."

"I understand," was her numb reply. Would she even want to work here without him?

Entering the security area, Casey was startled to see that Stan's office door was open. When she left yesterday, she'd made sure she locked it. As Casey drew closer, she heard typing. She poked her head inside and saw Gwyn. Right. Made sense. He had a master key to everything. Gwyn had called her early yesterday morning, demanding a full description of the attack and that she complete the incident report by Sunday afternoon.

"About time you got here," he grumbled. "I need you to handle some things."

Casey wanted to reply that this was her usual time, then thought better of it. "Sure."

"Stan's phone messages." Gwyn handed her the old-style, pink message slips that Stan and Amy still used. "I pulled the ones I'll deal with."

Casey flipped through the first few. "Do you want me to go through his emails too?"

"Already have. I forwarded you a bunch, and don't delete them. I want Stan to see everything when he comes back."

Barely listening to Gwyn prattle on about other tasks, Casey noticed that his dress shirt seemed too tight for him. His neck had all but disappeared beneath that big bald head. The weight gain had happened quickly. Her eyes widened as Gwyn slurped from Stan's *Old Fart, Big Heart* mug. How dare he use Stan's personal mug! She'd given it to him for Christmas a few years back.

"What with all the work on your plate," Gwyn droned on, "you should cut your evening shifts to just one a week. Have Marie and Anoop pick up the slack, and make sure you send the timesheets to payroll by deadline."

"Of course." He probably didn't know that she'd been helping Stan with timesheets for ages.

"The police sent more footage from the riot, which I've also forwarded to you. Study every frame and see if any of those shit-disturbers have been on our buses since that night. For all I know, one of them could be the maniac running around trying to kill my employees and burn my bloody office. Let me know what you find before the day's over."

Casey still wasn't convinced that the same man was responsible for the fires and the stabbings. "Two of them were spotted on Benny's bus, which was reported to the police."

"I know that, but I'm looking for more." Gwyn's hazel eyes flared and his complexion darkened. "I want every one of those bastards nailed, and if you can't do it, I'll find someone who can."

What was she supposed to do? Snap her fingers and make the bad guys magically appear?

"The police are on this, Gwyn. I'm doing two jobs as it is, and they have more time and resources."

"Regardless, take a few minutes at lunch to question staff." He straightened his crimson tie. "Look, Casey, I haven't had a single report from you. Have you even questioned drivers yet?"

She sighed. "I spoke with Ethan and Wesley, and they didn't see anyone. There was nothing to report."

"Not good enough." His eyes glowered. "You need to help find who's behind this, and if you're not interested in doing so, then maybe you should rethink your future here."

A second veiled threat to get rid of her. Was this jerk looking for an excuse? It was obvious that Gwyn had never liked her, but he was beginning to sound determined. If that was true, she had no intention of making it easy for him.

"I have a meeting in a few minutes." Gwyn swiveled back to the computer screen. "Keep this door locked when I'm not around."

"Of course." Casey stared at the man. Wasn't he going to ask for an update on Stan's condition or suggest sending flowers? "Nora said that Stan's going to be okay."

"I know." He tossed her an irritated glance. "Anything else?"

"No." Asshole. She charged out of the room, not bothering to shut the door.

Marie strolled into the office. The crow's feet around her eyes had deepened and her face was so pale that the freckles on her cheeks looked darker.

"What's the latest on Stan?" she asked Casey.

Casey highlighted her chat with Nora. "Gwyn wants you and Anoop to work more evening shifts while I do Stan's job."

"I'm already doing too many."

"I know. Take it up with the boss." She nodded toward Stan's office.

"Whatever." Marie went to her desk. "By the way, we were a half hour late getting in last night, so I'm adding overtime on my timesheet. Don't give me any grief about it."

"Are you always that bossy?" Gwyn entered the room and put on his jacket.

Furious eyes turned on him. "I just want what I'm entitled to."

"An ongoing theme with you." Gwyn headed for the exit. "Everyone needs to step up until Stan's back." He turned to Casey. "I want to see a revised work schedule before lunch." He glanced at Marie. "And I'll review all timesheets before you submit them."

He marched out of the security department, nearly smacking into Anoop who was on his way in.

"Just great," Casey muttered. "He's going to micro manage everything."

Even behind the glasses, Anoop's bloodshot eyes were hard to miss.

"Looks like graveyard's taking its toll," Marie said to him.

"I'm managing." He shrugged, turning to Casey. "Everything was quiet here last night."

"Good, thanks. I'm putting you back on the buses on evenings," Casey said. "Wayne and Zoltan can do graveyard patrols. I'll email you the revised schedule."

Anoop sighed. "Thanks."

"The rookies won't like that," Marie said.

"I know, but Gwyn expects more from all of us."

Casey sat down and got to work. After thirty minutes of struggling to prepare a schedule that would meet their needs and Gwyn's demands, she had to face reality. There simply weren't enough security people to go around.

In desperate need of a break, she switched to the camera footage Gwyn wanted reviewed. Surprisingly clear images showed a large placard being thrown at a crowd of anxious people scurrying out of the park. She figured that the bonfire and subsequent brawl had already begun at that point.

The sound of exploding firecrackers made some people scream. Parents carrying small children began to run. Judging from the angle, the camera was situated at the SkyTrain station near Town Center Park. Casey frequently stopped the footage to study faces. None were familiar.

When the footage ended, she opened the second attachment to find herself looking at Glen Drive, just a few yards east of her and Wesley's location that night. Casey scanned the crowd until a young woman's raven hair caught her attention. She sat forward and zoomed in, then took a quick intake of breath. Summer! She remembered Lou saying that he thought he'd seen her there. Casey zeroed in on the guy who had his arm draped over Summer's shoulder. Oh hell. Bloody Devon Price, and he was chugging a beer.

"For shit's sake!"

"What?" Marie asked.

Casey swiveled her chair around and looked from her to Anoop. "Summer was at the riot with her old boyfriend, Devon Price. She's right there on the footage!"

"Isn't that the kid who made trouble for us a while back?" Marie asked.

"The one and only." Devon's deceit and manipulative streak probably hadn't changed. "Which one of them should I kill first?"

"My daughter's only three." Anoop gave her a weak smile. "Not my area of expertise."

"I appreciate the sentiment," Marie said, "but you'll need a less volatile way to handle this."

"I can't believe she'd go out with that idiot again after the way things ended."

"Hate doesn't always last," Anoop offered.

"He's right," Marie added. "Tread carefully. If you trash him, Summer'll just dig in and rebel."

Marie would know. Two of her three kids were teenage girls and, based on her stories, already a handful.

"Has Summer been behaving differently?" Marie asked.

Casey hesitated before nodding. "She's been uncharacteristically cheerful and leaving the house all dressed up, supposedly to do a photoshoot for a friend's photography class."

Marie grinned. "You bought that?"

"I have my gullible moments, especially when it comes to parenting." Casey paused. "Summer came home drunk Saturday night, so I grounded her. She's been sulking ever since."

"You realize that won't stop her from seeing him, don't you?"

"I'm not that naïve." Casey sighed. "I made her talk to her mother yesterday."

Marie paused. "How'd that go?"

"Not well."

Summer had yelled, "You don't get it! This is all your fault!" to Rhonda. She'd then run out of the room, crying. When Casey picked up the phone, Rhonda was also crying and mumbling, "I don't know how much more I can take." Casey tried to reassure her that she and Lou would deal with this, but Rhonda sounded skeptical.

"Summer refused to give either of us the boyfriend's name," she told Marie. "I wanted to grab her phone and look it up, but it would have made things worse."

"Damn right it would have. You've got to be the grownup here, Casey."

Yeah well, that was getting bloody hard. With Devon back in Summer's life, what was she supposed to do? He must have just turned sixteen and acquired a learner's driving permit. Drivers with the mandatory L symbol on their vehicles weren't supposed to be on the road after midnight. If Casey caught him breaking that rule again, she could have his license suspended. But there'd be repercussions.

She continued playing the footage until Summer and Devon disappeared down a side street. The footage ended. Casey sat back in her chair and shook her head as Anoop handed her his timesheet.

"I gotta get more sleep. Only caught an hour before I had to take the kid to preschool and drop the wife off at work."

"Okay, and thanks."

Casey opened the final attachment. Slowing the action down, she watched looters charge inside a jewelry store just as someone fell. Oh god, was he the stabbing victim? Zooming in as far as she could, she saw a man dressed in black right behind him. The ball cap covered his forehead and shaded his eyes, but the jaw stubble was evident. She'd bet her life savings that this was the same person who stabbed Benny and Stan. His average height and build were just as witnesses described. Except for the stubble, there was nothing distinguishable about this man. The suspect turned and pushed through the crowd, then vanished around the corner.

Casey stared at the now frozen image. Why had he chosen that individual? What, if any, connection was there between this victim and her coworkers?

. . .

Gwyn charged into the security department, yelling into his phone. "I told the guy we'll pay him next month! If he keeps harassing us, then change suppliers."

He stomped into Stan's office. Bracing herself, Casey entered a minute later, to find him dabbing his brow with a handkerchief. Gwyn was the only man she knew under age seventy who used handkerchiefs. But a lot about Gwyn was a throwback to earlier times. He also believed that men made better security guards than women.

"I've brought you the revised schedule." She placed it on the desk. "Also reviewed the camera footage and saw something interesting."

As she told him about the victim and the man in black, Gwyn said, "He sounds crazy enough to torch my office."

"Or he could have nothing to do with what's happening here."

"For crying out loud, how many enemies do we have?"

A question Casey couldn't answer and definitely didn't want to discuss with him.

"I'll talk to the RCMP about a connection between the rally victim and the attacks on our people," he went on.

Casey hurried out of the room before Gwyn could dump more work on her. She wished she could discuss theories and motives with Stan. She could use his advice about Summer too. God, what would Lou say about the reappearance of Devon Price? Since Lou was home and Summer was at school, she might as well get this over with.

The second Lou answered the phone, she started talking.

She'd barely finished before Lou interrupted with, "How could she do that to us? Haven't we treated her with respect, put our trust in her?"

Casey let him rant. He had the right to be upset.

"I'll talk to her when she's home from school," Lou said.

"Wait till I get there, okay? We'll do it together. But there's something else we need to do first."

"What could be more important than that?"

A cooling-off period, for one. "A trip to the hospital. I need to talk to Stan. Since Benny's in the same ward, I thought you could come along." She listened to the silence, well aware that Lou loathed hospitals.

"Yeah," he said, his tone quiet. "I should see Benny."

"Pick you up in a half hour." Casey ended the call before he could change his mind.

THIRTEEN

For one reason or another, Casey had found herself inside three different hospitals in recent years, as visitor and patient. Unwanted images of last year's hospital stay after that psycho attacked her still flashed through her brain at times. Months before that, she'd been visiting her best friend, Kendal, who'd nearly died after an unexpected encounter with an enemy. And now Benny. Small wonder she felt uneasy here.

Lou did too. He gripped her hand and glanced up and down the corridor, as if in search of an escape route. The prospect of facing a seriously injured friend who was more of a father figure to him than his own dad had definitely ramped up his anxiety.

"It'll be okay," she murmured.

Lou's Adam's apple moved up and down. "I've heard he's not in good shape, mentally and physically."

"He will be. We just have to give him time." When they found Benny's room, she noticed Lou's cheeks turning red. "It's okay, Lou. I'm sure Benny won't expect a long chat."

Lou stood at the threshold. "Coming in?"

"Not yet. I need to see if Stan's alone and up for a chat. If he is, I'd better speak to him now before others show up."

Lou looked inside, then stepped back. "The beds are full," he mumbled. "Everyone seems to be sleeping."

"Maybe just dozing." She gently placed her hand on his arm. "Why don't you check on Benny. I won't be far away."

"Yeah." He swept his bangs to the side. "I can do this."

"See you in a bit."

Two doors down, Casey entered a room devoid of visitors. All four beds were occupied. The senior across from Stan was snoring. An elderly woman occupied the bed next to the snorer and stared at Casey with dull, hooded eyes.

Stan appeared to be the youngest patient in this room. Only now did she realize how white his beard had grown. After this disaster, would he actually consider retirement?

He looked up from his magazine and removed his reading glasses. "Ah. News from the front line. How goes the battle?"

"Lousy. How are you doing?" She pulled up a chair and sat down. "Nora says you're going home soon."

"Tomorrow, thank god."

"Excellent." She paused. "What about work? When will you be coming back?"

Stan smiled. "Gwyn's been that much fun, huh?"

"I truly want to strangle the man."

Stan's chuckle became a grimace. In a flash, he was smiling again, as if eager to convince her that he was perfectly fine.

"What's he done?"

By the time she finished, she was embarrassed "I sound like a whiny kid."

"With good reason. Gwyn has no business threatening your job like that. I'll have a word."

"Think he'll listen?"

Stan didn't answer right away. "I won't give him much choice."

"I didn't come by just to whine."

"I know that. So, what's up?"

Casey told him about the film footage. Evidence that he, Benny, and the riot victim were stabbed by the same individual.

"Gwyn said he would discuss it with the police, but I need to ask if you got a look at the suspect's face?"

Stan shook his head. "Just stubble and dark eyes, and I think he wore a black hoodie. Could be the same guy. Oh, and I remember bad breath and a funky smell, like he hadn't washed his clothes in weeks."

"Have you compared notes with Benny?"

"We talked briefly yesterday." Stan adjusted his blanket. "He doesn't recall much and I'm not sure he wants to." He paused. "Benny's in rough shape. Not himself."

She nodded, imagining how Lou must feel right now. "It's probably temporary. What with the surgery and everything, he's experienced a lot of trauma."

"All I know is that our jovial, easygoing coworker is now a frightened, disoriented victim." Stan lowered his gaze. "He kept rambling about how hard things have been since his wife died. Truth is, Casey, I'm not sure he'll be back."

She shook her head, scarcely able to grasp this possibility.

"MPT without Benny would be awful. No one else has his patience."

"I remember when you first trained as a driver. That was a special challenge for Benny," Stan said with a wink. "Hitting Gwyn's car on your way out of the yard was epic."

"I'll never forget it."

Gwyn had wanted to fire her on the spot, but Benny persuaded him to give her a second chance.

"Gwyn doesn't think I could ever do as good a job as you." Casey didn't add that she feared he was right. "I'm beginning to wonder if he not only expects me to fail but is setting me up to do exactly that so he can finally get rid of me."

"It won't happen."

"I'm not so sure." She paused. "I've already been suspended once. Remember my altercations with those twin teenage girls on the Granville Street route? Wouldn't surprise me if Gwyn's been keeping a list of all my transgressions."

"Don't worry, kiddo. I've got your back. Gwyn knows how much I depend on you. He's just in a weird state of mind right now. Worried, distracted, and paranoid. Doubt he means half of what he says."

"Thanks for saying that." Her face grew warm because she knew he meant it. "Has Gwyn come by to see Benny?"

"Just drivers and his kids, as far as I know. Man, his boys are one giant pain in the ass."

"What's happened?"

Stan glanced at the door. "A couple of days ago, the kids got into a shouting match in Benny's room. I could hear them from here. The nurse had to call security."

"What was the yelling about?"

"The boys wanted money but their sister said she'd given them enough."

"Poor Benny," Casey murmured. "Lou's with him now. I should pop by and say hello."

As Casey stood up she considered asking for advice about Summer, but Stan already looked worn out from talking.

"Keep me posted," he said. "My phone's here."

"Will do, and come back soon."

"That's the plan," he replied, "and try not to brood over Gwyn. I know you're doing a great job."

While she appreciated his confidence in her, Casey couldn't shake the feeling that she was letting him down. She wore this feeling with about as much comfort as a cold, wet scarf around her neck. Stan had to come back.

Casey said goodbye and left the room, her trepidation about seeing Benny escalating. She found Lou standing by Benny's bed. Drawing closer, Casey noted the bruises on Benny's face. His right eye was discolored and swollen. She hadn't realized how much of a beating he'd taken. The thought that this might have been payback for Wesley's behavior at the riot made her sick. She stifled her rising anger.

"Has he been asleep the whole time?" she whispered.

"He was awake for a couple of minutes." Lou's somber face turned to her. "Said something about being lost at sea."

"Did he mention his assailant?"

"I asked. That's when he started babbling about the sea."

"Who are you?" a voice demanded behind them.

Casey turned to see a younger version of Benny. Benny's youngest child had grown taller since she last saw him.

"You don't remember us, Reese? We've met at your dad's Boxing Day parties, though I think it's been about four years since we last saw you," she answered. "We're Casey and Lou from MPT."

The frown relaxed only a fraction. "Right. Well, don't expect him to go back to work."

Casey stared at the kid. No point in telling him that Benny liked his job and had tons of friends there. "Has your dad been able to talk about what happened?"

"Nah. Just says crazy shit."

Casey waited for Reese to elaborate but he didn't. "Even what sounds crazy could be a clue."

Reese scratched his cheek. "He was going on about a man in black and a green freak. Probably thinking about those dumb superhero movies he always watches. Probably expected to be rescued by one of 'em."

"That's not true," a woman said, entering the room.

Although it had been only a couple of years since Casey last saw Benny's daughter, Yvette looked much older than she recalled. No surprise, under the circumstances.

"Hello, Yvette," Casey said.

"Casey! Good to see you again." Yvette gave her a hug and turned to Lou. "Hi, Lou."

He nodded. "How're you holding up?"

"As best I can. You being here will mean a lot to Dad. Just before this nightmare happened, he told me how much he was looking forward to your wedding."

"It's still a month away," Lou said. "We're counting on him being there."

"I'm sure he will be." Yvette moved closer to Benny and leaned over. "How are you doing, Dad?"

"How do you think?" Reese snapped at her.

She spun around and glared at her youngest brother. "If you can't be more positive, then don't come by."

"Don't tell me what to do!"

Gaping at the kid, Casey felt Lou squeeze her hand, a warning to stay silent. Sometimes, he knew her too well. The patient across from Benny shifted in her bed and moaned softly.

"Keep raising your voice like that and you'll get kicked out again." Anger swept through Yvette's hushed tone. "You're here only for money anyway."

"I told you, we're almost out of food."

"Then stop buying takeout and start cooking. You won't get any more until Friday. If you want more, then get a job."

"Screw you." Reese stormed out of the room.

Yvette let out a long sigh and rubbed her forehead. "Sorry about that. My brother doesn't handle stress well, so he's nastier than usual. Dad's situation has brought out the worst in all of us, I'm afraid."

And clearly exposed some unresolved issues. "I understand," Casey replied. "This has to be incredibly tough on your family."

"Tough would be an understatement."

"Any word on Benny's progress?" Lou asked.

Yvette hesitated. "Dad's not healing as fast as they hoped. He's also having trouble dealing with reality."

"Yeah well, reality's a little ugly right now," Casey said. "My supervisor was also attacked. He's just two doors down."

"I heard, and that's terrible." Yvette hesitated. "There are rumors that the same man is responsible for both stabbings."

"Did the police tell you that?" Casey asked.

"Good lord no. They're not telling us anything. Dad's coworkers told me." Yvette watched her. "Have the cops said anything to you?"

"They're keeping us out of the loop," Casey answered, "which is beyond irritating."

Benny groaned. The undamaged eye opened partially.

"Hi, Dad."

"Yve?"

She placed her hand on his shoulder. "Are you feeling okay?"

He mumbled something Casey couldn't hear.

"Lou and Casey are here," Yvette said softly. "Do you want me to raise the bed?"

Benny barely nodded. While Yvette adjusted the bed, Casey glanced at Lou's pensive face.

"Hey, Benny," Casey said, grateful for the flicker of a smile.

"Haven't missed your wedding, have I?"

Lou smiled. "No. There's still plenty of time."

"Marriage is good," Benny murmured. "My wife was amazing." His voice quivered.

"It's okay, Dad." Yvette took his hand and stroked his head.

Casey edged closer. "Benny, do you remember anything about the man who attacked you?"

He nodded slowly. "Crazy eyes, like he wanted to kill me."

Crazy eyes? Like the goatee thug? "Did he have facial hair?"

Benny took his time answering. "Stubble, and B.O. Thought he was homeless."

Casey glanced at Lou, who raised his eyebrows. "How old would you say he was?" she asked.

Benny's eyelids began to droop. "Late thirties. Maybe older."

"Dad's tiring," Yvette said. "Maybe it's time to stop."

"Just one more question." She kept her gaze on Benny. "Was he dressed all in black?"

"Yeah," Benny answered, grimacing.

The pain twisting his expression was hard to watch.

"Are your meds wearing off, Dad?"

"Yeah."

Benny's oldest son, Max, appeared at the end of the bed. He was short and pudgy like Benny, but his face was more square-shaped than his father's.

"What's going on?" Max asked.

"Get a nurse," Yvette said. "Dad needs medication."

Max hurried out the door.

"We should go," Lou murmured. "Take care, Benny."

"Benny, were you able to tell the cops any of this?" Casey asked.

"Think so."

"Thanks, Benny."

"That's more than he's shared with us," Yvette said to her.

"I'll see what I can learn from the cops. The homeless angle could be important," Casey answered. "Thanks for letting me talk to him, Yvette."

"Whatever it takes to catch the bastard."

Casey and Lou slipped out and started down the hall. She told Lou about Stan's description of his assailant.

"Has to be the same guy," Lou said.

She spotted Max at the nurses's station. Judging from his loud, annoying tone, the kid was demanding rather than asking for help.

"You'd think the cops would give us a heads-up about a smelly man dressed in black," Lou muttered. "Unless they told Gwyn and he didn't bother to pass it along."

"He might not have done that on purpose," Casey said. "Stan said the man's frazzled and preoccupied."

"After all the crap Gwyn's dumped on you," Lou shot back, "why stick up for him?"

"I'm not. It's just that Gwyn's not coping well with all that's going on."

"He's probably more upset about his property and MPT's reputation than he is about us. The man needs to be held accountable for his mistakes and shitty attitude," Lou replied. "I totally get why someone would torch his stupid office."

Whoa, that was harsh, but saying so wouldn't help anything.

"If Gwyn won't give the drivers a description," Lou added, "then I will."

He picked up the pace and charged down the hall. Casey jogged to keep up, praying he would calm down before they confronted Summer.

FOURTEEN

On the way home from the hospital, Casey drove while Lou called his supervisor to describe Benny's assailant.

"The drivers need to know," Lou insisted. After a pause he said, "Yeah, fine." He hung up. "Asshole didn't even sound that interested."

"I get why you're upset," Casey said. "Maybe I should talk to Summer alone."

Lou let out a heavy sigh. "Fine. You talk and I'll listen."

She preferred that he not be there at all.

"I don't think she'll be straight with us," he added. "What will you do if you catch Summer in a lie?"

"Call her on it."

Lou shook his head. "It feels like we barely know her anymore."

He was right, in a way. How had it come to this? Friends had warned her that parenting someone else's teenager would be difficult. But she loved Summer and Rhonda. Rhonda had been a better mom to Casey than her own mother. She'd done the right thing by accepting Rhonda's request to become Summer's guardian. Who knew that parenting would make her feel more inept than anything else she'd been through, including divorce?

Lou pulled up to the house. "She'd better be home."

Casey's stomach clenched as she stepped out of the car. Summer's grounding meant that she was supposed to come straight home from school.

"Bet she denies being at the riot until you tell her about the CCTV footage." Lou barely opened the kitchen door before Cheyenne bolted past him down the steps and onto the grass to pee. "Bloody great. She's not home."

Irritation flared inside Casey. Waiting for the dog to return, she checked her phone. No messages. Damn it. Cheyenne trotted back inside and followed them upstairs. Lou banged on Summer's bedroom door and stepped inside.

"What are you doing?" Casey asked. "We already know she's not here."

"Looking to see if she's run away."

Casey froze. It hadn't occurred to her that Summer would do that, and she'd never leave without Cheyenne.

Lou stomped into the bathroom. "Her toothbrush and makeup are still here."

Casey collapsed against the door with relief. Cheyenne picked up a toy and looked at Casey with large, hopeful eyes.

"Where the freakin' hell is she?" Lou checked his watch. "It's nearly five."

"I'll call her."

"You seriously think she'll answer?"

"Worth a try." She scratched Cheyenne's head. "Why don't you go outside and throw a ball around with Cheyenne for a bit. You both need to work off some energy, and you'll be able to tell if she's walking home or getting a ride from her mystery man."

Lou gazed at the dog. "Let's go, girl."

Cheyenne scrambled downstairs while Casey headed upstairs into their top-floor apartment. She needed to regroup, figure out how to keep things from exploding. Kicking off her shoes, she greeted her sleepy guinea pig, Ralphie, then strolled to the bay window. The afternoon sunlight was heating up the room. She opened the window and saw Lou and Cheyenne. She was opening the second window when a small black car pulled up in front of the house. Summer emerged and shut the door. The vehicle peeled away.

"Where have you been?" Lou yelled at her.

"Detention! Caught skipping the stupid math class again."

As Cheyenne bounded up to her, Summer opened the gate and marched toward the house.

"You could have called!"

"They took my phone till it ended." She jogged up the porch steps.

Casey dashed downstairs, wondering why she hadn't called to say she was on her way home. By the time she reached the main floor, Lou was following Summer into the kitchen.

"I saw Devon Price drop you off," Lou said. "How could you possibly take up with that loser again?"

Casey's throat tightened. He was making things worse.

"He's not Devon!"

"Don't lie to me!"

"I'm *not*!" She dropped her backpack on the floor.

"Stop it, both of you!" Casey shouted. "Everyone, calm down." She flashed a warning glance at Lou. "Summer, just tell us who he is."

She opened the fridge. "He's Tyler, Devon's older brother."

Lou's eyebrows shot up as he turned to Casey. She recalled that Devon had a brother and two sisters. "Why didn't you tell us this from the start?"

Summer pulled out a can of pop, then slammed the fridge door. "Because you'd assume he was like Devon, which he's not."

Casey fought back the urge to say that sneaking around and breaking the law was exactly like Devon.

"It's almost Cheyenne's suppertime." Casey noticed that the dog sat expectantly by her empty dish. "Lou, will you feed her, please? The water bowl needs filling too."

He scooped a cup of dry food out of the large bag in the corner.

Casey sat down. "How long have you two been seeing each other?"

"A few weeks. He goes to school and works part-time." Summer opened the can and took a gulp. "We don't hang out every day."

But they were close. At the riot, they'd had their arms around each other. "Why didn't you tell me you were at the riot a couple weeks ago?"

Summer's vivid blue eyes narrowed. "Were you spying on me?"

"Of course not." As Casey told her about the camera footage, Summer began to fidget. "Why didn't you want me to know you were there?"

"It was no big deal." She took another drink.

"It *was* a big deal, thanks to all the violence. You should have left at the first sign of trouble," Lou grumbled. "A lot of people got hurt."

"I wasn't."

"That's not the point."

Summer glared at him. "It *is*."

"Lou, I'd like to talk to Summer alone, please. Could you start dinner?" She didn't like the challenge on his face. "This is girl stuff," Casey went on, "talking about boy stuff."

"Whatever."

When he left, Casey said, "Is Tyler more honest than his brother?"

"Totally."

Was that true, though? "Do you enjoy hanging out with him?"

Summer gave her a sharp look. "I wouldn't if I didn't. I'm not a total loser, you know."

"I know that. I'm just trying to understand. Come sit down "

Summer hesitated, then did so. "He's fun, okay? Mostly we just hang out and do stuff."

"What kind of stuff?" Whoops. The blunt tone wasn't intentional.

Summer shrugged. "Swimming, dirt biking, rock climbing."

Not so bad then, if that's all they did. "Sounds like an outdoors guy. Quite different than Devon."

"Tyler doesn't steal or try to take my clothes off, if that's what you're worried about."

She was, but she wasn't ready to admit it. "Your mother will be calling again on Sunday." Sometimes the weekly phone chats felt more like obligation than desire, but without them there'd be no communication at all. "I'm sure she'd like to know about Tyler."

"She won't approve, and I really wish she wouldn't call." Summer raised the can to her lips. "I don't need criticism from a murderer."

Casey sat back, stunned. She'd never heard this much disdain for Rhonda. Part of her wanted to admonish Summer, but that would send her storming out of the room. After Rhonda's imprisonment, they'd talked a lot and leaned on each other, desperate to create a new normal routine. She and Summer used to enjoy an open relationship, but candid conversations had become less frequent as time passed.

"I don't remember you sounding this harsh before," Casey said.

"It's what I've been thinking for a long time."

Casey didn't quite know where to go from here. "You still love your mom, don't you?"

Summer's mouth trembled. "She's a nut job."

"Summer!"

"You know it's true!" She jumped to her feet. "If she was sane, she wouldn't have been locked up in the first place."

Yes, her crime had centered on an unhinged, violent act, but Rhonda had shown so much remorse that Casey's own anger had turned to sorrow, pity, and finally compassion.

"We both know how deeply she regrets what she did."

"Don't stick up for her," Summer shot back.

"And don't ignore the truth, or disrespect her love for you."

"Mom turned your life upside down and you still do whatever she asks like some kind of puppet. It's so lame."

Casey tried to quell her annoyance. "I do what your mother asks because you are her daughter and this is her home. Despite everything, Rhonda's family to me."

"Is the loyalty worth it?" Summer crossed her arms. "You're just filling in space till she gets back, right? The moment she's out of prison, you'll move on. Buy a house, have a kid."

Summer wasn't wrong, but the filling space remark hurt. "This isn't about me, it's about you, and if you don't tell your mother what's going on, then I'll have to."

"Go ahead, I don't care." Summer's deep blue eyes glittered. "But don't expect me to talk to her or apologize. And I won't stop seeing Tyler. You can't lock me away."

"I can extend your grounding and hire a babysitter."

Summer sneered. "Yeah. That'll work."

Tempted to use words that couldn't be taken back, Casey took a breath instead and forced herself to reel the anger in. She was the adult here. She needed to take the high road, but right now the high road was a tough climb.

"Summer, you're a minor driving around with a kid who only has his learner's license, so let me be clear." Casey took another breath. "If you ever get in that car again late at night, I'll call the cops and talk to Tyler's mother."

Summer's hands dropped to her sides and her mouth fell open. "You'd actually be that mean?"

Was that how she saw it? "I'm trying to keep you safe and out of trouble."

"Why don't you just chain me up!" Summer stomped down the hall, muttering to herself.

Adrenalin soaring and heart pounding, Casey trailed behind. Summer slammed her door shut. Casey paused, then continued upstairs where she found Lou leaning against the wall outside their apartment.

"I stayed at the bottom of the staircase," he said. "Heard most of it."

Casey's shoulders sagged. She stepped inside and shut the door. "Where did all the animosity come from?"

"Yours or hers, or should I say ours?"

She slumped into her rocking chair. "Point taken."

"Maybe we shouldn't overlook the obvious."

"Which is?"

"Summer's a hormonal fourteen-year-old who sees her mom differently than she used to. The humiliation of Rhonda's incarceration is one thing, but there're more complicated issues now. Face it, aren't most teenage girls an emotional mess anyway?"

"Not all of them and not all the time, but Summer's had self-esteem problems since Rhonda's imprisonment." Casey paused.

"I can't help feeling that something else is going on with her." Something she wished she could identify.

Ralphie whistled. Casey lifted her guinea pig out of his cage and hugged him close, relishing the comfort of this small, warm critter who wasn't angry about anything.

. . .

Music boomed from Summer's bedroom and Casey's heart thumped with every beat. The 11:00 PM news had just come on. Summer was up late for a Monday night. Damn it, she knew the rules about noise. If the music didn't stop by eleven, Casey would have to knock on her door.

She was almost glad Lou had been called to work at the last minute. He, too, seemed relieved to leave the tension in this house. Casey had sensed that there was more he wanted to say about Summer but hadn't. They'd scarcely spoken all evening.

A grim anchorman peered into the camera. "We have breaking news. There's been another stabbing incident in Coquitlam tonight."

Casey inhaled sharply and turned her attention to the TV.

"Police report that a woman walking her dog near the Coquitlam Mall was stabbed by an unknown individual at approximately nine-thirty. The suspect was spotted fleeing the scene but hasn't yet been apprehended. Police are not confirming if this is the same person who killed a spectator during the riot, or who might be responsible for two attacks on Mainland Public Transit employees. Other sources believe that this is the work of a serial killer some are calling the Blade Man."

Casey hit the mute button. Felicity was the only person she knew who'd made that reference. Had the girl contacted them or had they found her through social media? Lord, what else had she told them?

She massaged her tingling neck. It appeared that the psycho wasn't targeting just MPT personnel. Location was the common ground, not the people. The suspect probably knew every damn shortcut and hiding spot in the area.

Casey moved to the bay window. Was Lou okay? Thank god Marie was riding with him. Wesley Axelson was also driving in Coquitlam tonight, unaccompanied by security personnel, at his insistence. Glimpsing the night sky, she worried and wondered. And then she called Lou.

"There's been another stabbing," Casey blurted. "Just heard it on the news."

"I know. Had to make a detour earlier."

"Why didn't you call me?"

"You had enough on your mind when I left."

"Has Wesley had any trouble?"

"Not that I know of, which is more than I can say here."

Casey flinched. "Why? What's going on?"

"Your three high school admirers are here, peppering Marie with questions," Lou said. "She's about ready to throw them off the bus."

Casey smiled. "She'll survive, but don't let the kids off in that area. In fact, I want to talk to Felicity. Can you get Marie to put her on the line?"

"Both of them are on the phone, but I'll have Marie call you. Lou paused. "Listen, I overheard the Friends talking. Seems that their buddy Travis is discreetly helping Anoop survey MPT property tonight, although I doubt Anoop's aware of this."

"For crying out loud! And why is Anoop there in the first place? I assigned one of the rookies. I bet Gwyn intervened."

"Wouldn't surprise me. See you later."

"Stay safe."

Music still blared from Summer's room. The two tenants at the back of the second floor wouldn't be happy. Casey hurried downstairs. As she reached Summer's door, the music stopped. She waited a few seconds, then crept back upstairs in time to hear her phone ring. She grabbed the phone and saw Marie's name on the screen.

"Hi, can you put Felicity on the line?"

"Something more important's come up. Del just got a call from Travis who said there's just been an explosion at MPT."

"What? You're kidding, right?"

"I wish. You'd better phone Anoop."

"On it." Another call came in. Gwyn.

"I need you at MPT right now!" he yelled. "The goddamn garage just exploded. Your incompetent guard saw nothing, so I'm firing his ass as soon as I get there."

"Anoop wasn't supposed to be working tonight," she replied. "He's already worked five straight shifts. I gave you the schedule, Gwyn."

"I didn't change it, so obviously your team's making other arrangements behind your back. Get them under control, Casey, or else." He hung up.

Irritation and fear raced through Casey as she fetched her jacket and purse. She rushed out of her apartment, stopping outside Summer's door. Should she tell her that she was heading out? No. Bad idea. Summer might invite Tyler over. Casey tiptoed down to the main floor, set the house alarm, then dashed outside.

FIFTEEN

The commotion at MPT forced Casey to park three blocks away. The cops had erected roadblocks to keep spectators and vehicles out of the area, not that there were many people around after midnight. MPT's entrance was on a side street, off the beaten path from the busier Lougheed Highway that stretched through several municipalities in Metro Vancouver.

Hoofing it down the sidewalk on this cool and cloudy night, Casey shivered. She doubted it would rain. Normally, she smelled the dampness just before it came. Tonight, she smelled smoke. The closer she came to the property the stronger the smell.

Firefighters were spraying water on bright, crackling flames still spurting through the garage's dilapidated roof. Emergency vehicles cluttered MPT's yard, where many buses were already parked for the night. A handful of spectators had begun to gather. More appeared to be coming from the condo towers at the end of the side street. Some appeared to have flung jackets over their PJs and wandered over here in flip-flops or crocs. Others wore slippers, personifying Vancouver casualness for pretty much any incident or event.

Casey turned back to the garage. At least the cinderblock walls were intact, but what about the contents? She listened to occasional shouts from firefighters and cops. The controlled chaos was both mesmerizing and horrifying. She spotted Gwyn Maddox near the entrance to the yard, talking with a cop.

"I can't believe this is happening," Anoop said as he drew nearer. "How could I have missed the arsonist? I walked through and around the garage just a couple of minutes earlier. Barely made it to the admin building before the explosion."

"Why were you patrolling?" she asked, hoping she sounded calmer than she felt. "Wayne was supposed to be here."

"He asked to swap shifts at the last minute."

Wayne had joined the security team only a month ago and had already called in sick twice.

"Firefighters said the back window was broken." Anoop adjusted his glasses. "But it wasn't when I'd walked by. After it happened, I ran back down there, but the gasoline smell was so strong I started choking. It was like the whole building had been splashed with it."

"Someone could have been watching you." Casey kept her voice low as she surveyed the spectators. "Waiting for you to move out of the way."

Anoop gazed at the ground. "I should have called you, but I tried searching for the suspect and then firefighters and cops and Gwyn showed up."

"It's all right. Don't lose sleep over this," Casey said. "If the guy was watching you, he'd make sure you couldn't see him."

"Mr. Verma *was* being watched," a voice behind them said.

Casey turned to find Travis's anxious face peering at her. His straight brown hair reached his shoulders. How long had the kid been standing there?

"What brings you here, Travis?"

"I drove out to Hedley's. He lives near here, and since I hadn't seen the yard in a while . . ." He shrugged.

"You're driving now? I thought you suffered from motion sickness."

"Not if I'm behind the wheel."

Casey folded her arms. "I heard that you've been monitoring the premises." Travis averted his gaze. Yeah. Busted, buddy. "Were you actually on the property?"

"No, I didn't even plan to get out of the car." He hesitated. "But then I spotted someone on the east side of the garage, just before it went up."

"Did you get a look at his face?"

"No. Sorry. At first, I thought it was just the shadow of a tree branch, but the movement didn't look right. After the explosion, I saw someone jump the fence and run down a side street."

"Did you try and find him?"

Travis fidgeted. "I should have, but the fire freaked me out."

"You did the right thing by staying put. The guy's dangerous." She noticed the way Travis's shoulders relaxed, as if he realized he wasn't in serious trouble for snooping around. "Could you tell if the individual was tall or short, thin or heavy set?"

"Short." Another hesitant glance. "Thing is, I think he was wearing a driver's uniform."

Casey glanced at Anoop, whose mouth fell open. "I didn't see any drivers before the garage lit up."

Casey absently watched a few flames, still sputtering for life. Why would a driver be dumb enough to wear his uniform while committing arson?

"Travis, you need to tell the cops what you saw."

Hedley rode up on a bicycle and stopped. "Travis texted me about the gar—"

His words were cut short by an exploding vehicle parked half a block down the street.

"Holy shit!" Travis yelled.

Spectators shouted and scattered while firefighters dashed toward the burning vehicle.

"My car!?" Gwyn Maddox ran toward his Mercedes.

"Oh no," Anoop murmured. "He'll blame me."

"He can't. You've been with me these past few minutes." Although Gwyn would probably try. Casey scanned the pedestrians, looking for anyone who might be leaving the area, especially one in a bus uniform. No one appeared to be.

The police shouted at Gwyn to stay back. He started arguing with them, but soon complied.

"Has anyone been hurt?" Hedley asked.

"Hope not," Casey answered, stepping forward for a closer look, but all she saw were firefighters and cops ordering people back.

"How could someone pull that off with all these people around?" Travis asked.

"Uh, Travis, we'd better go," Hedley said, watching Gwyn. "Maddox is heading this way."

All of the Friends were well aware that Gwyn wouldn't welcome their presence. They hurried off, merging with spectators as Gwyn bulldozed his way through another cluster of people.

"Casey!" Even under the streetlights, she could see red splotches on his pudgy round face. "First thing tomorrow, find out which of the companies around here have cameras. Someone must have the suspect on tape somewhere. And talk to witnesses before they leave." Gwyn glanced at the approaching cop. "For all we know, the slimeball arsonist is still here, watching his handiwork and plotting his next move to destroy me."

"We'll handle the interviews, sir," the cop said.

"*That* is my car." He pointed to the burning Mercedes. "And my garage! Miss Holland is my employee and a senior member of my security team. She's probably interviewed more people than you have. How old are you anyway? Barely twenty-five, I bet."

The awkward endorsement made Casey look away.

"Sir, I'm asking you and your team to let us do our job."

"For god's sake, we've assisted VPD a number of times, so let her damn well help," Gwyn retorted. "Witnesses could leave any minute. Do you have enough officers around to interview thirty or so people before they take off? I think not!"

The cop stared at him, then turned to Casey. "All right, but we'll require a full briefing when you're done."

"Sure."

"Brief me too," Gwyn demanded. "I expect results!"

She could practically hear the *or else* behind his words.

The cop didn't acknowledge him as he headed toward a cluster of folks near the burning vehicle.

"You didn't do your job," Gwyn said, pointing his finger at Anoop. "I should fire you right now!"

"I'm really sorry," Anoop mumbled.

Although Anoop was much taller than Gwyn, Anoop's manner made him seem smaller. No way would she let Gwyn roll over him.

"Gwyn, if you want all witnesses interviewed before they leave, then I really need his help. Anoop isn't your enemy. He's a valued member of the security team whose diplomacy and compassion make people want to talk to him, and we're short-staffed as it is, so please don't fire him."

Gwyn muttered a curse. "All right, for now. But if you two don't come through for me—the guy who signs your paychecks—then why should I keep either of you around? Guards aren't hard to replace."

For the first time, Casey began to truly understand Lou's desire to quit. With her experience, did Gwyn really believe she wouldn't find new employment quickly?

"One of my employees has to be behind this." Gwyn glared at her. "Tomorrow, start questioning every damn one of them if you have to. Judging from the endless gossip around here, somebody knows something."

Casey swallowed back her anger. "That doesn't mean they'll want to talk to me."

"Then make it clear there'll be serious repercussions if they don't." He stomped off.

Casey swore under her breath. No way in hell would she threaten colleagues, and no way would she tell him that someone in a driver's uniform was seen fleeing the scene. She couldn't be certain that an MPT driver had caused the explosion. What if the culprit had stolen a uniform to implicate a driver? Although it was hard to imagine why someone would do that.

"Anoop, there's a couple of people behind you," Casey said. "See if they saw anything."

"Okay."

ID in hand, Casey approached three people whose dark eyes, pointed noses, and thin mouths identified them as a family. Daughter, mother, and, based on his sparse, white hair and hunched shoulders, possibly the grandfather.

"Excuse me." She displayed her ID. "I work over there at Mainland Public Transport, and I was wondering if any of you saw someone near the car just before it exploded?"

All three shook their heads. "We did see a bus driver running down the street as we were heading here." The older man gestured toward the short street that led to the condo towers.

"Which way did he go?"

"Down that side street," the grandfather answered, "heading south."

Casey looked at the road that led to more industrial properties and connected with a busier street. There'd be many hiding places. She doubted anyone would find him now.

"Are you sure he was in a driver's uniform?"

"Yes," the woman replied. "I ride those buses all the time."

Oh hell. She'd been hoping there'd been a mistake. "Is it possible that he might have been chasing someone?"

"I didn't see anyone else." The woman looked at her companions, who shook their heads.

"Only one person was running," the girl said, "and he was fast."

"Did any of you see the driver's face?"

All three shook their heads.

"What driver?" Gwyn was suddenly next to Casey, his round face perspiring.

As the grandfather told him about the running driver, Casey stifled a groan.

"How long ago did you see him?" Gwyn asked.

The family looked at one another with puzzled expressions.

"Maybe ten, fifteen minutes ago," the grandfather answered.

"Thank you for the information." Gwyn took Casey by the arm and led her away. "Damn it! The suspect'll be long gone now. The only ones we can exonerate are the drivers who just pulled in and the ones still on the road. Although I suspect any driver could loan a uniform to an accomplice."

"The culprit could have stolen a uniform," Casey replied. "I can't picture a driver implicating himself that way. It's not that late. He'd have to know people would be around."

Gwyn frowned. "Why would the suspect want us to think he's a driver?"

"No idea," Casey answered. "All I know is that anyone can enter our building and locker rooms during business hours."

The lack of security during the day had concerned her and Stan for some time. While Gwyn had taken measures to improve security after 6:00 PM, he hadn't thought it necessary during regular business hours. Casey suspected that he and the other executives simply didn't want to be punching codes and swiping badges to go in and out of the building.

"A stranger wouldn't know where my office is located or what I drive," Gwyn said. "I want daily reports on everything you learn. Liaise with the cops."

Casey sighed. Right. She'd be about as welcome as head lice.

"No one's exempt from scrutiny, understand? Get a list of all current and former drivers and start establishing alibis."

Seriously? "There has to be a hundred names and I'm already doing two jobs."

"Stan should be back soon. Get other staff to help once you've cleared them." Gwyn wiped his brow again. "Find someone else besides Verma to patrol the premises tomorrow night. In fact, get me a list of the top three security firms and their rates. I need skilled, unbiased outsiders."

As Gwyn stomped off, Anoop approached Casey. "Bad news." He hesitated. "Someone saw a fairly short man in a driver's uniform run across this road, away from the garage."

She nodded. "I heard the same."

"Do you really think the arsonist's an employee?"

"Maybe." Not something she wanted to discuss right now. "Anoop, why don't you go home. There's no need for further patrols tonight. The fire department will be here a while."

"Thanks." He glanced up and down the street. "Good thing I parked on the street. The plan was to keep a low profile, not that it did much good."

"I'm not sure anyone could have stopped our firebug. If the suspect's familiar with MPT's schedule, then he'd know drivers would be returning and dispatchers were inside." Casey paused. "Gwyn's office was torched after 1:00 AM, but this one happened just after 11:00 PM, which means he doesn't care if employees are still around."

"Think he wants to hurt someone?" Anoop asked.

"Good question."

"Scary," Anoop murmured.

"Yeah." A knot twisted in Casey's gut.

SIXTEEN

When Stan entered the security department, Casey jumped out of her chair. Relief washed over her.

"You're back!" He looked pale, though, and wasn't moving fast.

The T-shirt and sweat pants totally caught her off guard. The only time Casey had seen Stan dress casually was during the occasional weekend shift. Even then it was jeans and a button shirt. This new look rattled her.

"Couldn't stay away from all the excitement." He smiled. "But I'm only part-time for now."

Three days ago, Casey had phoned him to discuss the arsons and whether the suspect was an employee or someone who wanted the world to think an employee was responsible. She'd also sought his advice on developing an effective strategy to carry out the internal investigation Gwyn demanded. Stan told her to hold off until he talked to Gwyn. Was this the reason he'd returned to work just five days after someone tried to slice him open?

"Have the police been in touch?" he asked.

"No, and I have a feeling they won't want to share."

"I'll see if Gwyn's heard anything."

While the HR and accounting staff were calling out greetings, Stan waved and assured everyone he was fine. Casey had her doubts. Had she or Gwyn given him the impression that she was in over her head?

Nora's comment that Stan might consider retirement weighed on her. With all of his kids married and having their own children, why wouldn't he consider it? On the other hand, Stan was one of those people who thrived on work. He didn't play golf, bowl, volunteer, or have any hobbies that she knew of. Casey couldn't imagine him ending his career because of one freak with a knife. Or was this what she needed to tell herself?

She followed him into his office.

"Holy shit." Stan gaped at the haphazard stacks of papers on his desk. "Gwyn's doing?"

"Yep. Your filing system confused him."

"Shut the door." Groaning slightly, Stan eased into his old chair. "Gwyn phoned yesterday to say he won't be coming in too often over the next few days."

It was the best news she'd had all week. "Good, because I think someone's out to destroy his company."

"Looks that way." Stan slowly leaned back in his chair. "Who hates him that much?"

"Should I list them on an Excel spreadsheet?" she remarked. "That way we can add more names as we think of them and alphabetize everything."

Stan smiled. "Sadly, you're not far off the mark."

"It's because a lot of staff are upset about you and Benny and feel that Gwyn hasn't done enough to protect us," Casey said. "To show that I'm doing what he wants, I've spoken to a couple of drivers about the fires." She paused. "I didn't tell you that Gwyn expects daily written reports of every interview and alibi that I can confirm."

"I'll be meeting with him shortly and have a word." Stan ran his hand over the brush cut that had begun to grow out. "The man's really rattled, Casey. Just between us, he's making noises about selling the company."

"You're joking."

"I don't think he'll follow through. Probably just an emotional response to the fires." Stan shifted in his seat. "I shouldn't have said anything. Must be the damn painkillers."

Different scenarios flashed through Casey's mind, some of them good, most of them bad. A new owner could be a positive change. But if Gwyn couldn't find a buyer, would he close the company? The thought of no more MPT frightened her. The more she thought about it, the more she realized that she truly wasn't ready to quit, let alone be forced out. Not yet anyway.

"You look stressed," Stan said. "Let's talk about something fun, like your wedding. It's just over three weeks away, right?"

"Yes." Casey appreciated his attempt to lighten the mood, but right now her wedding was the last thing on her mind. "Everything's pretty much done."

"Summer must be excited."

Casey's smile slipped. She couldn't help it.

"What's wrong?"

"Summer's feeling a lot of emotions these days, but excitement isn't one of them."

Stan sat back and crossed his arms. "What's going on?"

If there was anyone she could tell, it was Stan. He and Nora had raised four kids and had suffered through their share of bad boyfriends and broken curfews.

"She's been seeing her ex-boyfriend's brother behind my back, and she lied about not being at the riot. Gwyn had me review CCTV footage of that night. To my horror, I spotted her and Tyler drinking beer. A week later, Summer missed curfew and came home completely wasted."

"She's testing the waters like a typical teen. Stupid mistakes will happen," Stan replied. "Summer's got a good head on her shoulders and won't get herself in too deep, so be patient and supportive, but firm about your expectations."

"I'm trying, but she seems so troubled. Summer's showing a disturbing amount of disdain for her mother these days and I don't know why."

"Keep talking to her. Communication's crucial right now."

"I will, thanks, and enough about my problems." Casey shifted in her chair. "I've been thinking about all four attacks by this maniac they're calling the Blade Man."

Stan snorted. "I heard that dumb reference on the news."

Best not to mention that it originated with one of the Friends who might have talked to the media. Casey still hadn't had a chance to question Felicity.

"Here's the thing," she said. "How has the man always managed to escape on foot?"

Stan shrugged. "Maybe he has a car or a bike stashed close by."

"Or maybe he lives on the streets and knows every hiding spot in and around Town Center Park. You and Benny both said that he smelled bad."

"The RCMP came by again to ask a couple more questions, but didn't share theories."

"Did you see Benny before you left the hospital?"

"Briefly. We didn't talk about the incident." Stan cleared his throat. "Physically, he's doing better, but mentally he still seems a little out of it." His gaze drifted toward the bonsai. "Anyway, I'd better catch up on emails."

Casey understood his reluctance to discuss Benny. They'd both worked here for years and had deep mutual respect. "I need a coffee." She stood. "Want one?"

"No, thanks."

Downstairs, Casey entered the lunchroom and exchanged smiles with mechanic, Roberto de Luca. He broke away from the women he'd been chatting with and ambled toward her. Perpetually sexy, with his salt-and-pepper hair, gorgeous green eyes, and formidable muscles, Roberto rarely spent his coffee breaks alone, which was how the perennial bachelor liked it.

"How are you managing without the garage?" she asked him.

"Not bad. We've thrown up a makeshift work area, but the heavier work's being done off site."

Casey surveyed the room. A few employees were eating, but no one was close enough to overhear. "Any theories about who the firebug is?"

Roberto's smile faded. "Are you asking for yourself or Gwyn? 'Cause I heard that he wants you interrogating staff."

She should have known he'd be sensitive to this. Roberto had been a person of interest after a colleague's murder two years ago. The experience had nearly cost her their friendship. It had taken time to rebuild Roberto's trust. She wasn't about to lose it again.

"You're right. Gwyn asked but I'm only going through the motions to keep him quiet. I don't expect, or even want, anyone to say something that will put a coworker in an awkward position. Stan's back and he'll get Gwyn to stand down, I hope."

"Glad he's here." Roberto peered at her as if he was puzzling over something. "I know this sounds weird coming from me, but I actually think you should talk to staff. Everyone knows how pissed Gwyn is, and if you don't question people, then he could have the cops knocking on our doors. I know for a fact that most guys would rather talk to you than them." Roberto glanced around the room. "Come outside a minute."

Casey followed him as far as the staff parking lot.

Glancing at the sidewalk, he said, "Talk to Maurice. He was here when the garage went up. Hinted at seeing something, but he won't say what."

"Why was Maurice here so late?"

"Having coffee with a couple of drivers." Roberto paused. "It gives him something to do. He needs the distraction and the coffee."

"Distraction?"

Roberto looked around the lot. "Only a few of us know, but Maurice is in AA. This is the first job he's had in a while. He's a good mechanic and we don't want to lose him. But I'm pretty sure he's afraid that's exactly what will happen if he talks."

"Is he more worried about Gwyn or the cops?"

"Both. There were some incidents while he was living on the streets before he got sober." Roberto again glanced at the sidewalk. "As soon as the explosion happened, Maurice took off. I think he's worried that someone's gonna confront him about that night and I'd rather it be you." He pointed at the sidewalk. "He's at the smoking tree."

Smoking wasn't permitted on the premises, so employees usually congregated beneath the big oak tree on the wide strip of grass bordering the sidewalk.

"Just chat, don't interrogate, okay?" Roberto cautioned.

Casey hesitated. "Do you want to come with me? Put in a good word about my discretion?"

"Wish I could, but my break's up. Good luck."

Casey left the yard and headed for Maurice. With his back to the property, the thin, wiry man leaned against the tree and took a long drag on his cigarette.

She sauntered toward him. "Hello, Maurice."

He turned to her with a pensive expression. "Hey."

"How's Mainland treating you?"

"Good." He scratched the wisp of beard tracing his jawline.

She shoved her hands in her jeans pockets. "Crazy few days, huh?"

He shrugged. "I guess."

"It's not always this bad. I mean, we usually don't experience fires and knife attacks." She noted his guarded face. "Roberto thought it'd be okay to talk with you about the garage explosion Monday night. He said you were with the drivers when it happened, so I was wondering if you saw anything."

Maurice glanced up and down the street. "It scared the shit out of me and I took off."

Casey nodded. "As you left, did you happen to see anyone running by the garage or down the sidewalk?"

Maurice stood up straighter. "I don't want no cop knockin' on my door."

"Neither do I, but I'm worried that the suspect will try again and someone could wind up seriously hurt. If you have information, I won't tell the cops it came from you, I promise."

Bloodshot eyes studied her. "Those kinds of promises can break under pressure." The man's hand trembled as he took another drag on the cigarette. "I just want a nice, simple job. Don't need enemies."

Why was he worrying about making enemies, unless . . . "Witnesses described someone in a driver's uniform running from the property right after the garage went up." Based on the way he fidgeted, Casey sensed that she was onto something. "Did you see him too, Maurice?"

He shook his head. "Not a face." He hesitated. "But yeah, there was some guy in a uniform."

"Which direction did he go?"

"Came from behind the garage, climbed the fence, and ran across the road and down that side street." He pointed to the same short road the witnesses had told her about.

Only two or three drivers would be athletic enough to climb a six-foot fence. "Think you could you estimate his height or weight?"

"Average, I guess. About my height."

Maurice was shorter than most men, but Casey had learned never to contradict a man about his height. "What about hair color?"

"Didn't see hair at all. Might have been wearing a tuque." Maurice ground the cigarette into the sidewalk. "Gotta go."

"Thanks for telling me, and I won't break my promise."

Maurice shrugged. "Like I said, if the cops show up, I ain't saying nothin'."

"Understood." But had he told her everything he saw three nights ago?

SEVENTEEN

Casey paced around her living room, replaying her conversations with Maurice and Stan. Stan hadn't wanted to believe a driver was involved in the explosions, yet he couldn't ignore witness accounts.

She and Stan had agreed that only two drivers, Dimitri and Ethan, had the athletic ability and opportunity to run fast and scale fences. Stan jokingly said that Lou could probably jump a fence, which had caught her off guard.

"You know he wouldn't do that, right?" she'd blurted. "He may be ticked with Gwyn, but he'd never resort to crime and violence. Besides he was driving when the incidents happened."

"Relax." Stan laughed. "I'm just messin' with you."

She should have realized that, but the depth of Lou's anger was a sore spot. If Gwyn picked up on it, he'd target Lou.

She had managed to learn that, although Ethan had been driving when the Molotov cocktail set Gwyn's office on fire, he'd been working a day shift when the garage went up Monday night. Dimitri's schedule was a little more uncertain. He was supposed to work Monday night but apparently switched with someone else at the last minute. Stan planned to talk to Dimitri's supervisor about it.

"Isn't it possible that a uniform was stolen by someone who doesn't work here," Casey had said, "or that a former employee didn't hand his in?"

Stan thought they should focus on the most plausible angle first and had asked her not to share their discussion with anyone, including Lou. Part of her was relieved, but another part was worried that Lou and the security team would take offense at being kept out of the loop.

Lou emerged from the bathroom, rubbing his hair with a towel. "You're home earlier than I thought you'd be," he said.

"Stan showed up this morning. He's working part-time and said I should rest before tonight's shift."

Lou pulled out a frying pan. "Isn't it a little soon for him to be back?"

"Yeah, but he knows we need the extra help. For all I know, Gwyn badgered him into coming back because he doesn't think I can handle things."

"I'm making sausage and eggs for lunch," he said. "You want any?"

"No, I'll have what's left of the salad." She removed a container from the fridge. "Need to fit into my wedding dress."

Lou smiled as he drew her to him. "You'll look great no matter what."

Casey kissed his full, sensuous lips. With everything that had happened lately, they hadn't had nearly enough intimate time. At least his injuries had healed to the point where he wasn't wincing when he sat or stood.

"I plan to look better than great," she assured him. "I'm going for spectacular."

"You will be." He fetched the sausage and eggs. "Any leads on the firebug?"

"Not really." She poured a light balsamic vinaigrette over the salad.

"I've been getting texts from some of the drivers." He placed two sausages in the pan. "Word is that a guy in one of our uniforms was seen running from the garage." Lou turned to her. "You hear anything about that?"

So much for secrecy and discretion. Maurice and Anoop already knew. How many others? She wouldn't be surprised if Gwyn was going around muttering accusations. God knew the man wasn't all that rational lately.

"Stan doesn't want me discussing it with anyone."

Lou gently took her salad and placed it on the table. "It's not fair that we're all under suspicion." His face was close enough that she could count every freckle on his nose. Lou wrapped his arms around her. He kissed her forehead and massaged her shoulders. "Is the rumor true?"

Casey's body tingled. "You're not playing fair."

"True." Lou gently kneaded her shoulders. "But I need to know."

Oh lord, the massage felt incredible. Her resolve was melting, and since word was out anyway…"Witness accounts said the suspect hopped the fence and ran away pretty damn fast and, yeah, he was in a uniform."

"Are the witnesses reliable?"

"The ones I talked to recognized the MPT uniform. To the best of my knowledge, they have no connection to MPT and nothing against Gwyn." She left Maurice's name out of this. "Doubt they even know who he is."

"Maybe Gwyn and Stan should focus on ex-employees," Lou suggested. "Not everyone left under great circumstances or would have bothered to turn in their uniform."

In other words, leave his friends alone. "Stan wants to rule out current employees first."

Lou abandoned the massage to turn the sausages. "If a coworker did that, I'm not sure I blame him."

Casey started to reach for her salad, then stopped. "Excuse me?"

"Have you forgotten what it's like to be a driver?" His tone became edgy. "To be spit on, punched, and threatened every damn week while your employer does nothing to make things safer?"

"Of course I remember, but destroying MPT could throw every employee out of work. Gwyn's acquired more buses with cameras, and the alarm system's been upgraded. Using the security vehicle more often also helps, and yes, it's not enough, but it's better than it was."

"Yet here we are, in more danger than ever." Lou broke eggs into the frying pan. "Do you really think we should just accept this because of Gwyn's lame attempt to make things safer? Shit, Casey. Think about it. He doesn't even like you. Maybe we should both get the hell out of there."

Did Lou expect her to quit right now? Sure, Gwyn was an idiot, but Stan and the team needed her. "I'm saying that I understand your frustration, which is why Stan's lobbying harder for more improvements. But I really believe that we need to stick around and support our friends and coworkers until the arsonist and the Blade Man are caught."

Lou's solemn face relaxed a moment. "Okay."

But it wasn't okay. Not at all. Even if Lou knew which driver was involved, Casey had a feeling he wouldn't tell her. She picked up her salad and prodded a cherry tomato, realizing that she'd lost her appetite. The landline rang. Casey turned to the phone. Only telemarketers and Rhonda used this number. Rhonda called on Sundays and this was Thursday, yet something told her to pick it up.

"Hello, Casey."

"Rhonda?" Uh-oh. "Is everything all right?"

Rhonda cleared her throat. "There's something I need to tell you. I, uh, well, I've been putting it off, but it can't wait now."

The back of Casey's neck prickled. "What's wrong?"

"A few weeks ago, I found a lump in my breast." Rhonda sighed. "They sent me for tests, then a biopsy. The result wasn't good."

Casey tightened her grip on the phone. "Oh."

"Long story short, a mastectomy's coming up, but I don't know the exact day or if it'll be done here or in a hospital."

Oh hell. Casey sank into the rocking chair. "Is it an aggressive cancer? What's the prognosis?"

"Not sure."

Casey's mouth went dry. She wanted to ask how Rhonda was feeling, but it was a dumb question. How would anyone feel under those circumstances? "I wish you'd told me sooner."

"I didn't know how to deal with it. Still trying to process everything. And please don't tell Summer. My life has burdened her enough."

The tremor in her voice troubled Casey. She didn't know what to say. "I'm so sorry—"

"No. I'm the one who's sorry for being so short-tempered with you both. It's just that this has been hard to deal with."

"No kidding." Casey paused. "I should bring Summer to see you."

"No!" Rhonda sounded desperate. "I won't be able to hold it together and I have to, understand? I *cannot* fall apart or show any emotional weakness right now. After I've had time to heal, you two can come visit."

"But we won't be back from our honeymoon until the third week of July."

"That's okay."

Casey rubbed her forehead. Perspiration dampened her hair-line. "It's *not*, Rhonda. The wedding's still three and a half weeks away and the honeymoon's another two."

"Don't make me regret calling you."

Casey's eyes filled with tears. "Why did you call then?"

"Because." Rhonda let out a sob. "I had to tell someone."

Casey wiped the tears away. How could she persuade Rhonda that leaving her daughter in the dark was a horrible idea? "If there's anything I can do, promise you'll call, okay?"

"Sure." Another pause. "Is Summer all right? Did you find out the boyfriend's name?"

"We're working on it."

Could she possibly tell her the truth now? With the school year nearly over, Casey had no idea how they'd keep Summer out of trouble for two months. At least she'd be staying with Lou's mom during the honeymoon. But after that?

"If I don't get a chance to call before the wedding," Rhonda said, "I wish you and Lou all the love and luck in the world."

"Of course we'll talk before then."

"Take lots of pictures."

She hung up before Casey could say goodbye. Tears spilled down her cheeks. Suddenly, she was aware of Lou kneeling in front of her and removing the phone from her hand. Leaning into Lou, she cried. It wasn't just about Rhonda's cancer, but about the broken relationship between mother and daughter, about all the decisions and circumstances that made it so pain-fully clear that she, Rhonda, and Summer were still living with too much hurt.

"What's going on?" Lou asked.

Casey explained in two short sentences, then sniffled. "I know Rhonda's caused a lot of pain, but I also remember all the comfort and support she gave me in my teens. Breast cancer on top of a twenty-five-year prison sentence feels like a pretty damn harsh punishment, especially when any chance of parole's still seven years away."

"I know." Lou rubbed her back. "You were smart not to say anything about Tyler. Summer's fourteen. The relationship won't last."

"But it could last long enough to do some serious damage, even change her life forever." She shook her head. "Where have I gone wrong?"

"You haven't. You're doing a great job in a tough situation. You've been beating yourself up way too much."

Maybe, maybe not. Casey couldn't escape the feeling that she was failing this child a little more every year. How could she stop the downward spiral?

"Once the grounding is over, what do we do about Summer and Tyler?" Casey asked.

"Not sure," he replied, "but we'll figure it out."

Casey watched Ralphie snooze in his cage. He was a senior in guinea pig years and slept more now. How many more years did he have left? How much time did Rhonda have? Were things more dire than she'd admitted?

"Since we're both working tonight, should we have someone check in on Summer?" Lou asked.

"Good question." Casey paused. "Maybe Kendal could swing by. She often works Thursday evenings at the store, and I know she wouldn't mind. I'll give her a call."

"We should check out Tyler," he said. "See if he's as devious as his petty criminal brother."

"Yeah." Although the answer already seemed obvious.

EIGHTEEN

Casey was trying to read the article about the dog walker who'd been stabbed when Dimitri Klitou slammed the brakes for the third time. Dimitri had always been on the intense side, but his jumpy reactions to traffic were bordering on erratic. As they pulled out of MPT's yard, he'd complained loudly about having to drive near the hot zone. She could almost hear him thinking that the presence of a female security guard wouldn't make him any safer. Was Dimitri the firebug? Had his anger evolved into a destructive mission to destroy the company?

"Your driver seems kind of pissed," Del said from the seat behind her.

"Just tired and overworked," Casey answered.

The MPT Friends had boarded shortly after the bus left the yard tonight. Having warned the kids not to ride Coquitlam routes, Casey wasn't happy to see them. On the other hand, it did present an opportunity to ask Felicity a question.

"So, have any of you been talking to the news media?" Casey asked, keeping her tone casual.

Felicity glanced at Del and Lawrence, who was suddenly busy adjusting his Nikon.

"Why do you ask?" she replied, making a point of looking out the window.

Yep. The girl knew something. "I saw a reference to the Blade Man on the news." She stared at the squirming Felicity.

"You're the one who came up with the name. Who else did you tell?"

Felicity's porcelain face turned crimson. Lawrence kept his attention on his camera, while Del's serious gaze appeared to be studying Casey.

"I didn't contact them," Felicity blurted. "A journalist found our Facebook page, which is public, and read that we were there the night Mr. Lee was stabbed, so she messaged me."

"Our private group's separate and stays private," Del added.

Casey sure as hell hoped so.

Felicity shifted in her seat and turned her attention to Dimitri. "That cut on the driver's forehead still looks gross."

Okay, so the girl wanted to deflect the discussion. Maybe it didn't matter. There were bigger issues to focus on, like how best to protect MPT drivers. Dimitri's wound was a glaring reminder of how quickly things could go wrong. Casey had no idea if he'd been reprimanded for kicking the crap out of the goateed Bandana Boy, but his presence meant that supervisors were either critically short staffed or were siding with Dimitri's self-defense tactics. A number of drivers sure did and had been pretty vocal about the right to defend themselves through any means possible.

She resumed reading the piece about the latest stabbing victim. The reporter had written that the victim would likely make a full recovery from her injuries. *He came out of nowhere,* the victim was quoted as saying. *I didn't hear a thing. Just felt a sharp pain in my back and heard a man say something about a green freak. Guess he didn't like the color of my tracksuit.* Casey looked up. Green freak? Hadn't Benny's son heard his dad use the same phrase? Reese thought Benny had been babbling about the movies, but was there another reason?

Casey turned to the Friends. "Does the term *green freak* mean anything to you three?"

The trio looked at one another and shook their heads.

"What about in terms of superheroes?" Casey added.

Lawrence's eyes lit up. "The Green Lantern and the Green Hornet. And the Hulk turns green when his anger takes over. They've all been called freaks, but they were misunderstood."

Casey stared at him. "Uh-huh."

Del cleared his throat, his expression now troubled. "You know what else is green?"

An answer popped into Casey's head, one she didn't dare say out loud.

"MPT buses!" As if stunned by her own answer, Felicity's wispy eyebrows shot up.

"And drivers' uniforms," Del murmured.

There it was, the truth slapping her in the face. "My supervisor wasn't wearing green that night."

"But the security vehicle's green and has MPT's logo," Del answered. "Green must be the Blade Man's trigger."

"Which means none of us should wear it," Lawrence murmured, checking his clothing.

Felicity scanned her pink jacket and purple leggings. Even Del glanced at his brown hoodie and blue jeans.

"I'll warn Travis and Hedley," Felicity said, and soon started texting.

"What for?" Del asked. "Neither of them ride buses anymore."

Casey was tempted to say this wasn't true, but she didn't want to initiate a discussion about the Friends' group dynamics.

"They're worried about us, and more violence." Felicity frowned at him. "Hedley sent photos of the burning garage. Didn't you get them?"

"No."

Casey noticed Del's rigid posture. Did he and Hedley have a problem with each other?

"It's crazy that someone would kill over a color," Lawrence said to Casey.

"Yeah." Casey couldn't remember the color of the riot victim's clothing. She'd have to check the footage again.

"Mentally ill people are everywhere," Del remarked.

True. Far too many were fending for themselves on the streets. To seek shelter from bad weather and bad people, a few of the homeless rode buses without paying the fare. MPT drivers had learned not to press the issue.

"Witnesses said that the Blade Man who went after Mr. Lee was wearing all black clothing," Felicity said. "If he really is homeless, that's probably all he owns." She peered out the window. "We should watch for someone like that. I'll take this side. Maybe you guys should take the other side of the street, and Casey can watch the bus entrances."

Great. She'd been assigned to Team Friends. Casey glanced at the half-filled bus to see if anyone had overheard their conversation. Tonight's riders were a mix of middle-aged and young adults, most of them fixated on their phones.

"First," Casey said, "keep your voices down if you're talking about this stuff. Second, we're now in Maple Ridge, which isn't the Blade Man's turf as far as I know. And third, didn't I make clear that you three are not to go looking for suspects?"

"But we're safe here," she answered.

Casey's phone rang. It was retiree Wayne, who was patrolling MPT property tonight. Since Gwyn hadn't yet given any feedback about hiring a private security firm, she had to make do with the crew she had.

"Hey, Wayne. What's up?"

"I saw someone by the fence about five minutes ago," he replied in a hushed, nervous tone.

"The chain link one on the east side or the wooden one on the west?"

"Wooden one, by the flooring warehouse."

Shielded by trees and brushes, the west fence was difficult to see and offered many hiding spots. "Where are you now?"

"In the security department, looking out the window."

"Did you call the police?"

"Should I? I mean, he's probably gone now, right?"

Casey rolled her eyes. "How will we know for certain unless someone checks? He could be scoping out specific locations to set a fire."

"Oh, right." He paused. "Should I call them now?"

Dear lord. "Yes, and did you see what the person was wearing, by any chance?"

"No, I barely got a glimpse of the guy before I hightailed it inside. I mean, it wouldn't be good to confront an arsonist by myself, right?"

"Right. So make the call right now."

"I'll do that. Okeydokey."

Casey shook her head. A simple "ten-four" would suffice. When would the guy learn the codes or use a little common sense?

If Wayne had spotted the arsonist, then this ruled out Dimitri. Ethan was also on the road right now. Did either of them have an accomplice, though, or was the culprit someone else altogether? A former employee bent on revenge perhaps?

The timing of the arsons had been bothering her. If the suspect didn't want to risk getting caught, then why set fires while drivers were still returning to the yard? It would have been smarter to wait until three or four in the morning when everyone was long gone, like the graffiti artist had done. Why take so much risk?

Unless that was part of the game. Start with harmless spray-painting in the wee hours of the morning, then try a Molotov cocktail through an office window when nearly every employee had left. From there, blow up a garage when more people were around, followed by a car explosion practically in front of cops and firefighters. Was becoming more brazen part of the thrill? If so, what was coming next? The thought of someone getting hurt made Casey's stomach churn.

Dimitri pulled up to the next stop. An older Asian couple exited at the front. He was about to close the door when four teenage boys leapt on board. The boisterous group ambled down the aisle. None were staggering or slurring their words, and Casey didn't spot any alcohol. More importantly, none of them were the Bandana Boys. These guys were between thirteen and fifteen years old at most. Still, she remained alert. Dimitri glanced over his shoulder, his expression wary.

The boys gawked at Felicity, who seemed oblivious to their presence as she peered out the window and softly sang "Wheels on the Bus." One of the boys muttered something. The others smirked and slid into seats near the back.

"I see a guy in black!" Felicity pressed her nose against the window.

"Where?" Del raised his phone.

"The one who keeps looking at our bus. Oh, wait. He's wearing blue jeans."

"What did I say about staying out of this?" Casey glared at the Friends.

Felicity's face again bloomed with color. "Sorry."

Honestly, Casey wondered if something more was going on with that girl than immaturity and ADHD issues.

"We just want to help," Del said.

"Losers," one of the boys remarked loudly.

The Friends ignored him. Casey sensed that the trio were accustomed to verbal taunts. Felicity bounced slightly in her seat. So much for a calming ride.

"Bloody dorks," another of the teens said. "She looks like a ten-year-old on a fieldtrip."

As Felicity focused on her phone, her cheeks darkened even more. Casey turned and scowled at the foursome. A couple of them stared back but the other two looked away.

"Hey, little girl!" one of the guys called out. "Ain't you ever been on a bus before?"

Del slowly stood and scowled at the boys. Casey could see the storm building.

"I'll deal with this." Casey strolled toward the smirking foursome. Displaying her ID, she said, "Mainland Public Transport has zero tolerance for any form of harassment, including derogatory remarks. If you can't respect that, then you'll leave at the next stop. Understand?"

The smirks and smugness disappeared.

"Chill. We're just jokin' around," one of them said.

The bus pulled to a stop. Before she knew it, Dimitri was charging down the aisle, pointing at the boys. "You behave or get off! I don't need smartass punks on my bus!"

"I've got this, Dimitri," she said, annoyed by his intrusion.

He didn't look at her. "I should kick your asses out of here."

"He means it," Casey said. "So no trouble, all right?"

The tension between Dimitri and the boys continued. The bus was silent. A quick glance over her shoulder confirmed that every passenger was now watching the confrontation.

"Dimitri, the passengers need to get to their destinations and you have a schedule to keep," Casey murmured.

Dimitri stomped back down the aisle, muttering to himself. Casey sat near the boys and opened her notebook. She would be expected to write accurate details about Dimitri's confrontation, especially if the boys launched a formal complaint about perceived mistreatment. So, what was she supposed to say about Dimitri's behavior? If she reported a high level of aggression, Stan might be obligated to tell Dimitri's supervisor. Dimitri then would likely face a reprimand of some sort. They had enough enemies outside MPT. She sure didn't want to make one on the inside.

. . .

By the time Dimitri pulled into Mainland's yard at the end of their shift, Casey couldn't wait to go home. He'd remained edgy all evening and refused to speak to her after his altercation with the boys. She supposed she'd insulted Dimitri by telling him to do his job, but too bad. The teens hadn't caused further trouble and exited the bus shortly after the incident.

Lou had pulled into the yard just ahead of Dimitri and was waiting for her in the parking lot. Dimitri marched past him without saying a word.

"What happened?" he asked her.

Casey kept her answer brief.

"Guy's gonna create more trouble for himself., Lou said. "Did you hear from Kendal or Summer at all tonight?"

"No."

"Let's hope that no news is good news."

"Definitely."

Kendal had agreed to do a drive-by after her shift and look for any little black cars parked near the house. She said she'd only call if something was wrong. Casey had thought about phoning Summer, but was afraid she'd blurt out Rhonda's news. The cancer diagnosis had been in the back of Casey's mind all evening.

"I'll meet you at the car after I clock out," Lou said.

"Can you give me five minutes? I need to take a quick peek at CCTV footage from the riot. It could be important." She spotted Wayne emerging from the admin building. "And I need to talk to Wayne." She hurried toward him. "Any more action tonight?"

Wayne's double chin jiggled as he shook his head. "Cops checked things out but didn't find anyone." His gaze darted around the property. "Thing is," he whispered, "I can't shake the feeling that the perp's come back and is watching us right now. It's creepin' me out."

Casey studied the fence between MPT and the flooring warehouse. "Have you patrolled the yard since we last spoke?"

"I was about to."

"Okay, go ahead. I'll be here for a few minutes. Call if you spot anything."

"Okeydokey." Wayne started to leave, then stopped. "When will we get the security vehicle back? 'Cause I'd rather drive than walk out in the open."

No doubt. "Stan said the crime scene techs will release it tomorrow."

"Good. They find any DNA evidence from the perp?"

"They haven't said." Nor would they share that with an MPT employee.

Casey jogged upstairs. The entrance to security had had a new alarm system installed after Hedley was caught wandering through the building one evening last year. She swiped her badge and pressed the four-digit code.

Keeping the lights off, she glanced out the windows over-looking staff parking and the yard. The streetlights created too many shadows. If someone was truly watching the premises, he'd be almost impossible to spot.

Casey unlocked Stan's door and headed for the credenza, where a pair of binoculars were kept. She crept toward the window and spotted Wayne wandering down the center of the yard, midway between both fences. There was no lighting at all by the tall, wooden fence. Trees and overgrown bushes created more shadows.

Casey's shoulders tingled. Was Wayne right about someone being out there? She scanned the property twice. Nothing. Sighing, she moved to her desk and pulled up the footage of the riot.

"Casey?" Lou said from the doorway. "Ready to go?"

"Not yet. Come on in, but leave the lights off. Would you mind keeping an eye on the yard while I check something?" She handed him the binoculars. "Wayne thinks he saw someone lurking by the west fence a while ago. He called the cops but they didn't find anyone. The guy could still be out there, though, waiting for the right moment."

She found the camera footage of the man who was stabbed at the riot, froze the footage, and zoomed in. The victim wore a forest green polo shirt. "Well, damn."

"What?" Lou asked.

"The stabbing victim from the riot had been wearing a dark green polo shirt. The dog walker also wore green. A news article said that the dog walker heard her assailant say 'green freak'."

"No way." Lou peered at the footage. "Maybe Benny was quoting his assailant, a crazy nut who hates the color green."

Casey wondered if a green-hating street person was already in a law enforcement database for less serious crimes. Many homeless people with mental health issues caught the cops' attention, but a night in jail was no answer to their problems.

"Would you mind if we drove around the neighborhood a couple of times before heading home?" Casey asked. "If our firebug's around, maybe we can spot him."

"Casey, he's already proven to excel at hiding, and shouldn't we be getting back to Summer?"

"Just a couple of blocks, please? My gut says he's nearby."

"Five minutes, that's all." He yawned. "I'm beat."

"Me too, but I'd feel sick if another fire erupted partly because we couldn't be bothered to check out the area."

They headed back downstairs and outside.

Climbing into Lou's pickup, she said, "Turn right and start down that way. We're not just looking for pedestrians, but anyone sitting in a car. Let me know if any vehicle looks familiar."

Lou glanced at her. "Meaning one that belongs to a driver?"

Casey shrugged. "At this point, I'm not sure of anything."

"What would you do if we did spot someone?"

"Call the police and ask them to see if he's got arson paraphernalia in his car."

"Then what?"

"Nothing. We'd wait for them to do their thing."

He turned to her. "Think you'd be that patient?"

"Sure."

Lou snorted, but she let it go.

Minutes later, they'd covered the immediate area. Other than a group of young people ambling down the sidewalk, everything looked normal. But that didn't mean much. Someone could still be out there, watching and waiting.

NINETEEN

Casey couldn't stop yawning. The intense shift with Dimitri, frustrating discussions with Wayne, and camera footage review was more than enough activity for one night. It was just after two in the morning, and all she wanted to do was fall into bed. That they had to do this again for the next three nights was demoralizing. The only perk to driving home at this hour was the absence of traffic.

"If Gwyn hadn't insisted on expanding Coquitlam routes at night, we wouldn't have been exposed to some violent nut job," Lou muttered. "No one would have been pissed off enough to set fires."

Casey's eyes widened as she turned to him. So he really thought that a driver was responsible? She wanted to ask, but Lou's anger festered like an infected wound. She'd have to tread carefully.

"Do you think the fires are a message to Gwyn to smarten up, or that someone's truly out to destroy his company?"

"Does it matter?"

"Yes. The first option means that the fires will likely stop, if they haven't already. The second one means we could all be out of work within a few weeks if the whole admin building goes up. Gwyn might not want to rebuild."

Lou stared straight ahead. "Maybe the arsonist will stop once the Blade Man's arrested."

Casey's eyebrows rose. "You think the two are connected?"

"I think the arsonist's feeding off the fear and paranoia that the Blade Man's caused. That's why he's striking now," Lou said. "What I don't get is why it's so hard to find a knife-wielding nut who strikes in the same area every damn time."

"Wish I knew." She understood that stress and fatigue made him irritable, but ranting wouldn't help. "We're almost home." Casey touched his arm. "How about a massage to relax you?"

"After we make sure that Summer's actually home." He paused. "Do you remember where the Price boys live?"

Uh-oh. "Why?"

"I want to get Tyler's license plate number. Since we're out here in the middle of the night, might as well do it now."

"Do you even know the make of the car?"

"I got a good look at it when he dropped Summer off. Besides, how many little black cars would there be in the Prices's driveway?"

"Point taken," Casey remarked. "It's just a few blocks from here."

Soon they were in Tyler Price's neighborhood, assuming that the family still lived here. It was a poorer East Vancouver neighborhood reflected in the dilapidated homes, broken fences, and moss-covered roofs.

"I think that's it," Casey said, pointing to a single-story, clapboard house. "Black car's in the driveway."

Lou pulled up in front of the driveway but left the engine running. The yard was filled with old bikes, appliances, and assorted junk. It was the only house on the block with lights still on in the living room. The lack of blinds made it easy to spot two guys and two girls jumping around in some sort of frenzied dance, although she didn't hear any music.

"Neither of those girls is Summer," Lou said. "Looks like Tyler's getting some action on the side."

A third guy wandered past the window. Tall and thin, Casey wasn't sure if this was Tyler or Devon.

"Maybe not," she answered. "Two girls and three guys could mean that Tyler's the odd man out." She studied the group. "No sign of Summer."

"There's no dad around and the mom works nights, right?"

"That's what I remember."

The same guy stopped at the window, then disappeared.

"We've been spotted," Casey remarked.

"They're probably worried about cops." Lou turned to the small black car in the driveway. "Flashlight's in the glovebox. We need that plate number."

Casey retrieved the flashlight and shone it on the license plate. As she typed the number into her phone, a lanky figure strolled down the driveway.

"See any weapon?" Lou whispered.

"No, but stay alert. He might have a reason for taking his time."

The closer he came to the truck, the slower he moved.

"Sure looks like that shithead Devon," Lou murmured.

Casey held her breath as the kid approached her window. The resemblance to Devon was close, but now she could see that this guy's mouth was shorter, his lips fuller. "It's Tyler." She rolled down the window.

"Why are you watching our house?" he demanded.

"I understand why you don't recognize me, Tyler, given that Summer's never introduced us," Casey replied.

The kid stepped back, his expression wary, until recognition dawned. "You're Casey?"

"Yep. So how come you've been sneaking around, drinking alcohol with a minor?"

Tyler gaped at her. "What are you talking about?"

"I came across CCTV footage of you and Summer drinking at the riot. The cops might want to know the names of the underage beer guzzlers."

"What? No!" Tyler stepped back, as if afraid of being struck. "You can't do that."

"We sure as hell can if you don't answer our questions," Lou shot back.

"Summer wanted to go to the rally, not me."

"Why?" she asked.

"Something to do." He glanced up and down the street. "The beer was my idea, but she wanted one too. And it wasn't my idea to sneak around. Summer was the one who wanted to keep our relationship a secret."

"Sure," Lou remarked.

"Look, we're just friends. I wish it was more, so I do whatever she wants. Summer decides when we go out and where. Ask her if you don't believe me."

Was this sincerity or a desperate lie? Having been manipulated by Devon, maybe Summer had learned a thing or two.

"Does she know that you party with other girls?" Casey asked.

Tyler glanced over his shoulder. "They're with my brother and his friend. I asked Summer here but she said you grounded her. Anyway, she won't care if I'm with someone else."

"Dude, you seriously believe that?" Lou started to smile.

"Like I said, she's not my girlfriend. We just hang out."

"The footage showed you with your arm around her," Casey said.

"To protect her and keep her close," Tyler replied. "That night was insane. People looting and setting fires. A guy even got killed."

"Did you see it happen?"

"No. We were farther down the road."

Casey noticed that the dancers were now peering out the window. She turned to Lou. "We should go."

"No more speeding down our street," Lou said to Tyler, "and no more late curfews for Summer, got it?"

"I'll tell her. Can't guarantee she'll actually listen, though."

Tyler headed back to the house.

"I think he's telling the truth," Lou said as he cruised down the street. "Summer's independent and strong willed."

"True. Think he'll tell her about our chat?"

"Probably."

Summer would be upset over the invasion of her privacy, but wasn't it a guardian's responsibility to learn who she was spending time with? If Summer was truly calling the shots, that wasn't so terrible. But what exactly did she want from Tyler Price? The other troubling question was how much she herself had contributed to Summer's distrust?

When they arrived home, the only light on was the porch light.

"If he phoned her and she's pissed," Lou said, "we could be ambushed."

Casey hoped not. She was too tired to fight with anyone. They tiptoed up the creaky back steps, opened the door, and turned off the alarm.

"Silent so far," he whispered.

"It's fine. If Summer was up, Cheyenne would have greeted us at the door."

Casey followed Lou down the hallway, listening for sounds. At the second-floor landing, she and Lou paused outside Summer's door. All was quiet. As they crept upstairs and entered their apartment, Casey worried about what tomorrow would bring.

TWENTY

"**Y**ou wanted to see me?" Casey asked as she sat in front of Stan's desk.

"Yeah." He kept typing. "Gimme a sec."

Her supervisor looked far too pale. As much as Casey wanted Stan back on the job, perhaps his return was a mistake. It wasn't just his physical injury but the emotional trauma that concerned her. After the beating she took last year, Stan had insisted she seek counseling. She refused at first, then finally agreed. The sessions had proven helpful. When she suggested the same to Stan earlier today, he'd refused, stating that he wasn't seeking financial compensation for the missed work days.

Stan swiveled his chair to face her. "When I saw your note about the green theory, I called a friend with the Coquitlam RCMP. Seems they already knew about it."

Irritation swept through Casey. "Why didn't they tell us?"

"Probably because Gwyn and I haven't been at our desks much."

"And seconds-in-command aren't worth briefing?" Casey gripped the arm of the chair. "Or did they tell Gwyn but he didn't bother to tell me?"

"No idea." Stan's lips pinched together. "He hasn't mentioned the green theory to me."

"Our team and the drivers have a right to know, Stan. A description could save someone's life."

"Which is what I told my friend." Stan turned back to his screen. "He must have talked to the investigating officers because ten minutes ago I was emailed more details about their primary suspect."

Casey sat forward. "About bloody time."

"He's Charlie Applebee, also known as Charlie Apple," Stan read aloud. "Late thirties, Caucasian, dark hair, medium build, and usually unshaven. He's also a schizophrenic who rants about green monsters when he's off his meds."

"Is he homeless?"

"It looks that way, although officers haven't seen him in a while. Until three years ago, Applebee lived with his parents in Port Coquitlam. He had a run-in with the RCMP about that time and then his father died. His mother moved away, but Charlie stayed behind and started living on the streets. The mother claims she lost touch with him. Seems that Charlie doesn't like phones or living with others."

"The cops would know where the homeless hang out, though. Surely somebody knows something."

Stan shrugged. "They think he might have found a place to crash somewhere near Pinetree Way."

"Where Benny and the woman were attacked," Casey said. "The cops need to seriously search local neighborhoods."

"They're working on it." Stan gave her one of his measured stares. "Which is why we don't need to."

"But if we watch for Applebee, it'll increase the odds of spotting him."

"True." Stan scratched his beard and leaned his elbows on the desk. "My friend mentioned that Applebee likes crowds, probably because he'd be harder to spot that way."

"In daylight maybe, but you and Benny weren't in crowds, and he always seems to strike at night, or at least at dusk in the riot victim's case."

Gwyn barged in the room. His bald head glistened and his round face flushed as if he'd overexerted himself to come here. Casey wished he had the decency to knock before interrupting them.

"Didn't expect to see you today," Stan remarked.

Judging from the coolness of his tone and the unwelcome stare, he felt the same as she did.

"The insurance people want to meet." Gwyn zeroed in on Casey. "Why haven't I had a progress report on the firebug? You must've questioned staff by now and established at least some of the staff's alibis."

"There's nothing to report. No red flags anywhere."

"I find that hard to believe."

"I thought we agreed that daily reports weren't necessary," Stan said. "The cops don't want our help."

"This is about our own internal investigation." The lines around Gwyn's mouth deepened. "The cops don't have to know a damn thing about it."

The pair glared at each other for long seconds. Given Gwyn's perspiring brow and Stan's complexion, neither of them was in great shape. Casey worried that crap like this wouldn't help Stan heal.

"I still sign the paychecks," Gwyn added, his tone cold.

"Do you really want to play that card?" Stan asked, lowering his voice. "'Cause it seems to me that you need all the support you can get from supervisors, especially from one who's well connected to police jurisdictions all over the Lower Mainland."

Stan stared at his boss. "I'll be forced to withdraw my support if you keep treating my team like shit."

Casey held her breath. She'd never heard Stan threaten him like this before.

Gwyn blinked at him, then sank into the chair next to Casey and lowered his head. "I'm just trying to save my business from total annihilation. Is that so wrong?"

The resigned tone and downcast expression made Casey uneasy. Gwyn sat in silence for several long seconds before finally looking up.

"I worked my butt off to build something here," he said. "Started as a mechanic for BC Transit back in the day. Loved being around buses, riding them, working on engines." His bloodshot eyes peered at Casey. "Just like those damn kids who hung around the property."

"You mean the ones you called the cops on?" Stan asked.

"What?" Casey looked from Stan to Gwyn. "I knew they'd been banned from the premises, but I didn't know you involved the police."

"Gwyn didn't want the team to know," Stan replied.

She glared at Gwyn. "Why did you do that?"

"They were endangering themselves," Gwyn shot back. "One was nearly run over by a bus. Another was in the garage while mechanics were working. The last thing I needed was lawsuits from the parents of injured kids." He clasped his hands together. "Our insurance is about to go through the roof and we barely break even as it is. I might have to sell the company."

Casey and Stan exchanged worried glances.

"That's a bit drastic," Stan said. "Once the suspects are caught, things'll calm down."

"We'll see." He turned to Casey. "I'm willing to concede that the firebug might not be a current employee, so get a list of all missing uniforms, especially from those who left on bad terms."

"Can't your secretary just call the inventory clerk?" Stan asked.

"She's on medical leave for a few days."

Big surprise, Casey thought. Gwyn had probably driven her over the edge.

"Then call her yourself," Stan said.

"A request from me would raise suspicion," Gwyn retorted. "Casey can do it."

Stan's scowl wasn't easing the tension.

"Sure, no problem," Casey said. "I'll go see Angie."

"Good." Gwyn stretched out his legs.

"I've been thinking," Stan said. "A suspect list of current and former employees might not be enough."

"Meaning?" Gwyn asked.

"What about angry friends, family members, or riders? I've collected some hate mail over the past couple of years. One's from a fired employee's mother who demanded to know how they were going to pay their rent. She threatened to sue us for unlawful termination."

"You showed me that months ago and nothing came of it," Gwyn replied, "and I didn't see any new ones while you were away."

He checked his watch, then pushed himself out of the chair. "Give the cops the hate mail anyway. Maybe it'll lead to something." He left, shutting the door behind him.

"But it's old news," Casey mumbled to Stan. "If the cops show up at those peoples' door, it could trigger old resentments."

"Agreed. Our illustrious leader is not thinking rationally."

"You are, though, and you could be onto something with the angry friend, relative, or roommate angle." Watching Stan gaze at the bonsai plant on the corner of his desk, Casey realized that the poor guy seemed more depleted by the minute. "Why don't you go and get some rest. I can handle whatever comes up."

"Think I will. Thanks."

That he agreed so readily concerned her. Was Stan in worse shape than he was letting on?

Casey stepped out of his office. At the other end of the room, flustered human resources personnel were working hard. With all the resignations, medical leaves, and sudden vacations lately, their workload had to be soaring.

At her desk, Casey opened up a document on her PC as her phone pinged. A text message from Summer.

Can I have Tracy over for supper?

Sure.

Truthfully, Casey would have preferred a candid chat with Summer tonight, but it seemed right to cut her some slack. So far, there'd been no backlash about the confrontation with Tyler last night. Summer had left for school by the time Casey woke up this morning. If he'd told Summer about last night, she had chosen not to bring it up, for the moment.

Casey headed downstairs to the alcove where Angie handed out uniforms and maintained inventory. Her blue and green peacock curls looked like they hadn't seen a brush in a while. Angie got off the phone and swore under her breath.

"You seem a little frazzled," Casey said. "Have I come at a bad time?"

"I'm having my busiest month *ever*." The thick blue eyeliner around her pale eyes didn't hide the fatigue. "What can I do for you?"

"Sorry to add to your workload, but I've been asked to get a list of all missing uniforms from current and former employees for the past year."

Angie blew out a puff of air. "That'll take a bit of time to compile." She paused. "Is this about the fires?"

"I can't say."

Angie peered at her. "Word is that someone in a driver's uniform was seen running from the garage after it exploded. Gwyn thinks that one of our own did it, right?"

Ordinarily, she wouldn't take part in gossip, but Angie's chatty manner drew all sorts of information from people. She might have learned something interesting.

"There were several witnesses, including an employee, who saw someone in a uniform, yeah." Casey glanced at shelves of neatly folded shirts and cargo pants in the alcove behind Angie. "But the uniform could have been stolen."

"Totally." Angie looked down the hall toward the lockers and lunchroom, then beckoned Casey into the alcove. Once they were inside, Angie said, "Is Maurice one of the witnesses?"

"Sorry, but I've promised confidentiality." She made a point of appearing puzzled. "Why would you bring up his name?"

Angie hesitated. "Maurice spent time in jail not long before he started working here."

Casey tried not to show her surprise. "Really?"

"He's trying to clean up his life, but Roberto says he's having a tough time."

Like most women here, Angie adored Roberto. He loved gossip as much as Angie did.

"Between you and me," Angie whispered, "I wouldn't put it past him to take a uniform and do some damage."

"MPT gave him a job, though. Why would he do that?"

"Gwyn found out about his alcoholism and police record a little while back and wanted Maurice gone. But the guy's apparently a genius with engines, so his supervisor insisted that he stay. If Gwyn changes his mind, there could be a walk-off-the-job revolt. All the mechanics like him."

Gwyn hadn't mentioned Maurice as a suspect, so maybe it wasn't true. Or maybe he didn't want to single out the man without more evidence If Maurice believed that Gwyn was about to get rid of him, would he strike back? The arson attempts against Gwyn's office and car sure seemed personal. Yet Maurice didn't strike her as a vengeful hothead who acted on emotion. Besides, the garage fire had caused major problems for him and the other mechanics.

"You have to admit that a lot of staff are upset with Gwyn," Angie said. "For all I know, the arsons are a group effort."

Intriguing idea. "Any idea who might be in that group?"

Angie glanced over her shoulder. "Dimitri's still mad about the assaults on him and Benny. And Ethan has a buddy whose dad was a dispatcher until he got fired for always showing up late. It seems that the dad can't find another job."

"I remember him. Last name was Samuels." A middle-aged man who'd also been fond of badmouthing Gwyn, but that was over a year ago. "Can't recall his first name, though."

"Rick, I think."

Why would the guy wait to cause trouble now? More troubling was that Dimitri's and Ethan's names had come up again.

"I need to get going," Casey said, "but could you email me that list of missing uniforms sometime today?"

"I'll try." Her ruby lips pinched together. "If you visit Benny, say hi for me. I miss him."

Casey smiled. "Will do."

Another trip to the hospital wouldn't be a bad idea. She'd sure like to know if any drivers had dropped by. It was possible that the culprit could have let something slip, although Benny might not remember. Meanwhile, she would learn what she could about Rick Samuels.

Back at her desk, Casey's thoughts turned to Charlie Applebee, hater of green, lover of knives and crowds. She googled the City of Coquitlam. It wasn't long before she discovered that a high school track-and-field event would be held this weekend at the same stadium where the rally had taken place.

TWENTY-ONE

Casey approached Benny's bed, disconcerted by the puzzlement on his face. Only four days had passed since she last saw him. Granted it felt much longer, but surely he hadn't forgotten an old friend and coworker.

"Hi, Benny." As recognition dawned on his face, relief swept through her.

"Casey. Good to see you." He paused. "Not married yet, are you? I've lost track of time."

"It's still three weeks away. Angie says hi. She misses you."

His smile was the first she'd seen since before the attack. She pulled up a chair, grateful to see that the bruises on Benny's face had faded significantly.

"You look much better," Casey said.

"Gettin' there." He started to sit up but stopped.

Casey didn't want to upset Benny with talk about the attack or the fires, but Angie had sent her the names of six employees who'd reported lost uniforms over the past twelve months. No one had reported a stolen uniform. Five on the list were employees who'd quit in the past year. All were older and two of them were women. None would have been fit enough to hop tall fences and race down side streets.

The sixth person was Wesley Axelson, but Wes was far too large to match the description of the guy seen leaping the fence. Even Rick Samuels had turned out to be a dead end. A social media search revealed that the guy liked taking selfies and had gained a lot of weight since leaving MPT. He touted himself as an assistant manager in retail, with another selfie depicting his nametag and store logo. That left only Ethan and Dimitri as prime suspects, and she needed to know if either man had come by to see Benny.

"I guess a few drivers have dropped by to visit?" Casey asked.

"Yvette says there've been a few, but I don't remember much."

The patient in the bed opposite mumbled something in Italian. She kept her eyes closed, so it was hard to tell if she was dreaming or dozing. Casey had no idea if Benny managed to get any quality rest in this place.

"Hello, Casey."

She turned to find Yvette entering the room.

"Hi." Damn. She was hoping to talk to Benny alone. Unlike Benny, Yvette looked worse than she had a few days ago. Her hair hung in greasy strands. Dark smudges behind her glasses showed her fatigue. "Any idea when they'll be sending Benny home?"

"In a couple of days." She placed a backpack on the floor. "Hi, Dad. I brought you some clothes to wear home."

"Thanks. Can't wait to get out of here." He glanced at the mumbling patient.

"Hopefully our coworkers haven't overstayed their welcome. A lot of them are worried about you," Casey said.

"The huge man with red hair, Wesley, has dropped by, but never stays long," Yvette said. "And there's the good-looking Greek who was also injured. He seems angry about everything."

"Dimitri," Casey murmured. "Benny, has Ethan Carruthers come by? He's the guy who's lead singer in a band, remember?"

"Yeah. Haven't seen him."

"Neither have I," Yvette remarked.

"What about the mechanics? I know that Roberto's been worried about you."

"He came by at least once that I recall, and Maurice comes by a lot," Benny said.

"Is he the guy who reads the Bible to you?" Yvette asked.

Benny nodded. "Born-again Christian."

"I didn't realize he knew you that well," Casey remarked.

"He doesn't. I think he's trying to help in his own way."

Interesting. Maurice was small and wiry. She still had a hard time believing that he was the arsonist, but had she underestimated the depth of his anger at Gwyn for wanting him gone?

"The man gives me the creeps." Yvette shook her head. "Each time I see him, I think of last rites, and we're not a religious family."

"You talkin' about that old drunk?" Benny's eldest son Max sauntered into the room.

"He's cleaned up his act," Benny replied, "and he's in his forties, which isn't old."

Max shrugged and turned to Casey. "Have you learned any more about the crazy nut who ambushed him? The cops aren't telling us squat."

"Same at our end."

Max's jaw tightened. "Is that so?"

Casey didn't appreciate the facetious tone. She glanced at the Italian patient, who was still muttering to herself.

"Has anyone at MPT even bothered to get updates from the cops?" he asked.

She returned the kid's stare. "We've been overwhelmed with emergencies this week."

"I saw the garage fire on the news," Yvette said. "Looks like someone's targeting MPT's president."

"Possibly." Casey watched Max wander toward the window. Keeping his back to her, he looked outside.

"Can't say I blame them," Yvette answered. "Employees have suffered enough under that man."

"Don't talk like that," Benny said.

"Sorry, Dad, but the salary freeze and reduced hours over the last couple of years were just wrong, and when was the last time you had a Christmas bonus?" Yvette turned to Casey. "Dad was hoping to save something for Reese's education, but it hasn't worked out."

"It would have if he worked for TransLink," Max grumbled, keeping his back to them. "Misguided loyalty doesn't pay the bills."

Casey feared that she'd start an argument if she stayed much longer. Besides, there was little she could say to Benny in front of his family. "Benny, I should get going."

Max spun around. "You expect us to believe that the cops haven't told you about the wacko who's been running around stabbing anyone who wears green?"

Crap. "Where did you hear that?"

"I have my sources."

Like one of Benny's visitors? Word had gotten around about the green angle. Understandably, most of the drivers didn't want to wear uniforms to work, but their supervisors pointed out that it hadn't mattered in Stan's case. Drivers realized that the problem wasn't just the color they were wearing, but the green buses they were operating. They now felt as if they were stuck working inside a huge bull's-eye.

"I think you know more than you're saying," Max said.

Yvette tilted her head. "Is this true, Casey?"

Casey turned to Benny, who appeared to be drifting off. "There've been rumors and I'm not a big fan of those."

"Tell us anyway," Max said.

Better play along to stay on the family's good side. "There's a theory that the suspect is a mentally ill homeless person who lives in the area where Benny and others were attacked."

Max sneered. "Ya think?"

"Don't be an ass," Yvette snapped. "Casey's trying to help."

"All she's doing is stating the obvious."

"Stop." Benny opened his eyes, suddenly alert. "Leave her alone."

"It's okay, Dad." Yvette leaned over and patted his arm while she glared at her brother. "We'll accomplish more if we stay calm and work together."

"You keep telling yourself that," Max retorted.

Not for the first time, Casey thought about the angry friend or relative theory. As she observed Max, she began to wonder if that possibility was standing right here in this room. Max would have no trouble fitting into Benny's uniform. Having apprenticed as a mechanic, he also knew MPT's layout. The uniform Benny wore when he was stabbed would have been bloodied and unwearable now. But every driver had two, so where was the second one?

"Tell you what," Casey said, turning to Yvette. "I'll see what else I can dig up and then give you a call."

"Thanks," she replied. "I'll be staying at Dad's until he can look after himself. I'll give you my cell number."

"Benny, with your permission, I could open your locker and bring your belongings to your house," Casey said. "Stan has a list of all the combinations. Might be a good idea to check for leftover food too."

"Appreciate it," he mumbled, appearing to drift off.

Casey ignored Max's glowering eyes. Did he not believe that she wanted to help, or did he not want her ingratiating herself with his family? A guilty man would certainly be suspicious of her motives.

"The uniform he was wearing needs to be replaced," Casey said to Yvette. "If his spare's in his locker, I'll find out the size and see that he gets another one."

"Don't bother," Max muttered. "Doubt he'll be back at that shithole."

"That's Dad's decision, *not* yours," Yvette replied. "Honestly, I'm not sure he should be living with you two hotheads. Maybe he should sell the house and come live with me."

Max's hands curled into fists. "You just said that Dad should make his own decisions. What a hypocrite." He stomped out of the room.

"Sorry about all the hostility, Casey," Yvette said. "Needless to say, Dad's future is a controversial topic in our family."

"Don't worry about it. This is an incredibly stressful time for all of you."

She nodded. "My brothers are desperate to blame someone."

And Gwyn, as much as the Blade Man, was the best target. Another thought occurred to her. If Max had gotten hold of Benny's ID badge, he'd be able to get in and out of the admin building after hours. She twitched and shifted her feet.

"I understand," Casey said, starting toward the door. "I'll be in touch once I've emptied his locker."

"Thanks for your help." Yvette's downcast eyes didn't quite meet hers.

"You're welcome."

Casey hurried down the corridor, hoping she'd spot Max before he took off. She wanted to know the make of the vehicle he drove, and asking Yvette would have been awkward. The hospital wasn't large and there weren't many exits. The closest lot was near emergency. Casey maneuvered past visitors, patients, and hospital personnel until she reached the elevator. Its slow descent made her wish she'd taken the stairs.

Finally, the door slid open on the main floor. Casey started past the gift shop, then froze. Max was talking to Reese by the information desk a few yards beyond the shop and across the corridor. Their heads were close together, conversation low.

Casey ducked inside the shop and nodded to the clerk. She wandered close to the windows and peeked between the display of stuffed bears. Were the brothers working together, plotting revenge against MPT? If so, there might be evidence in their vehicles or in Benny's house.

Reese headed toward the elevator while Max marched to the nearest exit. The moment the elevator doors closed, Casey rushed out of the gift shop and through the waiting area in emergency. She made it outside just in time to see Max drive away in a silver Dodge Ram. No point in running after him for the license plate. She knew where he lived.

TWENTY-TWO

"Never thought I'd see the day when you and I would be working on the same bus," Lou said, as he followed Casey out of MPT's admin building.

"Neither did I."

She didn't mind that Marie had called in sick. She probably was. With three kids to support, Marie needed every penny she earned. None of the other security team members were available, and Stan didn't want Lou to drive in the Coquitlam hot zone without backup.

"Think Summer will behave without us around?" he asked.

"Hard to say. She was surprisingly calm after I told her about our late-night chat with Tyler. Didn't really say anything other than to confirm that he'd already told her about it." Still Summer's tell signs had made it clear she wasn't happy about the visit. "Just to be safe, I've asked Kendal to drive by again."

"She'll probably invite Tyler over tonight," Lou said, boarding the bus after her. "God knows what they'll get up to."

"I can't keep them separated, and setting more rules seems counterproductive."

As Casey reflected on Summer's behavior over recent weeks, she began to realize how long the secrecy had been going on. She regretted not recognizing the signs sooner.

"Have you given any more thought to telling her about Rhonda?" Lou asked.

"Still wrestling with it."

He adjusted the mirrors. "I know you don't want to hear this, but what if Rhonda doesn't have much time left? Would Summer forgive you for keeping her in the dark?"

"Probably not." The issue had been keeping her up nights.

Her greatest fear was that Rhonda would die alone and emotionally detached from her daughter. If she told Summer about the cancer, she'd betray Rhonda. If she didn't, then Summer would likely feel betrayed.

"It doesn't seem right to do it before her final exams and the wedding," Casey said.

"Rhonda will have had the surgery by then, though."

"I know."

The more Casey thought about it, the more she believed that Rhonda did know the date and location of her surgery. She just didn't want them to know, and Casey had no idea what to do about it.

She looked up at the cloudy sky. Rain wasn't unusual in June. She hoped their wedding day would be warm and dry, that she could put aside worry about Rhonda. She also prayed that the siege against MPT would be over by then. Wishing was one thing, though. Seeing it happen was something else.

Del, Felicity, and Lawrence boarded the bus for the second night in a row. Oh joy.

"Casey!" Felicity exclaimed. "You're working here tonight?"

"Yes." She barely cracked a smile. "You were expecting someone else?"

"Marie," Felicity answered, then clamped her hand over her mouth.

The sheepish glances between Lawrence and Del told her enough. It appeared that Del had hacked the database again. Why didn't that kid understand that he needed to stop?

"I see." She looked from one to the other. "What are you three doing back in Coquitlam?"

"We're going to hang with Travis."

"Does Marie have a cold or flu?" Lawrence asked. "There's a lot of that going around."

Good thing they were going to see Travis. Casey wasn't sure she could take another whole evening of chatter, questions, and more choruses of "Wheels on the Bus."

. . .

The bus was blissfully quiet for 10:30 on a Friday night. A dozen people were on board, and the MPT Friends had exited over two hours ago. The trio had shared thoughts about the Blade Man's frequent strikes, including the awful possibility that his violent rampage might not be finished. Their conversation had raised a frightening question. Who would be next?

Where was all the anger coming from? It wasn't just on the streets and at her workplace, but in her home and with Benny's family too. She didn't look forward to visiting Yvette tomorrow, but it had to be done.

Lou had been with her when she opened Benny's locker and found a pair of shoes, two science fiction paperbacks, and an umbrella. The absence of a uniform was disheartening. She shared her suspicions about Reese and Max with Lou, but to her surprise he didn't dismiss the theory. In fact, he told her that Max occasionally came by after Benny's shift to have a few beer with the guys.

"The last time Max joined us was two months ago. Max and Benny argued about MPT's lousy salaries. Benny told him that good friends were worth more than good money. Max didn't like that and left. Maybe the anger's grown into something more."

Without real proof, neither she nor Lou wanted to talk to the police yet. If cops started questioning the family, what would it do to Benny? He was so vulnerable right now. On the other hand, if Max was behind the arsons, he needed to be caught. If she found Benny's uniform in his house and that uniform smelled of gasoline or smoke, she'd let the cops know.

Casey brooded over this until they reached the hot zone and two guys in their late teens boarded the bus. Both glared at Lou and Casey. It took her only a few seconds to figure out why. One of them was Junior, the light blond Bandana Boy who'd cut his hand trying to climb through the bus window the night of the riot.

The boys took a seat at the back. Given the number of times she and MPT drivers had crossed paths with the Bandana Boys since the riot, they probably lived in the area. Judging from the hostile expressions, they weren't done sparring with MPT personnel either.

Casey scrolled through her phone until she found the photo she was looking for and showed it to Lou. "I don't know the dark-haired guy, but the blond kid tangled with us at the riot."

"The cops are probably still looking for vandals and looters," Lou said. "Call them."

As Casey did so, she turned to Junior, who was still glaring at her and saying something to his buddy. Junior stood and pulled a shiny blade from his pocket, then sat down again.

"Crap," she muttered. "He's got a knife."

Lou pressed the alarm and updated dispatch, who would notify the police. He pulled up to the next stop. Casey knew he wouldn't be moving until Junior was off the bus. Junior wasn't making any move either, which suited her just fine. But would he stay put until the cops arrived?

Casey sat in a seat reserved for seniors and the physically challenged, observing the boys until Del, Felicity, and Lawrence climbed on board. Damn it, their timing couldn't be worse.

"Thanks for waiting," Del said, turning to Casey. "Travis says hi."

Casey nodded. "Actually, we'll be stopped for a few minutes, so you might want to pick up a TransLink bus."

Del looked from him to Casey, then turned his attention to the passengers. "Problem?"

Her stomach knotted. Why couldn't they mind their own business for once? "If you three want to stay, don't sit near the back."

Junior and his buddy stayed in their seats, while Junior yelled out "Security bitch!" The buddy, about the same age as Junior, appeared to have no weapon, but his sneer and swagger suggested that he was all in with whatever Junior had in mind.

As if sensing trouble, a passenger left through the back exit. Another couple exited through the front. The Friends took seats near the middle, their attention swiveling from Casey to the boys and back again. Felicity raised her phone and began recording the boys. Casey wanted her to stop, but was reluctant to draw attention to the girl.

Lou stood. "Sorry, folks," he called out. "I've been asked to stay here a few minutes."

The remaining passengers barely looked up from their phones. Apparently, none of them were in a great hurry to reach their destination.

"Why?" Junior started down the aisle, followed by his buddy. "There's no good reason to keep us here." He scowled at Lou. "Get this bus moving."

He paused near the Friends, apparently unaware that he was being recorded. Felicity was sitting next to the window. Del was beside her and Lawrence in front of them.

Casey stood, her heartrate accelerating. "I've got this," she said to Lou.

"Careful," he murmured.

The passengers, most in their twenties or thirties, now watched the scene with cautious expressions. Displaying her badge, Casey reminded Junior that they'd met before. The kid's response was to show her his knife.

"Drop the knife on the floor right now," she said, stepping back. "Carrying a weapon on this bus is illegal. Do you understand?"

"Ya think I give a shit?" Junior shot back.

"I can take the driver," the buddy remarked. "He ain't nothin' to worry about."

Casey glanced over her shoulder at Lou, who was now standing right behind her, trying not to smile. The kid had no idea how well Lou could handle himself in one-on-one encounters. Although his injuries from the riot had healed, she preferred that he didn't acquire new ones. Lou crossed his arms. Casey put the badge in her pocket. She'd had defensive training, but that was some time ago. Even then, they'd been instructed to avoid confrontations where weapons were involved. Not always possible in real-life situations.

"Come on!" his buddy yelled. "Take her down, Liam! She's fat and old."

Liam. Okay then. Casey gritted her teeth. Thirty-three was *not* old and an extra twenty pounds was *not* fat. Liam adjusted his grip on the knife, then adjusted it again. Doubt flickered across his face.

"The cops are on their way, and you're being recorded on camera." Casey pointed at the camera in the ceiling. "Our dispatch office can also hear every word." Liam didn't need to know that their lousy sound system had probably already cut out.

"Cops won't touch minors," Liam said, sneering at her.

"Thanks to your part in the riot, they will," Casey replied. "You guys were all recorded."

"Bullshit. If they had anything, they would have arrested me that night."

"They didn't have the recordings then." She paused. "They do now."

Liam's cheeks flushed pink as his gaze darted among the passengers. He spotted Felicity with her phone raised.

"Hey!" He pointed the knife at her. "Shut that off!"

Liam reached past Del and tried to grab the phone. Del pushed Liam so hard that he lost his balance and fell, knocking the knife from his hand. Casey kicked the knife under a seat. As Liam got to his feet, Del tackled him to the floor. The buddy leapt on top of Del.

"Stop it!" Casey yelled. She and Lou hauled the buddy up. "Del, get up!"

As Del struggled to his feet, Liam swept the floor with his hands, apparently in search of the knife.

"Don't bother," Casey answered. "It's unreachable."

Lawrence pulled Del further back from an infuriated Liam.

"I'm gonna kill you, bitch!" Liam screamed at Casey.

"A death threat and assault with a weapon have serious consequences, regardless of age," Casey said, forcing herself to stay calm. "Think about what you're saying."

"You're being recorded everywhere, dude," Lou remarked, pinning the buddy's arms behind his back.

A quick survey of all those phones pointed at him transformed Liam's anger into twitchy agitation. Out the corner of her eye, Casey noticed two police cruisers pulling up. Seconds later, RCMP constables boarded the front and back exits. Liam jumped onto an empty seat and tried to squiggle his way through an open window.

"Seriously?" Casey remarked. "What is it with you and windows?"

After describing the kid's behavior at the riot and this latest incident, the cops shook their heads. One of them retrieved the knife while a second cop relieved Lou of Liam's buddy.

The third officer addressed the handful of people who remained on the bus. "We'd appreciate it if you could wait and talk to us about what happened here. I'll be with each of you shortly." He took hold of Liam's ankles. "Should I push you through?" the constable asked. "Landing on your head might knock some sense into you."

"That's police brutality!" Liam shouted.

"We could just drive the bus to the Coquitlam detachment," Casey remarked. "Let him hang out the window like a dog."

The officer smiled. "Wouldn't want you to go out of your way." He now gripped Liam's belt. "Back inside, young man." The cop didn't have to pull hard before Liam was safely in his grasp.

"Ow! I'm gonna charge you with assault, asshole!"

"Really? You brought a knife on board and threatened to kill someone, and you're yelling about brutality?"

The constable's scrutiny had the kid squirming so badly that Casey couldn't help grinning.

"We've seen CCTV footage of your activities at the riot on May 17th," the constable added. "I'll have to arrest you and contact your parents."

"You can't do that! I've got rights!"

"As does everyone here," the constable replied. "Let's go."

His colleague was already escorting the buddy off the bus.

Liam's defiance withered. "You can't call my parents!"

"You're a minor," Casey remarked.

"Look, I know something about that guy who got stabbed at the riot," he blurted.

The constable and Casey exchanged wary looks. Was the kid bluffing or telling the truth? Casey had to know.

"Prove it," she said.

The kid glanced at her, then turned back to the constable. "Only if you promise not to call my parents."

"Can't do that, son. The crimes you're being charged with are serious."

Liam lowered his head, his facial muscles tightening.

"What's your name?" the constable asked.

"Liam."

"We need to know what you saw that night, Liam."

As Liam shook his head, Casey heard Lou's heavy sigh.

"Should I call your folks right now?" the constable asked. "Won't be hard to track them down."

"You can't," Liam said, his expression worried.

"I can, and if you won't cooperate, then you should know that juvenile remand isn't a fun place."

Liam's face paled. "Listen, I saw the victim fall, all right?"

The constable peered at him. "What else?"

"The guy right behind him suddenly turned around and tried to move against the crowd that was swarming a jewelry store. It was weird. The guy wasn't interested in the store, but he sure reacted fast to the guy's fall. I, uh . . ." Liam's gaze darted around the bus. "I got the feeling that he had something to do with it, so I followed him."

Casey glanced at Lou, who frowned at Liam.

"Why follow him because of a feeling?" Casey waited for an answer, but the kid avoided her gaze. "You saw the man stab the victim, didn't you?"

"No. I , , . " Liam's Adam's apple moved up and down.

"Liam," the constable said, "did you see where he went?"

The kid hesitated before nodding. "Back down Glen Drive. Stayed there until he got to High Street, then cut through Westwood Village."

Casey was aware of the complex. There were commercial stores below several floors of condos.

"He dropped something in a garbage can," Liam added.

"Did you see what it was, by any chance?" the cop asked.

Liam cleared his throat. He appeared to deflate as his shoulders rounded. "A paper towel with blood on it."

And he hadn't shared this until now? Casey rolled her eyes.

"The riot was three weeks ago," Lou said. "Garbage would have been picked up."

"You should have let us know right away." The constable's stare made the kid squirm again.

Liam kept his eyes downcast as the constable ushered him off the bus. Casey noticed the Friends relaxing back in their seats, their faces animated as they whispered to one another. They'd gotten the excitement they'd been hoping for, more fodder for the chat group. Casey prepared herself for another talk with the trio about the importance of discretion.

TWENTY-THREE

Charlie Applebee wasn't a morning person, or so Casey had concluded. Each of his attacks had occurred in the early evening or after dark, so she saw no reason to attend the high school track meet until mid-afternoon. If the urge to kill someone wearing green overwhelmed Charlie, he could show up today. Given that two constables were patrolling the area, the RCMP thought so too. Many people were here on this warm, sunny Saturday. Unfortunately, one of the competing teams was wearing green, as were their supporters. Charlie would have his pick in this crowd.

Going after adults at night was one thing, but would he be crazy enough to attack kids in daylight? As it was, the whole green-hating angle made little sense. Grass was green. Trees were green. As far as Casey knew, the nut didn't go around stabbing bushes and leaves. On the other hand, maybe he did. Who knew how deep the crazy went?

Scanning the stadium, she observed the partially covered bleachers opposite her. To the left of the bleachers, people were lining up to buy food. Even from here, she detected the smell of frying onions. She strolled past the high jump area and started around the south end of the track, paying close attention to the athletes in green. Another constable strolled past the concession stand, his head swiveling back and forth as he surveyed the crowd.

Using her small, lightweight binoculars, Casey zeroed in on the javelin area by the stadium's east perimeter. So far, there was no sign of any man dressed in black. A teen cleared the high jump bar and the crowd cheered. Casey turned her attention to the hurdlers preparing to race until her ringing phone distracted her.

Rhonda. Casey's body went still. A second call in two days couldn't be good.

"Rhonda?" She moved away from the noise. "Are you okay?"

"You tell me."

Casey flinched. "What do you mean?"

"I called Summer a few minutes ago to say hi and she didn't sound happy to hear from me." Rhonda paused. "What's up with my daughter and what have you learned about the boy-friend?"

Crap. Not a good time to get into it. "I learned that he's not a boyfriend, but just a kid she hangs with. There's no romantic involvement."

"Are you sure? Have you met him? What's his name? What grade is he in?"

Casey sighed. "I've met Tyler and he's not horrible. He's a year or two older than Summer."

A starting pistol went off and the race was underway.

"Where are you?" Rhonda asked.

"Doing surveillance at a track-and-field event." The crowd grew louder. Casey raised her voice. "Have you found out when your surgery will be?"

"This week, I think."

"No exact date?"

"Not yet."

Was this true? Not that Casey wanted to confront her right now. "You'll survive this, Rhonda."

"If you say so."

Not the most optimistic of attitudes. "Have you reconsidered keeping this from Summer?"

"No."

How could she convince Rhonda to confide in her daughter? After surgery, there could be months of radiation or chemo treatments. More pain and anguish. She shouldn't have to endure that alone.

"Casey, I have to go. I'm sorry."

"No, Rhonda. Wait. We love you. You know that, right?" Casey heard the desperation in her own voice, but didn't know how to stop. "Summer's attitude is a defense mechanism. She misses you so much that she can't express it without falling apart."

Rhonda didn't answer right away. "Thank you for taking good care of my daughter." Her voice cracked. "I'll never be able to repay you."

"I'm not running a tab, Rhonda. Never will."

Rhonda hung up, leaving Casey with the phone pressed to her ear, her hand shaking. While she fretted about Rhonda, it took several seconds to realize that a man in black was rummaging through a garbage can just a few yards away.

Casey's mouth grew dry and her heartbeat accelerated. Giving the man a wide berth, she circled the area until she saw his heavily lined face and long gray-and-white beard. Not Charlie. She shoved the phone in her pocket. His stained and torn clothes branded him as homeless. He picked up a half-eaten hot dog, studied it a moment, then crammed the food into his mouth. She'd seen this type of activity so often in Vancouver

196 Debra Purdy Kong

that it hardly fazed her anymore. Casey removed a nearly full water bottle from her backpack.

"Excuse me." She said strolling up to the guy. The man chew faster, as if afraid she'd demand the hot dog back. "Would you like this?"

The man swallowed his food. Swollen, gnarled fingers wrapped around the bottle. "Thanks."

She tried not to stare at the splotch of mustard in his mustache. "How's it going?"

His tentative smile exposed three gaps where the upper teeth should be. "Just waking up means it's a good day, mostly."

A sense of humor. Good. He might be open to talking. She glanced around. No sign of anyone else dressed in black. "Were you at the union rally three weeks ago? Bet there were plenty of cans and bottles to collect that night."

"Bottles were all broke."

Casey nodded. "I guess they would be. Did you hear about the stabbing on Glen Drive?"

He squinted at her. "You a cop?"

"No, I work for Mainland Public Transport. Two of our employees were stabbed near here."

"Don't know nothin' about that." He went back to rummaging.

"Their attacker wore black clothing." Casey raised her voice over the cheering crowd. "Word is that he's a man named Charlie Applebee."

The old man's eyebrows rose. "Charlie Apple did that?" He rubbed the bristles on his cheek.

"You know him?"

Wariness flooded the man's face, as if he'd just realized his mistake.

"It's okay," Casey said. "The police already know who he is. They're the ones who told us. What we don't know is where Charlie hides out." She removed her wallet and pulled out a ten-dollar bill. "Any idea where that might be?"

The old man stared at it hungrily. "Wish I did."

"Can you tell me about him?" She held the bill out.

He grabbed the money and shoved it into his pocket. "Well, he likes to eat apples. That's why we call him Charlie Apple."

"Does he like to eat the green ones?"

"Sure, that's their natural color. He likes natural green, like in plants and grass and what-not."

Casey thought about this. "But not green clothing, for instance?"

"Never that. No way." The old man chuckled. "One time, he broke a store window and butchered a St. Paddy's Day display. He avoids the holiday altogether now." The old man's expression grew somber. "Charlie once said that people in green are evil spirits pretending to be trees. 'Course, he was probably off his meds when he said it."

"Meds?"

The old man nodded. "Charlie's been hearing voices a long time, he told me once. Talks to 'em too. Doubt Charlie even knows what normal feels like."

Schizophrenia perhaps? "How long have you known him?"

He scratched his chin. "Started seeing him on the streets about four years ago, I guess, give or take." The man took a gulp of water. "When things get bad, Charlie wanders the streets all night, arguing with hisself, or maybe the voices in his head."

Casey noticed a young couple with a stroller, staring at the old man in disdain. "Think he'll show up today?"

"Charlie likes crowds, but one look at the cops and he'll vanish." He wiped his mouth with the back of his hand, but it only smeared the mustard stain. "If Charlie's stabbing people, he's probably laying low. The man's crazy, but he ain't stupid."

True, or he would have been caught by now. "Does Charlie have favorite hangouts?"

The old guy lifted a slightly mashed juice box out of the garbage and dropped it in his bag. "He likes the mall on rainy days,"

"What about sunny days like this?"

He gave her a lopsided grin. "Look for him in the trees. That's where he feels safe. Charlie has agility. Climbs faster than anyone I know."

Casey gazed up at the enormous trees around the stadium's perimeter. She supposed he could have climbed a tree the night he stabbed Benny, then waited for the commotion to die down. But what about Stan? She couldn't remember if there'd been trees nearby or not.

"If Charlie's living on the streets, where would he hide if there are no trees around?"

"Don't think he's on the streets right now. Least I haven't seen him a while. Word is he's got a place somewhere around here, though I don't know where, I swear that's a fact."

"When was the last time you saw him?"

"At the park 'n ride about a month ago." The old man wiped sweat from his forehead. "Seen him there a few times over the past year. Guess you could call that a hangout."

There was one not far from here. Most of the bays belonged to TransLink, but one was reserved for MPT buses. Casey again scanned the grounds. "Does Charlie ever wear anything other than black?"

"Not that I've seen." He peered at her. "Don't go after him yourself, miss. If Charlie's carrying a knife, then you best stay well away."

She flashed a grim smile. "That's the plan."

TWENTY-FOUR

Benny Lee's quiet, residential street in South Burnaby was populated by modest, older homes. Judging from the grassy yards and many large trees, this neighborhood was a well-established testament to a time when single-family homes were affordable for average-income earners. Casey wouldn't be surprised if some of the homeowners had lived here for over forty years. These days, new owners would have to be double-income professionals, probably with enormous mortgages. Even Benny's older home on an average-sized lot would be worth well over a million bucks. No wonder Yvette wanted him to sell.

Glancing at the bag containing his personal belongings, she wondered if Benny truly was having doubts about driving a bus again. Should she persuade him to stay, convince him that he'd make a great supervisor? Benny never saw himself as management material, though. Could be a hard sell, seeing as how staff disillusionment, fear, and anger were at an all-time high.

These days, everyone was looking over their shoulder, praying they wouldn't be on MPT property when the next explosion went off. And most employees believed there'd be another one. If it did happen, Gwyn would blame her, maybe fire her on the spot. As much as she loathed his tactics and brusque manner, she knew in her heart that she really wanted to stay with MPT, at least until most of her friends had moved on.

Casey parked across the street from Benny's house. Max's Dodge Ram wasn't here. If she was lucky, Reese wouldn't be home either. Benny's SUV was in the driveway, which meant that either Yvette or the brothers had ventured onto MPT property to pick it up. A newer model Toyota RAV was parked behind Benny's vehicle. Probably Yvette's. So, what did Reese drive?

She collected Benny's belongings and stepped out of the car. The light blue paint and white trim on Benny's house was streaked with grime in places and the lawn needed mowing. Ivy vines had spread across the cracked concrete walkway. Max and Reese should have been doing more to help around the house, the lazy jerks.

Children's happy shouts came from the backyard. Casey had phoned Yvette earlier to say she'd be coming by. Yvette told her to come around back, as she'd be working there. Casey headed down the side of the house, noting the detached garage to her left and the small dirt-encrusted window. Peeking through the window, she saw boxes, tools, bicycles, old appliances, and other junk everywhere. A perfect hiding place for arson paraphernalia like gas cans and glass jars.

Casey unlatched a gate and entered the backyard. "Hello?"

Two preschoolers were playing on the grass, Yvette was sweeping the patio. She looked up as Casey ambled toward her.

"Hi, Casey."

Dark circles still haunted her eyes and her black hair was gathered in a lopsided ponytail. She looked a lot like her mother before the cancer took hold. Casey had met Yvette's mom at a Christmas party shortly after she joined MPT. She remembered a warm vivacious woman, half Caucasian and half Chinese. Yvette had many of her mother's features—large brown eyes and high cheekbones—but her skin was paler.

"Thanks for bringing Dad's things."

"You're welcome. There weren't any valuables." Casey glanced at the bag. "Is Benny excited about coming home?"

"Relieved and anxious mainly. He's still quite weak, so it looks like I'll be staying here a while. Honestly, I wish he'd move in with me. This place is a pigsty, thanks to my bloody brothers."

Casey noticed the open back door. "I take it they aren't here?"

"They took off the moment I asked them to do some chores."

"That sucks." Casey glanced at the house. "Would you mind if I used your washroom? I'll leave the bag inside."

"Go ahead, but excuse the mess. The bathroom's next on my to-do list, but I needed a break from the inside work."

"I know what that's like. Lou and I are caretakers for the old, large house we live in."

She nodded. "Dad told me about your situation." Yvette paused. "All that responsibility must be hard."

"Sometimes."

Benny was one of the few people who knew how betrayed she'd once felt by Rhonda's violent act, and her trepidation when Rhonda asked her to continue living in the house and become Summer's legal guardian. She wished she could tell him about Rhonda's decision to keep her illness from Summer. Benny would have sound advice.

"A couple of months ago, Dad told me that you sold your father's home," Yvette said. "Was it difficult to let go of the house you were raised in?"

Why was she asking? Had Yvette given more thought to persuading Benny to sell his home?

"Not really," Casey answered. "After Dad died, I and my first husband moved in. When we split up, he stayed and paid rent until I was ready to sell. By that time any connection I felt for the place was gone."

"I know what you mean." Yvette watched her kids chase each other around the yard. "I haven't lived here in ages, but Dad still loves this place. Doesn't want to leave, even though selling it would give him more than enough to live on without ever having to work again. I know he looks and acts much younger than he is, but Dad will be sixty-five next year."

"Oh, I didn't realize." It sounded like Yvette had already discussed this with Benny.

"I think memories of Mom keep him here." Sadness crept over Yvette's face. "Maybe he's afraid the memories will fade away if he leaves."

"Benny's got a good head on his shoulders," Casey said. "Once he's stronger, he'll be able to weigh the pros and cons."

"I hope so."

Casey climbed the back steps, grateful that Yvette was staying outside. She entered the dated but pristine kitchen that smelled of Pine Sol. Benny's place was the standard design of the 70's. Three bedrooms and a bathroom on one side of the house, living and dining area and kitchen on the other.

Casey started down the hallway, recalling that the first bedroom door on the right was Reese's. At the last party, Benny mentioned that Max had turned the basement into his own suite. Casey hurried past the bathroom on the left and scooted into the master bedroom to find dated black lacquer furniture against ivory walls. The only bright colors in the room came from a desk next to the dresser, where tea candles and dried flowers were neatly arranged around a photo of Benny's wife.

Casey placed the bag on Benny's bed, then searched the open closet. No uniform. She rushed back down the hall and opened the closet by the front door. Nothing there either. A car door slammed in front of the house. Footsteps stomped toward the door.

She dashed into the bathroom just as the front door banged shut. Heavy footsteps clumped into the kitchen. Through the partially open window, Casey heard Reese's voice but couldn't tell what he was saying. She was tempted to go back and check the bureau drawers but she'd been gone long enough.

Casey headed back down the hall, pausing at Reese's door. Tempted as she was to peek inside, Reese was too tall and thin to fit into Benny's uniform, so it was unlikely he'd have it. But what about Max and the basement suite?

Back outside, Casey strolled toward them. Reese's startled expression turned to annoyance. "What are you doing here?"

Despite the kid's wiry frame, there was something formidable about him that went beyond the hostile attitude.

"Don't be rude." Yvette scowled at her brother. "Casey was kind enough to drop off Dad's belongings."

Casey didn't like his skeptical stare.

"Learn anything about this freak they're calling the Blade Man?" Reese asked her.

Casey cringed. She was reluctant to update them, partly because the cops wouldn't appreciate her sharing information they'd disclosed to Stan, but also because she didn't know what Max or Reese would do with that knowledge.

"Your expression tells me you know something," Yvette said.

"The suspect's name is Charlie Applebee and he was homeless, but might not be anymore." She saw the surprised glances exchanged between Reese and Yvette. "I talked to a homeless man this afternoon who knows Charlie. He said that Charlie hates the color green and likes to climb trees, which might be how he got away after he attacked Benny. I told the investigating officer about it an hour ago."

"What did the officer say?" Yvette asked.

"That I had no business interfering in their investigation."

"Seems that you're doing a better job than they are," Yvette said. "Keep going."

Casey hesitated. "I could wind up in a lot of trouble."

"Dad told me about your crime-solving skills." Yvette's expression grew intense. "He said that when people you care about are hurt, you'll do whatever it takes to get justice. We desperately need that, Casey."

Man, she was really pouring it on. "Searching for justice also resulted in serious repercussions."

"Just think about it, okay? I know Dad would be grateful," Yvette said. "Which reminds me, I have some injury forms that I helped him complete. Would you mind delivering them to your HR department for me?"

"Sure. I could look them over if you'd like," Casey replied. "I don't know if Benny told you, but I was on medical leave last summer. The paperwork was daunting, to say the least."

"I remember him talking about it," Yvette replied. "He was really worried. Said you were attacked by a home invasion suspect and had to postpone your wedding."

"Yeah. The guy's trial is this fall."

It frustrated her not to have received full closure yet. Benny's injuries were a painful reminder of the horrible things some people did to one another. And of the lack of proactive support for people like Charlie Applebee.

"Oh god, you made me realize something." What little color Yvette had on her cheeks drained away. "Dad might have to face his attacker in court one day."

"Not for a while," Casey answered. "The system doesn't move quickly."

"Which means this nightmare won't end quickly for Dad." She shook her head. "He'll stew over it."

"I found that going back to my normal routine, and staying busy really helped, especially when I was surrounded by friends."

Yvette appeared to be assessing her, as if trying to decide if the statement was helpful or not. "Let's get the papers. The sooner we submit them, the sooner Dad'll receive financial assistance."

"Which you'll control, no doubt," Reese grumbled. Without waiting for her response, he headed inside.

Yvette sighed and also started toward the kitchen door. "The forms are in my purse."

Casey glanced at the basement window overlooking the backyard. "Would you like me to stay here and watch the kids?"

"As long as the gate's closed, they'll be fine." She started up the stairs. "Better they're out here than getting underfoot inside."

"The latch didn't quite close properly. I'll check it and catch up with you inside."

"Thanks."

Casey ambled toward the gate, stopping to kick a wayward soccer ball back to the kids. Yvette was just entering the house when Casey opened the gate and hurried down the side. Scrunching down, she cupped her hands around her eyes and peered through the basement window into an open living and kitchen area scattered with dirty dishes. Clothing, a guitar, and other items cluttered the living room, but she didn't see any uniform.

She hurried to the back of the house and peered through that window. Same view, different angle, and still no uniform in sight. Unfortunately, Max's bedroom wasn't visible from this angle, but maybe it didn't matter. Max could just as easily keep the uniform in his truck.

Casey entered the kitchen, where Yvette had spread the contents of a large vinyl bag over the table. Rap music blaring behind Reese's door set Casey on edge.

"I must have left the forms in my car," Yvette said, "and I need Dad's health and work ID numbers from his wallet, which I put in his bureau."

"I'll fetch it for you, if you like."

"I appreciate it. His wallet's in the top drawer."

"By the way, have you found Benny's second uniform yet? It wasn't in his locker."

"Honestly, I haven't had time to look, but go ahead if you want." Yvette grabbed her car keys and hurried outside.

Perfect, although she doubted that the invitation extended to Max's basement suite. Casey hurried down the hallway and shut Benny's bedroom door to muffle the music. She glanced at the shrine, hoping that her invasion of Benny's privacy would be forgiven.

Opening the top drawer, Casey found herself staring at a mish-mash of socks and underwear. Good lord. The colorful briefs and brightly striped socks were far more information than she wanted.

Casey located the wallet quickly and peeked inside. His ID badge wasn't there. Nor was it on top of the bureau. She opened the other drawers. A missing uniform and badge. Not good. Casey was pulling open the fourth drawer when the door banged open.

"What the hell are you doing?" Reese glared at her.

Casey jumped. "I could ask you the same thing, banging the door open like that. Yvette asked me to get your dad's wallet, and I asked her if I could look for his uniform so I could get him another one in the correct size."

"Don't bother."

Casey returned his glare. "A lot of us don't want him to quit, Reese. We love Benny, and I know he loves his job."

Yvette appeared. "What's going on?"

"Caught her going through Dad's stuff," he replied. "Claimed to be looking for Dad's wallet and uniform."

"She is, and how dare you accuse our guest of anything."

Muttering a few swear words, Reese left the room.

Yvette sighed. "I'm not sure he'll ever grow up."

"Don't worry about it." Casey hesitated. "Look, I may sound naïve and overly optimistic, but I can't stand the idea of some violent freak scaring Benny out of a job he loves. I don't think your dad would want to leave under those circumstances."

"True, but what's the sense in returning until management takes more steps to protect drivers?" Yvette gazed at the papers in her hand. "If Dad sold this house, he could work part-time on his own terms."

This was the second time she'd raised the topic. Casey liked Yvette but didn't know her well. Teachers didn't earn a lot of money, and Casey couldn't remember what Yvette's husband did for a living. Was it possible she wanted to sell Benny's house to help with her own debts?

"Let's take the forms to the kitchen table." Yvette picked up Benny's wallet and headed down the hall.

"Yvette, do you know what happened to Benny's ID badge? I didn't notice it in his wallet or in his room, and it wasn't in his locker either. He wore it on a lanyard."

"I don't remember seeing it among the personal items the hospital gave me, but couldn't he just get another?"

"Yeah. It's just that those badges allow drivers access to our administration building after hours. Gwyn will freak out if he learns that it's missing, and probably blame me and Stan for not knowing about it earlier."

Yvette grimaced. "Maybe Dad lost it during the scuffle on the bus. Badges are only clipped to lanyards, right? It could have fallen on the floor and slipped under the seat or something."

"Right." Casey nodded. "I'll check it out." But what if one of Benny's sons had taken it?

Reese's door was again closed, the music still blaring. If he'd helped Max set those fires, then her question about Benny's uniform would be a red flag. And if this was true, then what would the boys do about it?

After Yvette filled in Benny's personal information, Casey took the sheets and headed for the front door. She tried not to stare at the clutter of mugs, plates, and beer bottles strewn about the living room.

"Thanks for coming by," Yvette said.

"You're welcome. I'll call Benny later in the week."

"He'd like that." Yvette's smile cracked and her expression grew solemn. "I don't want to belabor the point, but please help us find that Charlie psycho before he strikes again. There's been enough pain."

"I'll do what I can." She'd already taken a few steps down that slippery slope, but to go any further filled her with misgiving.

Casey strolled down the walkway, noting the older model, dark-green Honda Accord now parked out front. Must belong to Reese. She slowed her pace past the vehicle, noting the food wrappers in the back seat.

As Casey memorized the license plate, she could almost feel Reese's eyes on her from his bedroom window. She didn't care. The jerk needed to know that suspicion worked both ways. The entire security team would soon be watching for Max's and Reese's vehicles. If the brothers were responsible for the fires and decided to do more damage, she'd make sure they were caught. She just hoped Denny would forgive her.

TWENTY-FIVE

"**Y**our bachelorette spa day's all set for next Saturday," Kendal was saying on the phone, "but I'm worried you'll have to work. In fact, didn't you have a shift tonight?"

"It's been a rough week, so Stan gave me the night off." Seated on the cushion seat in her living room's bay window, Casey stretched out her legs and told Kendal about busting Liam, the conversation with the homeless man, and her visit with Yvette.

"Look, one more punk off the streets is a win, Casey. You're making progress."

"Meanwhile, morale's crumbling at work. Another driver quit, along with our part-time guard, Zoltan."

"Sounds like that spa day can't come soon enough. Meanwhile, how about a movie tonight?"

"Thanks, but I should stay here with Summer. By the way, I found out who she's been sneaking around with."

On hearing about Tyler Price, Kendal gave a low whistle. "Is he as sneaky as his loser brother?"

Kendal knew all about Devon. He'd shoplifted from the department store where she worked as a loss prevention officer. No one had realized what he'd done until Summer confessed days later.

"I don't think Tyler is as bad, but I could be wrong."

"I wonder how Devon feels about Tyler seeing his ex."

"No idea, but I'd be happier if the relationship ended soon."

"As long as you want it to end, then it probably won't," Kendal remarked. "Summer's highly intuitive."

"Tell me about it."

Summer had spent the entire evening in her room, declining Casey's request to join her for dinner. Punishment worked both ways, she supposed. Who knew how long the sulky silent treatment would last?

"There's something else," Casey mumbled.

While Casey told her about Rhonda's cancer diagnosis, she looked out the window. The sun had set a while ago. Casey gazed at the large weeping willow taking up most of the front yard.

"I don't know what to do, Kendal. It feels wrong to keep Rhonda's illness from her."

"Wait till the surgery's over, then reassess things. If it goes well for her, then Rhonda might feel optimistic enough to have a change of heart."

Through the willow tree's branches, Casey saw a small black vehicle pull up in front of the house. As Cheyenne and Summer rushed toward the car, Casey leapt to her feet.

"Holy shit! A car pulled up and Summer's getting inside with her dog!"

"Stay cool. Hysterics won't help, and don't hang up."

Phone still in hand, Casey ran out of the apartment and bounded down the stairs. She flung the front door open and dashed outside as the car took off.

"Damn it! She's gone."

"Okay, calm down," Kendal said. "You have some choices here."

"Is one of them killing Tyler Price?" She rushed back inside. "Because I'm up for that."

"Come on, girlfriend. Take a moment and breathe."

Casey preferred action. "I should call the cops and have her picked up. The guy only has his learner's license. Shouldn't even have a nonfamily member alone in the car."

"You'll be fanning the flames."

"Kendal, I'm about ready to start a friggin' bonfire!" She jogged up the porch steps and shut the door. She wanted to slam it, but that would disturb the tenants.

"Come on, Casey. Think this through."

Casey was too busy hyperventilating to try. "I should drive to his house, see if they're there."

"And if they are?"

"I'll bring her back home. Ground her for life. I don't know."

"Uh-huh," Kendal replied. "Maybe it's time to think about family counseling."

Casey's phone beeped. "I've got another call."

"Let me know what happens."

"Okay." She forced herself to slow her breathing before answering.

"It's me," Lou said. "The Blade Man's struck again."

"Oh no! Who?"

"Wesley, but he's okay. Deflected the knife with his arm, so he just needs a few stitches. He also managed to kick the freak in the face. Sent him flying right off the bus. Wes closed the door and called the cops, but the guy took off before they got there."

"So, Charlie Apple got a little payback. Good." Casey stepped into her apartment and leaned against the door. "Did Wes get a look at his face?"

"Said he had a three-or-four day stubble and bags under his

eyes. Late thirties or older. Definitely the Blade Man."

"Yep," Casey replied. "I was watching the news an hour ago, and there was a shooting in another part of Coquitlam tonight. Doubt there's much manpower left to search for Charlie. Anyway, something else has happened."

Casey paced the room as she told him about Summer's disappearance.

Lou muttered a couple of obscenities. "Did you call her?"

"Haven't had a chance. I was on the phone with Kendal when she took off, and then you called."

"If you get voice mail, leave a message. Tell her you'll send the cops after Tyler if she doesn't come home right away. Maybe we should have a talk with Tyler's mother."

Casey had a feeling that would make things worse. "I'll drive by the place. See what's what."

She peered out the bay window, wishing the car would pull up and Summer would return. A horrible thought struck her. "She took Cheyenne, Lou. What if she's run away?"

"Check her room."

Casey swallowed her rising fear.

. . .

Casey sat in her Tercel, staring at the Prices's rundown home. The lights were off, driveway empty. At least she'd found Summer's clothes and toiletries still in her room. But things were far from okay. It was time to do something.

Casey dialed 9-1-1. This wasn't a real emergency, but it could be if Tyler was in an accident. She provided a brief explanation about a young driver currently on the road with her fourteen-year-old ward. Gave them the license plate number and the make and model.

Tired and demoralized, she drove back home and parked at her usual spot at the back of the house. The porch and kitchen lights were on just as she'd left them. Lights from the tenants' studio suites on the second floor were off.

Lord, how the hell was she supposed to survive the rest of Summer's teen years? Ages eleven to fourteen had been challenging enough. Summer would be twenty-one when Rhonda was released from prison, provided she made parole, or lived that long.

Casey trudged up the back steps. Once inside, she turned off the alarm and listened to the silence. As she started down the hall, strobing lights flashed through the rectangle of thick, amber glass next to the front door. With trepidation and hope, she jogged down the hall and opened the door.

A patrol car was parked in front of a familiar black vehicle. The fence and bedraggled hedge kept her from seeing everything. Casey hurried down the steps, onto the walkway. At the gate, she saw Tyler. A cop stood in front of him. Summer and Cheyenne weren't there. Was Summer already inside or had Tyler dropped her off somewhere? Casey ran inside and jogged upstairs.

Without bothering to knock, she barged into the room. Summer stood at the window. She kept her back to Casey while Cheyenne padded up to her, tail wagging. Casey scratched the dog's head.

"What have you done?" Summer turned around, her face pinched with anger.

"What I told you I'd do," she answered. "You broke my rules and he broke the law. Did you think there wouldn't be consequences?"

"We just went to get ice cream and take Cheyenne for a walk. You said I should take her out more."

"At ten-thirty at night and without letting me know?"

"I called but the line was busy. Didn't know how long you'd be, so I left. Figured we'd be back before you even noticed."

"If you'd knocked, I would have answered."

Summer turned back to the window. "Whatever."

"Do you honestly believe that rules don't matter?"

"Sure, why not?" She kept her back to Casey. "It's in my genes, right?"

Casey was taken aback. "What does that mean?"

"Nothing. Forget it."

Casey shut the door. "I want to know."

Slowly, Summer turned around and folded her arms across her chest. "It means that my biological mom was a junkie and the mom who raised me wound up in jail 'cause she lost her mind and killed someone. Even my grandmother, who hasn't broken any laws that I know of, is crazy." Summer's eyes glistened. "You can't escape your genes. Ask my biology teacher."

Did Summer truly believe she was destined for a life of trouble and misery because of her bloodline?

"Summer, you're not a slave to genes, your family history, or your upbringing. You're more than capable of making better decisions than they did."

"Decisions about what?" Her eyes blazed. "I don't have a life!"

"What are you talking about? You have friends and volunteer work, and us."

"*You?*" The tears began to spill. "You and Lou are so busy with your own lives that you act like I don't exist."

So, Summer was acting out because she wasn't spending more time with the adults? Casey didn't buy it.

"How many times have I asked you to join me for dinner, and how many times have I asked how you're doing only to get a one-word answer before you dash off somewhere?" Casey couldn't stop the rising anger. "Why couldn't you have taken two minutes to tell me about Tyler and how he was a friend that you went places with? Why didn't you tell me how you felt? I would have made time."

"Tyler makes time for me without me having to ask and come up with a reason. You're the one I practically have to make an appointment with."

Casey sat on the bed and rested her elbow on her knees. Was all this really her fault? She shook her head. No. Not all of it, but Summer seemed intent on putting everything on her.

"Maybe Lou and I should have taken you rock climbing or hiking, or all the things that Tyler does with you, but we had no idea you were even interested. Until you quit the swim team a while back, your life was focused on that and school. You have good friends now, and I didn't want to curb your social life by making you spend time with us. Honestly, I assumed you preferred their company to ours."

Summer shrugged. "Doesn't matter. None of it matters. Not school or volunteering or Tyler. Nothing."

What was happening? Was this depression? Anxiety? Grief? Perhaps Kendal was right about family counseling.

"Sweetie, it *does* matter. I'm sorry if you've been unhappy and felt isolated, but running around breaking rules doesn't solve anything."

"I told you, it's in my DNA." Summer sat beside her, wiping the tears from her face. "What if I can't help doing something really bad like both of my mothers?"

Was this truly the source of her angst and rebelliousness? Casey didn't know how to answer her. She did know that Summer's self-esteem and confidence had taken a beating since Rhonda's incarceration. It appeared that the scars hadn't healed as much as Casey thought.

"You've got Lou and his family's support," Summer went on. "All I've got is a bitchy grandma, a dead biological mother, and her sister—the one who raised me for eleven whole years—in prison." The tears streamed down her face.

"You have me and Lou and his family too. We all love you, Summer."

Summer cried harder. Casey handed her a tissue and put her arm around her as her own face grew warm. Cheyenne sat before them, her large brown eyes looking from Summer to her and back to Summer. The dog's eyebrows twitched and rose inquisitively before she finally slumped onto the floor and rested her snout on her paws.

As Summer calmed down, she said, "When Mom gets out, I don't want to live with her. We'll drive each other insane."

"You don't have to think about that right now," Casey said softly. "I know it's unfair to have to deal with situations you didn't create, and of course you have doubts about the future. But Lou and I will always be here for you, and your mother loves you, so please don't dismiss her. She might not be around forever."

Uh-oh. She shouldn't have said that. Judging from Summer's scrutiny, her intuition was on full alert.

"What do you mean, she might not be around forever?"

Damn. "It's just that none of us are getting any younger and prison ages a person fast."

Summer's dark blue eyes stared at her. "Is she okay?"

How on earth was she supposed to respond to that? "I'm sure she's fine."

"No." Summer frowned. "Something's wrong. I heard it in Mom's voice the last couple of times she called. Now I hear it in yours." She edged closer to Casey until her face was only inches away. "What's going on?"

"I don't . . . I can't." Casey watched Cheyenne. "Rhonda made me promise not to say anything."

"If you don't tell me, I'll call the prison right now, or I'll have Tyler drive me out there tomorrow and cause a lot of shit, I swear."

"Don't." Casey looked up. "Please."

"Watch me."

"Summer—"

"Tell me!" Summer gripped her hand. "What's going on with Mom?"

Casey sighed. Rhonda would never forgive her for this. She'd figure out how to live with that later.

"Your mom has breast cancer and is scheduled for a mastectomy very soon."

Summer. "That means chopping it off, right?"

"It's a careful, surgical procedure." While Casey explained the possibility of radiation or chemotherapy treatments afterward, Summer's shocked expression didn't change. More tears slid down her cheeks.

"Your mother swore me to secrecy because she was afraid it would upset you, and what with final exams coming up, she wanted to spare you the worry."

Summer leaned into Casey and began to sob. While Casey felt terrible, she was also relieved that Summer's anger was overridden by sorrow and perhaps fear for Rhonda.

Summer was on her second tissue when Casey's phone rang. Stan. Was he calling about Wesley? Had they caught Charlie Applebee? With one arm around Summer, she answered.

"There's been another explosion at Mainland," Stan said. "One of the buses. Looks like a Molotov cocktail was pushed through a partially open window."

"For crying out loud. Anyone hurt?"

"No one was around."

"This is getting ridiculous. Why hasn't this person been caught? I thought Wayne was patrolling the place."

"He left about an hour ago. Said he had a bad headache."

"Just great. He should have called me and not bothered you."

"It's fine. One of the dispatchers on a smoke break thought he saw someone running down the sidewalk and went after him, but he lost the suspect. The cops are searching the area now."

Casey took a deep breath. "Tell them that they need to look for a silver Dodge Ram and a dark-green, older model Honda Accord."

"Why?" Stan asked.

Casey tightened her grip on the phone. "They belong to Benny's sons." She swallowed back the fear that Benny would see this as a betrayal of their friendship. "The boys are furious with Gwyn for what happened to their father."

"I remember the anger I heard in the hospital," Stan replied. "Have you got any evidence to back that up?"

"No, but Benny's second uniform isn't in his locker. I was at his house late this afternoon and looked through his room and a hall closet. It wasn't there. Yvette hasn't seen it either." Casey paused. "Max is about Benny's size, and since he apprenticed at the garage he knows the layout. None of Benny's kids think he should come back to work. Also, Benny's ID badge is missing. Yvette said it wasn't with his belongings that the hospital gave her."

"I have it," Stan said. "Cops found it under Benny's seat when they were searching through the bus. I found it in my desk drawer, so I guess they gave it to Gwyn."

"Geez, it would have been nice if he'd told me," she replied. "I still think we need to take a closer look at the brothers."

"Yeah. Damn." Stan let out a long puff of air. "I'll talk to the cops, but without proof I'm not giving them any names, and you should let Lou know that he'll be coming back to chaos again."

"Right. He told me that Wesley was attacked tonight. Did you know?"

"Yeah, but since he's okay, I didn't want to bother you on your night off."

"I appreciate that, but this siege is relentless, Stan. It has to stop."

"Agreed. The firebug and Charlie Applebee will be caught soon, don't worry." Stan paused. "Stay strong, kiddo. You're needed."

So it seemed. She held Summer a little bit tighter.

TWENTY-SIX

Dressed in blue jeans and a light gray jacket, Casey strolled along the northern perimeter of Coquitlam Park 'n Ride. She kept her distance from people waiting at the long rectangular loop of bus bays. She didn't mind the contrast to yesterday's warm sunny weather. Her umbrella would shield her face, should Charlie Applebee show up and notice her. His appearance was a long shot, but she had to try, not just because of Yvette's plea but because social media had taken to warning people about MPT's "safety issues."

Stan had forwarded an email from Gwyn this morning, containing stats that showed a sharp drop in ridership over the past month. Gwyn apparently expected the team to step up and help find the Blade Man or he'd be forced to reevaluate the entire security team's future. So, here she was hanging out at the frigging park 'n ride at noon on a soggy Sunday. None of the dozen people waiting for a bus were dressed completely in black. One teenage girl's height and shoulder-length hair reminded Casey of Summer.

Poor Summer. She'd looked exhausted this morning and wanted to know exactly when Rhonda's surgery would take place. Casey promised to help her find answers when she returned from this mission. She doubted they'd be successful.

A man dressed in black emerged from the SkyTrain exit near the far end of the park 'n ride. Casey removed the binoculars from her bag as a TransLink bus pulled in. The man hastened toward the bus. A look through the binoculars showed that his jacket was actually navy blue and that dark blond hair poked out from under his hooded jacket. Not Charlie Applebee.

Casey scanned the area. The Coquitlam Center Mall was right across the street on the north side of Lougheed Highway. The old guy she'd met yesterday said that Charlie hung out there on rainy days. Might as well check it out to appease the boss.

At the intersection, Casey crossed the busy, multi-lane thoroughfare and walked through the mall's rapidly filling parking lot. Rainy days always attracted shoppers. Entering the complex, she tried to determine where someone like Charlie would hang out without attracting too much attention. A food court perhaps?

Noting every male face who wore a dark jacket or hoodie, Casey made her way down a fairly short corridor, then turned right. She despised crowded malls. The bright lights, chatter, and canned music had triggered migraines in the past. She wouldn't stay long. Signs pointed to the food court upstairs. As Casey rode the escalator, her phone rang. Summer.

"Hi, I'm at a mall in Coquitlam," Casey said, adopting her most cheerful voice. "Need anything?"

"I called the hospitals to see if she's scheduled for the surgery, but they wouldn't tell me anything, and I'm family! How unfair is that?"

"I understand, honey, but to them you're a stranger asking about a prison inmate. I'll try and learn more when I'm done here. Right now, I'm searching for the suspect in the knife attacks. Rumor is he hangs out here."

"The Blade Man?"

Casey sighed. "That's the one."

"He's a dangerous freak. Be careful."

"I will, and I'll call as soon as I can."

Casey stepped off the escalator and headed north to where four corridors converged into one large open area with seating around TV screens. Groups of people, mostly elderly men, were gathered in front of the TVs showing news and a baseball game. Grandmothers were also seated, along with moms and babies. It was a place where Charlie could observe people without anyone paying much notice.

While she studied all of the male passersby who appeared to be alone, Casey tried to block out snippets of conversations and whining kids. She ambled past store windows, pausing now and then to glimpse the displays.

By the time she completed a full circle of the open area, she'd identified three men in black. One of them made the back of her neck tingle. In his late thirties, she noted the stubble and dark bruise on his cheek, possibly put there by Wesley's boot. Casey's gut told her this was the guy, and her adrenalin surged. Charlie Applebee wasn't watching TV but focusing on the shoppers. Casey could almost feel his anxiety as he stared at a girl in bright green tights and a green-and-black plaid skirt. She looked all of ten years old.

Would he actually go after a child? Was he carrying the knife now? Even in this crowd, the child was vulnerable. Casey started toward the girl, but a group of teens cut in front of her. Swearing silently, she dodged them, then watched the girl and the adult accompanying her—probably her mother—enter a store.

Charlie stood, then looked over his shoulder and surveyed the crowd. Casey pretended to browse a jewelry case embedded in the wall next to the store's entrance. What next? If she called mall security and they approached Charlie, he'd probably go nuts and lash out at anyone within reach. As long as he stayed calm, the chance of disaster lessened. An RCMP presence could also make things unravel fast. Wouldn't it be safer for everyone if she called after he left the mall?

Casey inhaled sharply as a security guard wandered toward the open area, seemingly oblivious to Charlie's presence. Charlie, however, noticed him. While Charlie stood still, Casey stopped breathing altogether. The guard turned down the north corridor and ambled away from him. Charlie's body relaxed. He turned around in time to see the mother and daughter emerge from the store and head toward the mall's exit.

Charlie started after them. Her heart racing, Casey began to maneuver her way among the shoppers, determined not to lose sight of him.

Charlie barged outside, keeping his pace brisk as if he had purpose. The falling rain gave Casey an excuse to raise her umbrella. Mother and daughter hurried through the parking lot. Charlie looked over his shoulder, prompting Casey to lower her head. Raising the umbrella again, she saw the mother unlock a blue SUV. Charlie edged closer and Casey moved faster, prepared to beat him with the damn umbrella if necessary. The mother opened the SUV's passenger door. The girl scrambled inside while her mom jogged to the driver's side. The engine started.

Shoving his hands in his pockets, Charlie marched past the parked vehicles and headed away from the mall toward High Street. Although rain had begun to pound the asphalt, Casey decided to keep following him. If he was heading home, maybe she could give the police an address. Again, she thought about calling them now, but if they came charging in too soon, they risked losing Charlie again. He'd proven himself an expert at vanishing on his own turf.

Charlie turned off High Street and made a right onto Glen Drive, the exact spot where she and Wesley had been trapped during the riot three weeks ago. The busted store windows had been replaced and everything looked normal again. But when Charlie was around, things were far from normal.

On the yellow light, Charlie jogged across the road to the north side of Glen. Casey stayed half a block behind him. A lull in traffic allowed her to dart across Glen and jog down the sidewalk until she reached the short, narrow road Charlie had taken. There was no sign of him. She rushed down the road to an open area adjacent to a building on her left, identified as Glen Pine Pavilion. To the right was a parking lot and the busier Pinetree Way. She stood there a moment, scanning the area. Where had he gone?

She hurried to Pinetree and spotted Charlie at the Pinetree and Guildford Avenue intersection. Casey was still half a block away when the light changed and Charlie crossed the road, heading east. Casey again began to jog, but by the time she got there the light was red. Head down, Charlie kept walking.

Waiting for the light to change, she glanced at people coming and going from the aquatic center on the northwest corner. More poured out of the SkyTrain exit on the northeast corner. From here, she saw where Benny's bus had been stopped that terrible night. The area was more lively and active in daylight. Despite the rain, plenty of pedestrians were around.

Charlie slowed his pace, turned, and looked at traffic. Without hesitating, he darted across the street toward Town Center Park. Finally, the light changed. While Casey was crossing the road, Charlie disappeared behind the Evergreen Cultural Center. By the time she reached the trail he'd taken, there was no sign of him.

Trees and bushes kept her from seeing a clear view of any-one. She scanned the area repeatedly until she spotted Charlie threading his way among the trees and still heading east. Casey kept to the sidewalk, maintaining her distance while she fol-lowed.

Farther down the block, two women, each pushing a stroller, emerged from a trail. Charlie appeared behind them, far enough back to not attract their attention. Neither woman wore green, thank heaven.

Casey found herself in a residential area with three-story condos facing the park. The women crossed Guildford and went south down Pipeline Road. Charlie also crossed, but rather than tail the women, he crossed Pipeline and continued east.

Guildford had now become Ozada Avenue, a narrower, two-lane road with far less traffic. Charlie glanced over his shoulder and picked up the pace. Did he realize he was being followed or was it paranoia? Casey stayed on the north side of Ozada. Char-lie could have spotted her easily, but he seemed intent on get-ting somewhere pretty quick.

Charlie turned right onto Grosvenor Drive. Dashing across Ozada, Casey trailed after him past older one- and two-story detached homes. About six houses down, Charlie crossed the road and hurried down the driveway of a home with pale yellow paint. The yard had been mowed, but the lack of plants and fencing made the place appear barren, as if the homeowner had no real interest in the property. An old Camry was parked in front of the detached, single-car garage.

By the time Casey strolled past the house, Charlie had disap-peared. She slowed her pace, observing two narrow, horizontal windows just above ground level at the front and a short stair-well and door off the driveway.

Well, damn. If Charlie lived in the basement suite, it explained how he'd eluded the cops. No one would be aware of his comings and goings, except possibly the people living upstairs. So, who lived above him? Casey was about to call 9-1-1 when a woman stepped out from behind stacks of boxes in the garage.

TWENTY-SEVEN

The forties-something woman was carrying one of the boxes out of the garage. She spotted Casey, smiled tentatively, and continued toward her at a leisurely pace.

"Hello," Casey said as quietly as possible. Approaching the woman, she displayed her ID, praying that Charlie wouldn't open his door. "My name's Casey Holland. I'm a security officer with Mainland Public Transport."

The woman's brows scrunched, her confusion obvious.

"What can I do for you?"

"This'll sound weird, but may I ask if you own this house?"

"I rent the top floor. Why?"

"Who rents the basement suite?"

"Charlie Applebee." Her confusion turned to wariness. "Is something wrong?"

"I think so." Casey glanced at the door, half expecting him to burst out, knife in hand. "Who owns the house?"

"Charlie's mother." She paused. "I'm Janet, by the way."

"Nice to meet you." Casey kept her gaze on the basement door. "Where does Charlie's mother live?"

"In Chilliwack, but since it's over an hour away she never visits. The lady remarried after Charlie's father died a while back. She bought this place a few months ago so Charlie wouldn't have to stay on the streets. He has no income, so she rents the top floor to help with the mortgage, I guess."

"Then her last name isn't Applebee anymore?"

"It's Slater."

That could explain why the cops hadn't been able to locate Charlie.

Casey stepped closer and murmured, "We have good reason to believe that Charlie's behind several stabbing incidents in the area. Two of the victims are my coworkers. The RCMP's been looking for him and I need to call them, but first I want to get you safely out of the way."

Janet gasped. "Good lord. Charlie has mental health issues, but to try and kill someone? I can't believe this."

"So, he's never given you any trouble?"

"I've only been here four months." She shrugged. "My brother's bipolar, so I have a lot of sympathy for people like Charlie. Besides, the rent's cheap."

"Have you noticed any changes in his mood or behavior?"

She bit her lower lip. "Lately, he seems more agitated than usual. I've heard him talking to himself, yelling actually. He could be having trouble with his medication, or stopped taking it altogether."

"Have you seen him coming and going at night?"

"No, I'm a nurse and I've been working nights."

"I should call 9-1-1 now," Casey said. "It'd be safer if we left the property before the cops show up."

"I'll get my keys."

As she hurried upstairs, Casey stepped into the garage to make the call. No way did she want Charlie overhearing this. Casey was still on the line when Janet returned. Casey was following her to the Camry when a loud crash from inside the basement suite startled her.

The door flung open and Charlie stood there, brandishing a knife with a six-inch blade. The fire in his eyes frightened Casey.

"I seen you watching me!" he shouted at her. "Get outta here!"

"Oh god," Casey said to the 9-1-1 dispatcher. "He's spotted us."

"Leave the premises right now," the dispatcher said.

"Charlie, just calm down." Janet opened the car door. "Nobody wants to hurt you."

"Liar!"

Janet slid behind the wheel and shut the door. As she leaned over and unlocked the passenger door, Charlie raised the knife.

"No one's gonna get me!"

Casey flung herself inside just as Janet began peeling backward down the driveway. Charlie ran after them.

Casey looked over her shoulder. "Watch out!"

Janet slammed the brakes, barely avoiding a boy racing along on his bicycle. Charlie leapt onto the hood, his face twisting with rage.

"No!" Janet hit the gas again.

Charlie tried to keep a grip as Janet backed the car onto the road.

"I'll kill you!" he screamed.

Janet stopped in the middle of the road and tried to shift out of reverse, but her hand was shaking too much. Charlie stabbed the windshield. Spittle ran down his chin and his bloodshot eyes bulged. Casey's entire body clenched. Part of her wanted to jump out and flee, but outrunning Charlie wouldn't work. His adrenalin would give him superhuman speed.

Charlie sat on his butt and kicked the windshield. Janet gaped at him and didn't move. Casey reached over and blasted the horn, but this stopped Charlie for only a moment before he resumed kicking.

"He's going to break it," Janet whimpered.

"Back the car up!" Casey yelled, but Janet remained frozen in place. "Come on! It might throw him off."

A couple of pedestrians stood gawking farther down the sidewalk. One of them was on the phone. One block ahead, an RCMP cruiser turned onto the road. In the side mirror, Casey saw another cruiser approaching from behind. At that moment, Janet chose to hit the gas. Still in reverse, the car lurched backward.

"Janet, stop! The cops are here!" She clamped her hand on Janet's arm, but she kept going. "You're gonna crash into the cops!"

Janet slammed the brakes. The jolt caused Charlie to lose his grip and roll off the hood. He sprang up. Still clutching the knife, he pounded on Janet's side window with one hand and tried to stab it with the other. She screamed.

"Drop your weapon!" a constable shouted. "On the ground! Now!"

Charlie kept attacking the glass, his face a mottled crimson beneath the heavy stubble. A third police cruiser arrived. Within seconds, the cops were surrounding him, their weapons drawn, yet Charlie seemed oblivious.

"Put the weapon down now!" the officer shouted again.

Casey hoped to hell that Charlie didn't notice the residents gathering on their lawns. One of the constables edged closer, catching Charlie's attention.

"Get down on the ground!" the constable yelled.

Charlie raised the knife and was about ready to lunge for the cop when he was tasered. It didn't faze him. Charlie cursed and slashed the air. A second taser blast jolted him backward. The knife fell from his hand and he recoiled, collapsing on the ground. Charlie tried to get to his knees, but the cops were on him. Casey held her breath as Charlie continued to put up a fight until he was eventually restrained. It took four cops and many long, tense seconds to control the Blade Man.

While Janet wept, Casey reached over and turned off the ignition. She closed her eyes in relief.

TWENTY-EIGHT

"**E**xcellent work, kiddo." Stan leaned his elbows on the desk. "You went above and beyond to find Applebee, though I totally get why the RCMP gave you hell for following him in the first place."

Casey huffed and crossed her arms. "If I hadn't, he'd still be out there stabbing people."

"True." Stan gave her a long look. "But did you have to put yourself in that much danger?"

"Didn't think I was. Charlie was inside while I was practically whispering to the upstairs tenant in the driveway. I had to warn her what could happen once I called the cops."

"I just wish you'd found a better way."

"I wish one had presented itself." She didn't want to talk about Charlie Applebee anymore. "I spoke with Benny's daughter yesterday. Benny's home but he was asleep when I called. Yvette was happy to hear about Charlie's arrest."

"I bet. My RCMP contact confirmed that Applebee never leaves the Tri-Cities, so just as we thought, he's not the firebug." Stan frowned. "Unfortunately, I didn't get a chance to tell Gwyn before he went on TV and told the world that Charlie's likely responsible for all of MPT's problems. The idiot's ignoring evidence to the contrary simply to get the ridership back."

"I saw him on the news," Casey remarked. "The smug attitude makes me wonder if the arsonist wants to put him in his place, so to speak."

"Agreed, and I told Gwyn as much this morning. Now he wants us to keep up surveillance 'cause he thinks more of you are now available for graveyard patrols."

Casey slumped back in her chair. "The team needs rest, Stan, and I know other issues are waiting to be dealt with."

"Which I told him, but he's not listening."

"Why am I not surprised?"

"There's been progress on other fronts," Stan said. "Cops tracked down two people behind the Facebook threats. One of them is that Liam kid you busted the other night. The other is the buddy who was with him." Stan scratched his beard. "Both have alibis for all of the arsons. Seems they work part-time at a McDonald's that's open twenty-four hours a day."

"Great." She shook her head. "Benny's sons are back on top of my suspect list. Did you tell the cops about them?"

"Yeah, and I've been strongly advised not to have further contact with the family."

"Bull crap. We have every right to visit Benny, and won't it look strange to Yvette if we ignore Benny now that he's home? The sons could become suspicious."

"Good point." Stan tapped his pencil. "I'll stop by to see Benny on my way home, then let you know if anything should be done to watch the brothers."

"All right. Who's on graveyard patrol tonight?"

"Marie."

Casey grinned. "She'll love that."

. . .

Slouched behind the wheel of his truck, Lou yawned as he turned to Casey. "How long are we supposed to stay on surveillance?"

"Until Stan tells us to leave."

"But we've been here over two hours, and it's after midnight. I'm bagged."

"Me too."

Casey hadn't intended to bring Lou along, but when he heard what she was up to tonight, he volunteered to keep her company.

"I'm still surprised he okayed this," Lou said.

Casey wasn't. Stan had told her that the brothers were hostile when he showed up at Benny's place earlier this evening. He'd also overheard them talking about meeting up somewhere to-night. She'd proposed the stakeout and he'd agreed, reluctantly.

"He wouldn't have if he didn't think the brothers could be our arsonists," she said. "Desperate times, desperate measures."

"Then shouldn't the cops be doing this?"

"Doubt they have the manpower."

Not that MPT did either, but she was especially grateful that Anoop was also here. Stan wanted both brothers watched, and if they took off at separate times then, two tails would be need-ed. Anoop seemed eager to earn extra cash and do whatever he could to get back into Gwyn's good books. Catching an arsonist would certainly accomplish that.

"It's Monday night," Lou said. "What are the odds that Max and Reese will go out now?"

"High, if they're the arsonists."

"Want more coffee?" Lou asked, lifting the thermos.

"Sure, thanks."

He poured her a cup. "Looking forward to your bachelorette spa thing this weekend?"

"Definitely." She sipped the coffee. "It'll be fun, but if we haven't found our firebug by then, I'll feel guilty about taking time off."

"You've worked hard." Lou took a sip. "MPT can't stop us from enjoying our down time or going on our honeymoon. I won't feel one bit of guilt."

His attitude still bothered her. Maybe it would improve once Benny returned to work. But what if he didn't return, or he did but without the same easygoing optimism that the drivers counted on? No. Don't dwell on it. Time for happier thoughts.

"What have the guys planned for your stag?"

"Dunno. They want it to be a surprise."

"Uh-oh. You aren't going to wind up in a diaper handcuffed to a bus bench, are you? I wouldn't put it past some of the guys."

"I had better not be."

Casey smiled as she observed Benny's house. "Only two and a half weeks to go."

She couldn't wait for their wedding. Kendal's mom had offered the use of her large home for the ceremony and reception.

"Hope Benny can make it," Lou murmured.

"Me too."

But she had her doubts. Casey hadn't had the heart to share Stan's concern about Benny's weak and disoriented state. He said that Benny barely smiled at the news of Charlie Applebee's arrest. Casey feared that Benny's kids wouldn't want him at the wedding. Hanging with coworkers on a happy occasion might trigger a desire to stay employed.

"Looks like Yvette's leaving." Casey watched her step outside and head for her SUV. "Strange that she'd go out this late on a weeknight."

"Max and Reese are there to watch the kids, who are probably asleep anyway."

"I just had an ugly thought." Lou paused. "If her brothers wanted to destroy MPT, would Yvette help them?"

"I don't think so." She watched Yvette back her SUV out of the driveway. "Yvette wants Benny to sell the house and move in with her. She's not a fan of Gwyn's either. Still, I can't believe she'd actually help them commit a serious crime like arson."

"Maybe not. But would she turn them in if she found out? Help them hide evidence?"

Truthfully, Casey didn't know. Despite Yvette's arguments with her brothers and her disdain for their laziness, they were family. How far would Yvette go to protect them?

Lou sighed again. "I'll fall asleep if I have to stay here much longer."

She'd warned him that might happen, but pointing it out now wouldn't go over well.

"Surveillance takes focus and patience, Lou."

"Patience?" He grinned. "You?"

"I'm getting better. Haven't you noticed?"

"Now that you mention it, yeah." Lou took another sip of coffee. "You've been more patient with Summer than I have."

She squeezed his hand. "Trust me, it takes a lot of effort, especially after her latest hissy fit. Can't blame her for being upset over that last phone call with Rhonda."

Lou nodded. "She shouldn't have refused to see Summer."

After Rhonda's heated discussion with Summer, she'd called Casey, and yelled, "Why did you go against my wishes and tell her? How could you do that to me?"

So, Casey told her the brutal truth, that Summer was lost and still angry with Rhonda, and now terrified that she would turn out like the rest of the Stubbs women. Despite Rhonda's swearing and heartbroken sobs, Casey had pressed on.

"Do you want to spend your time raging at me or fixing things with your daughter before she really stops caring?"

Thank heaven Rhonda backed down and agreed to let Summer visit as soon as arrangements could be made. Rhonda's continuing vagueness about her surgery only compounded the stress. Casey sensed that she really was keeping the details from them, but confronting her about it wouldn't help. As things stood, there'd be plenty more tears and drama when mother and daughter met face-to-face.

"You okay?" Lou asked, stroking her hair.

"Yeah," she murmured. "Thinking about Rhonda."

"I understand, but try to focus on happier stuff, like how we'll soon be on a tropical beach."

"Good idea." Casey drained her coffee and rubbed her sleepy eyes. "Let's hope we can get through these next few days without any more disasters."

. . .

Casey's cellphone rang, startling her. She hadn't realized she'd dozed off.

"Pretty spiffy surveillance work, Sherlock," Lou remarked.

"What time is it?"

"Just after 1:00 AM."

"I thought you'd be the one to fall asleep," she mumbled.

"Well, one of us had to stay awake."

She glared at him. "You should have woken me."

"Thought you could use the rest."

She wasn't surprised to see Stan's name on her screen, given that he was helping Marie patrol for part of the evening.

"What's up?"

"We've got action here. Someone's sneaking down the admin building's west side. Can you and Anoop swing by and cover the side streets? I've called the cops, but until they arrive I don't want Marie handling things alone. God knows what our trespasser's up to."

"Okay, en route." She turned to Lou. "Stan thinks the arsonist might be on the property." She noted that Max's truck was missing. "Max is gone!" Yvette had returned, though.

"I know. Anoop was eager to follow him so I said sure. Max left by himself, which means Reese must still be inside."

Lou started the engine. "We're heading to Mainland?"

"Yep. I need to tell Anoop to get over there fast. Stan wants all of us cruising the side streets." Casey brushed cheese and cracker crumbs off her shirt. "This is the messiest surveillance I've ever been on."

"One of the most restful too, I bet."

"Until now." She dialed Anoop.

TWENTY-NINE

As Lou sped toward Mainland Public Transport, Casey watched for patrol cars. She wasn't worried about being stopped. In fact, she wanted their help. Glancing at the night sky, she could almost feel the heavy clouds swell and prepare to spill. Moist air filled her lungs. Her phone rang and Marie's name appeared on her screen.

"What's happening?" Casey asked.

"We haven't found anyone. He may have left," Marie murmured. "Stan's at the back of the yard. I'm working my way around the admin building, but he wants you to take a close look at the front of the property before you check the side streets."

"Sure. Have you noticed a silver Dodge Ram near the place?"

"Wait." Marie's voice became strained. "I hear glass breaking."

Casey sat up straighter. "Where?"

"Northeast corner of the admin building, main floor."

"Get away from there!"

"I'm on—"

An enormous explosion blasted Casey's ear. "Marie!" No response. "Marie!"

"Whoa, I heard that from here." Lou reached for his phone. "I'll call 9-1-1."

"Marie, are you there? Talk to me!" Casey gripped the phone.

"Oh god."

She hung up and phoned Stan. The phone rang five times before he answered. It sounded like he was running.

"I was talking to Marie when something exploded," Casey blurted. "She's not responding to me. Lou's talking to a 9-1-1 operator. Can you see her?"

"Not yet!" He wheezed as if struggling to catch his breath. "What's your twenty?"

"Couple minutes away." Lord, he shouldn't be running like that. "Stan, be careful."

"Copy that!" Stan gasped for breath. "Search the area."

She was on the phone with Anoop, two blocks from MPT, when Lou hit the brakes and pulled over, his eyes on the rear-view mirror. "Someone's running down the sidewalk."

In her side mirror, Casey didn't see anyone. She opened the door and stepped out, spotting him instantly.

"Anoop, the suspect's running north on Bedford Road," she replied. "How fast can you get there?"

"Nearly there now."

"We'll take the next street over in case he tries to cut through." Casey hopped in the truck. "Watch for any vehicles. He might have one waiting, and stay on the line."

"Ten-four."

"Cops and fire department are on their way," he said.

"If the suspect's heading toward Lougheed, maybe we can cut him off."

"I couldn't tell if he was in a driver's uniform," Lou said.

"Neither could I, but it doesn't matter. It's the same culprit and sooner or later we'll find out if he's one of us or not."

Lou turned down a dimly lit street populated by industrial buildings. Each property was surrounded by a high chain link fence. Bushes and hedges provided a buffer from Lougheed

Highway traffic. They also offered plenty of hiding places.

Casey put her phone on speaker. "Anoop, see anyone?"

"Afraid not."

"Must be cutting through properties. With all those fences, he'd have to be quite the athlete." Something niggled in the back of her mind but she couldn't quite get her head around it. "When you're sure he's gone, take the next street over, on the east side."

"Ten-four."

Casey scanned every parked car, worried that the suspect might already be hiding in one of them. She heard sirens.

"Any sign of a silver Dodge Ram?" she asked Lou.

"No."

"I still don't see anyone," Anoop said over the phone.

"Damn it." She sighed. "I'll call Stan on Lou's phone. Stay on the line."

Lou handed it to her. It took five rings before Stan finally answered.

"What's happening?" Casey asked. "Is Marie okay?"

"I'm with her now. She's conscious, barely. There's some bad cuts from glass on her back and left arm. Fire department got here pretty quick and I can hear the ambulance coming."

Lou leaned forward and squinted at the windshield. "I see someone."

Following his gaze, Casey also thought she saw movement.

"One block down?" she asked Lou.

"Yeah." He hit the gas.

"Stan, tell the cops we're in pursuit of someone dressed in dark clothing." After Casey provided the street name, she turned to her own phone. "Anoop, did you hear that?"

"Yes. En route."

"Put me on speaker," Stan said.

As Casey did so, Lou said, "He's turning the corner!" Lou sped down the road, slowing just enough to make a right turn. "Where'd he go?"

"There!" Casey pointed to the property halfway down the block. "He's hopping the fence. Pull over! I'm going after him."

"No!" Stan yelled. "Cops'll be there any second."

She did as ordered, but feared they were losing precious seconds. Lou stopped in front of the property's padlocked gate. Anoop approached from the other direction.

"He disappeared." She switched phones. "Anoop, do you see anything?"

"No."

Casey peered at every shrub, every foot of vacant asphalt, and every visible corner of the building. A patrol car sped up to them. By the time she finished updating the officer, she was exasperated. The suspect had probably gotten away, and the cop didn't seem overly eager to jump the fence and search on foot.

"Leave the area, ma'am," the officer said. "We'll take it from here."

"Do as he says!" Stan's voice rang out. "And tell Anoop he can go home. I'm hanging up now."

"Fine." She ended the call but kept staring at the property, alert to any sign of movement.

Lou took his phone back. "Come on, Casey. Stan'll need us."

She nodded. "Anoop, we're heading over to Mainland. Stan said you can go home, and thanks for your help tonight. I really appreciate it."

"No problem. I hope Marie will be okay."

"Me too."

The closer they got to MPT, the smokier the air became. Since the entrance was once again cordoned off, two buses were parked on the side street. A barrier at the end of the road kept Lou from getting closer to Mainland.

"Looks like we'll have to walk in," he said.

Casey stole another glance at the sky. The dense clouds felt heavier. Two news vans approached the police barriers. Once Lou had parked the truck, she marched toward the premises, gaping at the smoke billowing from the northeast corner of the admin building.

A handful of coworkers and other spectators waited on the sidewalk. Stan was as close to the building as was permitted. Casey noticed the way his shoulders rounded as he spoke on the phone. Was he talking to Gwyn? Demolishing the idiot's delusion that their problems had been solved?

"I'm gonna talk to the drivers a minute," Lou said.

"Okay."

Casey hurried toward Stan and tried not to gag on the stench of gasoline. She caught sight of Marie in the ambulance just before they closed the doors. Stan ended his call.

A shudder rippled through her and she hugged herself. "I was afraid it was only a matter of time before one of us was hurt."

"Yeah." Stan released a huff of air. "Gwyn wants to come by but I talked him out of it." He shook his head. "The torched room was his temporary office. Don't see how Benny's sons could have known that unless they have an informer on the inside."

Casey thought of the Friends and everything they knew. "If Del can hack our emails, maybe they can too." She paused. "A few days ago, I learned that the Friends have a private Facebook group for sharing MPT stuff. That could also have been hacked."

Stan rolled his eyes. "Talk to those kids, see if any new

members have joined or if there's been any strange activity with their accounts."

"Sure." Stan's haggard look concerned her. This latest fiasco wouldn't help his recovery. "Why don't you go home? I'll stay here a bit longer."

"I don't think any of us needs to stay. Doubt our firebug will be back tonight." Stan looked up and down the street. "I want to see if the cops have found any evidence."

Still hugging herself, Casey watched the firefighters work. God, when would this nightmare end? Craig Hedley rode up on a bicycle. No surprise that at least one of the Friends would appear. Stepping onto the road, she waved him down.

"Hedley? Were you or any of the Friends watching the property tonight?"

"No. I found out what happened from a video on the net."

"Who posted the video?"

"Dunno. Assumed it was a passerby."

Or the culprit. "When was it posted?"

"About a half hour ago, give or take. Anyway, I jumped on the bike and raced here." He looked around. "Was anyone hurt?"

Even under the streetlights, Hedley looked flushed and sweaty as he surveyed the damage.

"Marie Crenshaw." Casey cleared her throat as the smell of gasoline and smoke again wafted over her.

"That sucks. Will she be okay?"

"Hope so." Casey observed the cops talking to spectators. Stan was with Lou and the drivers. "You didn't happen to see anyone in dark clothing, or even a driver's uniform, leaving the area as you got here, did you?"

"No." He frowned. "Why?"

Casey shook her head. "Doesn't matter."

He looked at his phone. "Mind if I take a couple of photos

for Travis? I'll stay out of the way, especially if your president's around. Is he?"

"No," Casey murmured, observing spectators recording the action. "Go ahead with the photos. Everyone else is." She paused. "Listen, have you or your friends accepted new members to your Facebook group over the past couple of months?"

"No, it's still just the five of us. Why?"

She ignored the question "Any requests to join, or strange activity with your accounts?"

"Not that I know of." Hedley peered at her. "Is this about the threats on MPT's page?"

"Mostly, it's about this." She nodded toward the fire.

Hedley hesitated. "Yeah. Well, I hope you find the asshole."

While he was riding off, Lou joined her. "From what I've heard, the cops haven't found the suspect. Probably long gone by now."

Casey plunked her hands on her hips. "How is that bloody possible?"

"Must have had a car waiting a few streets over and took a shortcut through the properties to get to it." He looked around. "Haven't seen any silver Dodge Rams or green Hondas around either."

Stan came up to her. "Did I see Craig Hedley talking to you?"

"Yeah. Apparently this latest disaster's already shown up on social media and Hedley came to get a firsthand look. I asked him about the Facebook group and he said there's been no new requests to join or weird account activity."

"Not that he'd be completely honest." Stan looked down the street. "Kid probably came to gloat."

Casey frowned. "Why would he do that?"

"I never told you this because Gwyn didn't want anyone else

to know," Stan said, gazing down the street. "But last summer, after he caught Hedley wandering toward the executive offices, Gwyn had him charged with trespassing. His parents came to see Gwyn and things got a little ugly."

"What a jerk," Lou remarked.

Staring at the spot where Hedley stopped his bike, Casey realized that the kid had appeared after two of the explosions. He'd been wearing shorts and a light blue jacket tonight, but he'd also been sporting a backpack. And hadn't she gotten a whiff of gasoline while she was talking with him?

"Uh-oh."

"It's never good when you say that," Lou remarked.

"No kidding," Stan said. "What's wrong?"

"What if Hedley didn't come from home tonight? What if he'd been here all along?" She noted their blank expressions. "You just provided a motive and I admit it's weak, but he could be behind this. The guy knows MPT's layout well."

The thing that had been niggling in the back of Casey's mind sprang forward, making her blood race. "And Hedley's into fitness. Teaches classes, for god's sake."

"Why would a trespassing charge cause him to act out a year later?" Lou asked, "and in such an extreme way?"

"For one thing, the longer he waited the less likely he'd be considered a suspect. It could explain why Hedley distanced himself from the Friends, pretending to lose interest when he was actually plotting revenge," Casey replied. "Secondly, he's been really busy with school, which is over now, and third, he saw the knife attacks as an opportunity to add to Gwyn's trouble and anxiety."

"I agree with Lou," Stan said. "To commit arson over a lousy trespassing charge just doesn't make sense."

"The Lee brothers' motive is stronger," Lou added.

"Maybe, but Hedley brought up Gwyn's name tonight, asked me if he was here and I told him no. I also got a whiff of gasoline while talking to him. Thought the breeze was carrying the smell from the building, but what if it came from Hedley?"

"Freakin' hell." Stan scowled at the street.

"I suppose he could have stolen a uniform by entering the building during office hours and making his way to the guys' locker room," Lou said. "If there's only clothing inside, most of us leave our lockers unlocked. Benny often did it when he on a break in the lunchroom."

"I'll talk to Del and find out what he knows," Casey said.

"Bad idea," Stan replied. "He could be a co-conspirator."

"I don't think so. He and Hedley have been at odds and don't talk. Now I'm wondering if Del suspects something."

"What about the other Friends?" Lou asked.

"More complicated. Felicity and Travis are closer to Hedley," Casey answered. "I doubt they'd help him commit crime, but covering for him is another issue, especially if they really don't know what's going on. Maybe Del can clue me in if I talk to him alone."

"Is he capable of keeping a secret?" Stan asked.

Casey thought about this. "He'd better be."

THIRTY

As Lou drove the bus down Lougheed Highway, Casey stared out the window without really seeing anything. She was too busy stewing over Hedley. Online research showed that every photo or video posted about last night's explosion popped up after Hedley claimed he saw it.

Casey knew she'd been on the phone with Marie at 1:05 AM when it happened. That was roughly the same time Hedley claimed he saw a social media posting. But what if he'd been here, recording it himself?

Stan had shared her suspicion about Hedley with the police, but who knew if they would take it seriously. She just hoped that Del could give her some insights into the guy. When she invited him to meet her tonight he'd been eager to oblige until he was told that he had to come alone.

"This is a highly sensitive matter," she'd insisted, "and I need your discretion. We can decide what to tell the others later." Casey knew he would agree. He'd be too curious not to.

Del boarded the bus and sat next to her. "Hey, Casey." His black hair looked damp and was tied back in a short ponytail. The smell of soap wafted off him. "I heard they caught the Blade Man right at his own house. Must be a huge relief."

"It is, and thanks for coming to see me on short notice." She didn't want to discuss her experience with Charlie Applebee. Happily, the cops hadn't told the media that she'd been there.

"I'm surprised that you're working with your fiancé again," Del said, glancing at the few passengers. "Thought that was against the rules."

Stan had little choice, given that Marie was in the hospital and Anoop and Wayne were unavailable. Although Applebee was off the streets, several Bandana Boys were still out there, and Stan didn't want Lou ambushed.

"How do you know about that rule?"

Del cleared his throat. "Must've heard someone mention it. Anyway, pretty awful about last night, eh?"

Good. The opening she needed. "Yep."

"Is Marie okay? Will she be back at work soon?"

"She'll be fine, but I don't know when she'll be back."

The flying glass hadn't done serious damage, but Marie had injured her left hip, arm, and shoulder when she hit the ground.

"Did you see it happen?" Del asked.

"No, we arrived shortly afterward." Casey paused. "Hedley came by."

"Yeah, Felicity said he'd texted."

Casey waited, but Del didn't add anything. She didn't expect him to. "You don't seem to communicate directly with Hedley. Is there a reason for that?"

Del's smile faded and his glance bounced from passenger to passenger. "He lost interest in the group after college started."

She wasn't ready to add that he sure seemed interested in it now. "Why? Hedley seemed passionate about it."

Del shrugged. "I think he was kind of jealous."

"Of what?"

"That I got along with MPT employees better than he did and have better computer skills. He's also super sensitive. Takes things personally."

Casey glanced at the two older women quietly chatting across the aisle. "I just learned that there were some repercussions after Hedley was caught wandering through the admin building after hours last year. Do you think that might have something to do with his loss of interest?"

"Maybe." Del paused. "I warned him that it was a stupid move, but Hedley wanted to prove he could get inside anytime."

"Gwyn upgraded our alarm system after that, but I never heard Hedley explain how he bypassed the old system in the first place."

"He didn't bypass it, he'd been watching staff press the digits on the keypad," Del answered. "I told him it was wrong, and he stopped talking to me after that."

Del looked like he wanted to say something more. Instead, he stared out the window.

"Does Hedley hold grudges?"

He turned sharply. "Why do you ask?"

"Curiosity mainly."

Del's facial muscles tightened. "You didn't want Lawrence and Felicity here because they stay in touch with him, right?"

"Something like that. Would you say that he's renewed his interested in MPT?"

"Maybe. Hedley's been asking Felicity for inside info about MPT."

"What kind of info?"

He rubbed his hands on his jeans. "Who's going where and when."

"Drivers?"

Del's mouth opened and closed. His tawny complexion turned a couple of shades darker, and he swept long black bangs from his forehead.

"Del?" She kept a gentle tone. "I need to know."

He cleared his throat. "Gwyn."

She was afraid he'd say that. "I'm going to share a theory, but it stays between us, promise?"

Dark chocolate eyes zeroed in on her. "Yes."

"Since the damage to MPT seems directed at Gwyn, I can't help wondering if Hedley's involved and the fires are some sort of payback for the trespassing charge and being banned from MPT."

The color on Del's face deepened. "I can't believe he'd do something as bad as arson. That's really messed up."

"Agreed, but Hedley showed up at MPT after both explosions, which might make the police wonder how solid his alibis are." Leaning closer, she lowered her voice. "If he becomes their prime suspect, the police will want to talk to you and the others. I'm sure you know that withholding information could mean trouble for all of you."

Del fidgeted. He brushed his fingers through his bangs again. Good. He was beginning to understand the stakes. She wanted him to think about this a minute, to weigh the pros and cons of his decisions.

"Anything you can tell me about him might help me understand the guy better. Maybe I can do something to stop the destruction, without involving the cops, before somebody dies."

Del glanced behind him as if worried about eavesdroppers. "Did you know that Hedley was originally accepted at UBC?"

"No."

"He was excited about studying medicine, but plans fell apart after the trespassing charge. Hedley wouldn't discuss the details, but I know he lost a big scholarship that would have covered a lot of his first-year tuition."

"Yikes."

Admission to the University of British Columbia was fiercely competitive. It was one of the few institutions in Western Canada that offered medical training. Did Stan know this part of the story?

"That would have made Hedley furious, no doubt."

"Yep. His parents weren't happy with the trouble he caused and withdrew their offer to pay for his education once the scholarship money was spent. So they sold their house and moved to the Okanagan. It's why Hedley rents a basement suite and goes to Douglas College. Felicity says he supports himself on whatever jobs he can get." Del paused as Lou stopped the bus for more passengers. "It's changed him."

The loss of an expensive education would certainly be a stronger motive, especially for a hyper-sensitive kid who took things personally.

Del's phone rang. "It's Felicity."

"Can it wait till you're off the bus? We're pretty much finished anyway." Casey didn't like his hesitancy. "Look, based on what I've seen, Felicity's really into Hedley. If you tell her about this meeting, you might upset her."

Resignation swept across Del's face. It was hard to tell if this was because he couldn't trust his friend or because he didn't approve of her feelings for Hedley.

"Got it," he mumbled.

Del stood as Lou pulled up to the next stop. The moment he exited, Casey called Stan.

. . .

An uneventful two-hour ride had lulled Casey into a drowsy, relaxed state until her phone rang. The caller identified himself as a Vancouver officer who was investigating the arsons.

"Your supervisor, Mr. Cordaseto, gave me your number."

Casey sat up straighter. There were only five passengers on board. Not surprising, given that it was nearly midnight. "What can I do for you?"

"I went to Mr. Craig Hedley's residence this evening, but the roommate said he packed a duffel bag and drove away an hour ago. The roommate claimed he didn't know where Mr. Hedley went or when he'd be back. Couldn't even confirm if he would be back."

Crap. So why was he calling her? "I have no idea where Hedley would be."

"I understand that, but Mr. Hedley had a visitor just before he left. An young Indo-Canadian male. Your supervisor says you know who he is."

Casey's stomach sank. Damn it, why had Del gone there?

"His name's Del Darzi, one of our regular riders and part of a group of teens who call themselves the MPT Friends."

She provided a brief history of the Friends' relationship with MPT, but admitted that she didn't know Del's address or phone number, just the name of the high school he attended.

"Any idea why Mr. Darzi would show up late at night to Mr. Hedley's home?" the cop asked. "The roommate said the two were arguing."

Oh boy. "I'm afraid it's about a conversation Del and I had earlier tonight." After she told him what Del had revealed, the long silence that followed sent her heartbeat quickening.

"Miss Holland, I strongly suggest you avoid further chats with the MPT Friends until we've spoken with Mr. Hedley."

His authoritative tone irritated her. "Just trying to help."

"I think you've helped enough." He hung up.

While Lou pulled up to the next stop, Casey ranted about Del and her chat with the cop.

"He has a point, you know," Lou said. "If you can't trust the Friends, then you need to isolate yourself from them."

"Not before I have a few choice words with Del. I'm tempted to call him right now."

Lou merged back into traffic. "You don't seriously think he'll answer."

"Probably not." She slumped into a nearby seat.

The best way to get answers would be through the Friends' chattiest, most gullible member, Felicity. After her parents' first met with Stan, they gave him their contact information and address, should an emergency arise. In Casey's view, an emergency was unfolding right now. Calling them at this time of night, though, wouldn't be smart.

"I know that look," Lou remarked. "You're planning something."

Casey responded with a dismissive wave. Why say anything when he'd only try to talk her out of it?

THIRTY-ONE

Parked in front of Felicity's house, Casey waited for her to come home from school. Although the school was only three blocks from here, she couldn't risk being seen by Del and Lawrence. Coming here was a gamble, but since Felicity didn't seem to have any extracurricular activities, a part-time job, or friends other than Del and Lawrence, Casey thought it a safe bet that she'd be here soon.

It was highly possible that the cops had already talked to the Friends and probably their parents, so technically she wasn't interfering. She truly believed that Felicity would confide in her about Hedley and share info that she wouldn't tell the cops. The challenge would be in persuading Felicity to help find him. If the girl was protecting Hedley, persuasion could turn into a forceful ultimatum. Not a great strategy, but a necessary last resort.

Casey spotted Felicity ambling down the sidewalk, staring at her phone. Casey stepped out of the car. She was only a few steps away before Felicity finally looked up.

"Casey!" Her eyes widened. "I was just reading about the Blade Man on my phone. Were you there when they caught him? A couple of people said he tried to attack two women in a car."

"Actually, I'm here to talk about Hedley," Casey said. "Do you know where he is? I really need to speak with him, and he's apparently vanished."

As anticipated, the direct approach caught Felicity off guard. Her complexion blanched.

"The police came to our house before school this morning and asked me the same thing. Went to Del's and Lawrence's place too." She stared at Casey. "Did you give them our names?"

"Felicity, I'm not answering your question until you answer mine, truthfully."

"I don't know where he is!" Felicity's high-pitched whine grated on Casey. "And there's no way Hedley would have set those fires."

Arguing would be a waste of time. Besides, she needed the girl's cooperation. "Then we need to help clear his name, which means talking with him. Do you know where Hedley likes to hang out or where he'd go if he was in trouble?"

Felicity blinked at the sidewalk and tugged on the ends of her light red hair. "There's a couple of coffee places with WiFi, but you should ask Travis. They're good friends."

Casey had planned to do exactly that, but a better idea was forming. "How good?"

"They grew up on the same street," Felicity answered. "Hedley's a year older than Travis."

"Can you do me a favor and call Del?"

"Why?"

Casey didn't want to say that Del probably wouldn't take her call. Under the circumstances, Travis probably wouldn't either.

"I'll explain once he's on the line."

Felicity made the call. "Hi, it's me."

"Thanks." Casey snatched the phone from her, ignoring the girl's gasp.

"This is Casey." She put the phone on speaker. "Don't hang up or I'll have Felicity show me where you live." Emboldened by his silence, she added, "Why did you go see Hedley when I asked you not to?"

"You didn't say not to." Del cleared his throat. "You just said not to tell him about our conversation, which I didn't."

"What conversation?" Felicity asked.

Casey turned away. "Then why go there at all?"

"I needed to know if he started the fires."

How could such a smart kid be so stupid? "Did you seriously think he'd confess?"

"No, but I can always tell when he's lying."

"Was he?"

"Yeah."

"No!" Felicity blurted. "Hedley wouldn't do that."

"It's true," Del mumbled, "and it's all my fault."

Casey's eyebrows rose. "How so?"

"We had a fight earlier this year. I told Hedley that he'd changed and didn't deserve to be in charge." He cleared his throat. "He lost it and accused me of taking over his group."

"You shouldn't have said that." Felicity stepped closer to the phone. "You know how sensitive Hedley is, and I know what that's like, trust me. Hedley's a good person who's had a really tough year. He needs us."

No doubt about it, the girl had a major crush on the guy.

"Del, did you tell Hedley that the cops are looking for him?"

"No, I swear."

"Then what did you say?"

"I asked if he'd seen anyone suspicious near the explosions. He said he wasn't around when any of them happened, except for Mr. Maddox's car. Then he kicked me out."

"I heard that you argued with Hedley last night," Casey said.

"Yeah." He paused. "He thought I was accusing him."

"Great," Casey muttered. "That's why he took off so fast."

"The cop pretty much said the same thing to my parents. Now I'm stuck doing extra chores all weekend. Look, I'm really sorry. If I'd known . . ." His voice trailed off.

Casey heard his sincerity and remorse. It was the leverage she needed. "How about you and the others help me find him?"

"We can do that," Del replied. "Right, Felicity?"

The girl shifted her feet. "I guess so."

Her lack of enthusiasm bothered Casey. She'd need to keep the girl close by so she couldn't warn Hedley.

"Would he go to his parents in the Okanagan?" Casey asked.

"No, they don't talk to one another," Felicity answered.

"What about other family or college friends?"

"Just Travis," she replied. "Poor guy's kind of a loner."

Casey struggled to maintain an impassive expression. "Do you think Travis will help us clear Hedley's name?"

"I think so," Felicity murmured, "but he and I haven't talked since the cops came to my house."

Casey studied her. "If he's protecting Hedley from the police, then they'll both wind up in trouble."

Felicity's face blanched once again. "Del?" She leaned closer to the phone Casey held out for her. "What do we do?"

"I'll call him," Del offered, "and say that something urgent's come up about Hedley. He'll want to know what it is. Lawrence is on his way to my place now."

"Thank you." Casey turned to Felicity. "You mentioned a couple of coffee shops that Hedley goes to. Maybe we should start looking there."

Felicity shrugged. "He could have left the city."

"Don't think so." Del's tone became more somber. "When Hedley's on a mission, he won't quit until he's finished what he started."

Casey stared at the phone. "Meaning he's not done with MPT until it's burned to the ground?"

More silence, and then a quiet, "Maybe."

Just great. "Del, when you call Travis, don't mention me."

"What if Travis tells Hedley?" Del asked. "They're probably staying in touch."

"Not much we can do about that," Casey replied. Maybe it would be enough to make Hedley think twice about setting more fires. "Call my cell as soon as the meeting's arranged." She handed Felicity's phone back. "You should probably tell your parents that you'll be out for a while."

"They won't be home till seven, anyway," she mumbled.

"Okay." But finding Hedley could take a lot longer than that.

. . .

The moment Casey spotted Del heading down the sidewalk with Lawrence and Travis in tow, she felt like an overburdened school teacher about to embark on a tedious field trip. As the boys drew nearer, Travis looked up, spotted Casey, and faltered. His slowing pace told her that Del had indeed not mentioned her presence. Would the kid turn and bolt when he learned why he'd been summoned?

"Hi, guys." She opened the back door.

Given that Travis was six inches taller than Del, the glare he directed at Del had to be intimidating. "What's going on?"

"We need your help finding Hedley," Casey answered.

Travis stepped back and shoved his hands in his pockets.

"You should have told me, Del."

Del looked down, his black bangs falling over his eyes. Casey noticed that Travis didn't ask why they needed to find Hedley.

"Sorry, but Casey asked me not to."

"You do every damn thing she tells you to?"

"That's not fair," Lawrence said. "All we want to do is help Hedley."

Travis shook his head.

"You might have heard that the police want to question him about the MPT arsons," Casey said, noting the way Travis pinched his lips and avoided eye contact.

"We don't think he did it," Felicity blurted. "We just want to help clear his name."

Lawrence adjusted his glasses. Casey had no idea if he believed in Hedley's innocence or not, but he'd been even quieter than normal and certainly seemed uncomfortable.

"Hedley didn't set the fires," Travis said, his gaze now fixed on Casey. "He wouldn't do that."

"Then help us prove his innocence," Casey replied. "Do you know where he is?"

"No."

"Can you text him and ask him to meet with us? Make sure he understands that we just want to help."

"I've been trying to get hold of him for two hours, but he's not answering," Travis said.

"We really need to find him before the cops do," Casey said.

Travis's gaze darted from one friend to the other. "Fine. Whatever."

Not the most reassuring commitment, Casey thought, but it was better than nothing.

THIRTY-TWO

After their visit to the third internet café, Casey felt a headache coming on. Felicity's constant chatter only made things worse. Who knew whether the girl was excited or nervous, but this trip had become a test of patience that Casey was about to fail. A few coffee shop employees had recognized Hedley from Felicity's phone photos, but no one had seen him this week.

"How's the motion sickness, Travis?" Casey asked as she drove to the next place on their list. The kid sat behind the passenger's seat, his head almost hanging out the open window. Good thing his hair was in a ponytail. If he barfed in her car, though, she'd be ticked.

"I'm okay."

Maybe, but Casey had a bigger worry. Each time they checked out a café, Travis texted someone. He'd tried to hide it from her, but she'd spotted him twice. The kid was probably texting Hedley, but a confrontation wouldn't get her anywhere. She needed him to lower his guard.

"Travis, I meant to ask you something about the night Gwyn's car was torched. You said you were helping with surveillance, correct?"

"Yeah. Why?"

She understood the caution in his voice. "I've been reluctant to mention this, but my prime suspect is a guy who drives a silver Dodge Ram. I was wondering if you saw it that night."

Travis's expression brightened. "Might have. Who owns it?"

Casey pulled into a coffee shop parking lot and turned off the engine. "He's related to an employee, but as this is only a suspicion of mine, I don't want to say more."

The optimistic glances between the Friends made Casey feel a tinge of guilt. To raise hope that Hedley might not be the arsonist bordered on unethical, but she needed these kids' cooperation. She'd repair her moral compass after Hedley was caught.

"Travis, are you sure you don't know where Hedley is?"

Travis's body seemed to close in on itself as his shoulders hunched and his neck shortened. He reminded her of a retreating turtle.

"I wouldn't be here if I knew where Hedley was, and since there's another suspect, why waste time driving around?"

"I think he's still in Vancouver somewhere, not that far from MPT," Del said.

"Me too." Lawrence remarked.

Travis slumped further down and looked out the window.

"Do you know where Hedley's been at some point during the last twenty-four hours?" Casey asked.

Travis bit his lower lip as his complexion paled.

"Dude," Del said, "you gotta tell us what you know."

"I need some air."

As Travis opened the car door, Del grabbed his phone from his hand. Short and slight as he was, the kid was incredibly fast.

"Hey!" Travis tried to grab it back, but Del tossed it to Casey.

Casey read his play-by-play account of their café stops. She noted that Hedley had responded once with a thumbs-up emoji. She looked at Travis. "I see that you did ask him to meet with us."

"It's not going to happen. Hedley believes you think he's guilty and won't give him a fair chance."

The spiteful glance he tossed Casey irritated the crap out of her. "Is he at your house now?"

"No."

"Where, then?" He lowered his head and said nothing. "Do you want to be charged as an accessory to the arsons? How would your parents feel about that?"

Travis took a deep breath.

"Look, if any of you are withholding information, the cops could get ticked off enough to charge all of you as accessories. I'm not fooling around here. Your long friendship and history is well documented on social media."

Lawrence said, "Do what's right, Travis." His jaw tightened. "The arsons are getting more dangerous. Someone could die."

"If the cops think we're helping him, we're in deep shit," Del added. "My dad's already pissed that they came to our house."

Travis slowly looked up and swallowed hard. "Hedley stayed at my place last night, but I swear I don't know where he is now."

"When did he show up?" Casey asked.

"About one-thirty in the morning. Slept in the basement and left early. My parents didn't know."

"Did he say where he was going?"

"No. Wouldn't tell me if he was coming back either."

Casey studied his pensive face. She couldn't tell if he was telling the truth or not, but judging from his cohorts' skeptical expressions, they had their doubts.

"I think he's planning a final major blow-up before he disappears," Del said, fixing his deep brown eyes on Travis. "Has he hinted at something?"

Travis shook his head.

"Are you sure?" Casey asked.

"Yes!" Panic swept across Travis's face. "Hedley knows I can't handle pressure." Travis crossed his arms over his stomach and leaned forward. "I feel sick."

Casey turned to the Friends. "Do you guys think Hedley would physically harm Mr. Maddox?"

"No way," Felicity replied.

Lawrence shrugged and looked at Del. "What do you think?"

Del tucked his hair behind his ears and sighed. "Hedley took a swing at me when I went to his place. So yeah, violence is possible, and I think he'll target Mr. Maddox."

Felicity's face reddened. "He must be really stressed."

"Totally losing it." Lawrence nodded.

"If I don't text him soon, he'll know something's up." Travis could barely look at Casey. "We have an arrangement."

Casey handed him his phone, shoving back a desire to smack the idiot. "Let Hedley know we've checked out this coffee shop and are deciding on the next location."

As Travis began texting, Casey forced herself to stay calm. She hoped that Gwyn had truly made himself scarce. If Hedley couldn't find him, would he take it out on more MPT property and personnel? Were any of them safe? She started her own text.

"You're aren't contacting the cops, are you?" Travis asked.

"No."

She didn't need freaked out teens who'd take off if they thought the police were coming for them. And she sure didn't need more grief from the cops about involving herself in the search for Hedley. Stan would know what to do. While Casey texted him, Travis opened the door and puked onto the asphalt.

THIRTY-THREE

Casey pulled into MPT's nearly empty parking lot.

"This is so awesome!" Felicity said, her enthusiasm revived by Stan's invitation. "I can't wait to meet your supervisor."

Awesome wasn't the word Casey would choose. She understood Stan's desire to question the Friends. If anyone could pull more information from these kids it was him. After spending two hours with this bunch, Casey had had enough. Medication had dulled her headache, but if this evening went on much longer it could come back with a vengeance.

Travis's stomach seemed to have settled, although he wasn't as enthusiastic about meeting Stan as the others were. Casey wasn't sure why he'd even agreed to it, given that Stan said no one was under any obligation to attend. Maybe Travis's curiosity about MPT's inner sanctum trumped his reservations about the meeting, not to mention their promise to not involve the police in this discussion.

Stan had spoken with each of the Friends' parents, explaining who he was and why he wanted to speak with their kids. None had accepted his invitation to attend the meeting and only Felicity's parents wanted to be put on speaker phone. Stan assured the parents that their kids weren't in trouble and that he was only asking for assistance in locating their friend who might have information about a crime. Stan could be exceedingly diplomatic when he wanted to be.

Casey held the door open for Felicity, who bounded inside, her eyes wide as she looked up and down the corridor. She was like a kid on her first trip to Disneyland. The guys were trying to act cooler, but their animated faces gave them away.

"This place is amazing," Felicity said, turning full circle.

Tempted as she was to roll her eyes, Casey refrained. "It's a hallway."

An empty one, for now. It was just after six and administrative staff had gone home. The building was pretty much empty.

"This way," Casey said, gesturing toward the lunchroom.

Del's smile faded. "We're not going to Mr. Cordaseto's office?"

"The upper floor's restricted to most staff, let alone visitors. And how would you know where it is anyway?" At least he had the decency to blush and look away.

Casey sighed. The kid probably knew the building's layout as well as she did. What hadn't Del hacked into?

"I guess Mr. Maddox isn't around," Travis remarked.

"Correct."

And thank god for that. Even if Gwyn agreed to this meeting, he wouldn't hesitate to take charge. Casey was leading the group toward the lunchroom when she noticed Travis staring at the taped-off door at the end of the hall.

"Travis?"

"The explosion that hurt your coworker happened down there, right?" He nodded toward a closed door at the end of the corridor. "In that room?"

"Yes."

Insurance investigators had come and gone, but who knew when renovations would start? Room by room, MPT had become a damaged, frightening place to work.

Casey spotted Del raising his phone. "No pictures, please." She crossed her arms. "Everyone, keep your phones in your pockets."

Reluctantly, they did as they were told.

Casey led them into the lunchroom, where Stan was sitting at one of the larger tables. Even sitting down, the former football player was an imposing figure. The Friends gaped at him. Lawrence cleaned his glasses with a tiny cloth while Travis's paling face revealed his misgivings about this meeting.

After introductions were made, Felicity surveyed the microwave, coffee machine, scuffed linoleum floor, and plastic chairs.

"This is really nice," she said.

Casey tried not to smile at Stan's mystified expression.

"Have a seat, everybody," he said.

The boys noticed two drivers eating at a table across the room. The drivers returned their stares until the boys turned away and sat down.

Once everyone was seated, Stan said, "If it's okay with you, I'll record our conversation. My memory's not that great. I would also ask that each of you place your phones on the table. You're welcome to record the discussion or to put your parents on speakerphone or FaceTime. Whatever works."

Felicity tapped her phone and spoke to her mother. Del and Lawrence also began recording.

Travis placed his phone on the table, but made no move to record anything. "I can't stay long. Got chores at home."

Stan gave a quick smile. "Me too."

Leaning forward, he stated the date and time with a formality and seriousness that caused the Friends to exchange worried glances. Was it finally dawning on them that this discussion would be a bit more serious than they thought?

"Please note that this is just an informal exchange of information," he said. "But I do need to know how many of you have enough computer skills to hack our databases."

Felicity's cheeks flushed pink. "Not me."

"I hope you're telling the truth, Felicity," her mother's voice burst out of the phone.

"I am, Mom. Totally."

"I have the skills," Del answered. "No one else here does as far as I know."

"Thank you," Stan replied. "I understand that Craig Hedley's a competent hacker too. Is he as good as you?"

Del shifted in his chair. "He wasn't, but we haven't talked about that in nearly a year, so I really don't know."

Stan kept his gaze on Del. "Did either of you ever hack into personnel files to learn employee addresses or other personal information?"

Del turned to his cohorts, whose frozen expressions made it clear they'd be of little help. The resignation clouding his face reminded Casey of the ethical dilemma she'd helped create. This kid was being asked if he'd committed a crime, and she'd delivered him straight to his interrogator.

He bit his lower lip. "I thought we were here to talk about Hedley."

"It's related," Casey replied. "Please tell the truth, Del."

"Am I in trouble?" he murmured.

Stan peered at him. "Not if you're honest with me. As I said, this is just an informal fact-finding mission."

"Yeah. Okay." His dark eyes barely met Stan's. "I hacked into a database with personal info, but just one time, I swear."

Through the phone, Felicity's mother murmured something Casey couldn't quite hear, but her comment made Felicity's shoulders hunch closer to her ears.

"Did you find Gwyn Maddox's home address?" Stan asked.

Del's forehead glistened. "Yeah."

The other three Friends exchanged surprised glances.

"Didn't tell anyone," he added.

"Okay, people." Stan paused. "Tell me everything you've learned through those databases."

Felicity squirmed while Lawrence turned the recording off on his phone. Travis was the only one who seemed to relax a little. Maybe he hadn't been in the loop.

"Felicity," her mother said through the phone, "tell Mr Cordaseto everything you know, darling."

The girl bit her lower lip. "Mostly, we know work schedules."

"And how much employees earn," Lawrence added.

Dark patches appeared on Del's tawny face. Elbows on the table, his clasped hands rested against his mouth.

Stan nodded. "What else?"

All eyes were again focusing on Del. He lowered his hands and began to speak. The kid's knowledge of employee performance reviews, disciplinary actions, and incident reports was more aggravating than surprising, and unnerving. By the time Del was finished, Casey could smell his deodorant.

"Thank you for telling me," Stan said, "but you do understand that you've broken the law."

"Yes," Del murmured. "I promise it won't happen again."

"We didn't want to hurt anybody." Felicity's voice wavered and her eyes became glassy.

"I believe you," her mother said over the phone."

"So do I." Stan's gaze drifted to each of them. "Because your intent wasn't malicious, we won't press charges, but I need to know if Hedley knew that Mr. Maddox was using that first-floor corner office."

Travis, who'd been adjusting his ponytail, stopped moving. Casey also noticed that Del was staring at him.

"Travis?" she asked quietly.

"What? Nothing!" His petrified face started to crack. "Uh, do I need a lawyer?"

"Have you committed a serious crime?" Stan replied.

"No!" Travis cleared his throat. "Like I told Casey, Hedley showed up at my place last night and only stayed for a few hours. Del's visit had freaked him out and he was worried he'd be blamed for the fires."

"Did Hedley know where Mr. Maddox's temporary office was located?" Stan asked.

Travis seemed to think this over. "I guess."

"Were you telling the truth when you said that he left your place?" Casey asked.

"Yes!"

"Did the police question you?" Stan asked.

He nodded. "And my parents. I didn't tell any of them that he'd been in the basement."

The anguish and guilt on his face almost made Casey feel sorry for him.

A message popped up on his phone screen. Travis leaned forward and swore.

"What is it?" Stan asked, his voice low.

"Hedley wants to know where I am. He says something big's about to go down."

THIRTY-FOUR

Stan rose, but not that quickly, Casey noticed. His abdominal wound was still healing.

"Let's get these folks off the premises and some place safe," he said.

"Felicity, do what he says!" her mother shouted. "I'm coming to get you."

"'Kay."

Everyone pushed back their chairs and stood.

"Travis, tell Hedley that you're en route to another coffee shop but you're not sure which one yet," Stan added.

Travis began texting as he shuffled toward the door.

"We need to evacuate, guys," Stan shouted to the drivers. "Arsonist might be on the premises."

"No!" Felicity shook her head. "Hedley wouldn't do that."

"He might." Del's gaze darted around the room.

"Stay calm, everyone. It'll be fine." Stan raised his hand. "Let's move."

The drivers lost no time packing up and heading out. Casey noticed the Friends' strained, fearful expressions. She also noticed Stan's demeanor—he had things well in hand. They both knew that the next few minutes would be unpredictable and dangerous, which was why he was already describing the situation to a 9-1-1 operator. As he spoke, he gestured to the kids to follow him.

"Let's go, guys," Casey said.

Stan held the phone away from his ear while the Friends entered the hallway. "Casey, get dispatch to help you make sure the building's clear and meet us outside."

"Ten-four."

As Stan followed the Friends into the corridor and toward the exit, she turned the other way and ran to the communications room. Within seconds, she and both dispatchers began a search. The dispatchers would take the main floor while Casey headed upstairs.

Few people ever used the old, unreliable elevator at this end of the building. Casey dashed for the staircase at the far end of the corridor. She was passing by the lunchroom when glass shattered inside the room.

She halted in her tracks. "What the hell?"

An explosion knocked her off balance. Casey smacked into the wall and fell. Her ears rang. Smoke wafted into the corridor. Squinting behind her, she slowly propped herself up, aware that the dispatchers were suddenly beside her.

"Casey!" one of them said, leaning over her. "Are you all right?" Their voices sounded muffled.

"Yeah." Feeling woozy, she let them help her to her feet. The stench of gasoline made her stomach roil. "You guys okay?"

"Yep, we were searching locker rooms when the blast hit."

Casey checked herself for any sign of blood. Nothing. She coughed as smoke began to fill the corridor.

Stan charged toward her. "Are you hurt?"

"No." Though she'd probably wind up with a couple of bruises. "Where are the kids?"

"On the sidewalk across the street."

Stan ushered her outside and instructed the dispatchers to stay with the kids. There was still plenty of light on this warm, mid-June evening. Hedley shouldn't be hard to spot. Casey rubbed her aching arm. Her throat felt blackened and parched, as if she'd swallowed a teaspoon of powdery charcoal.

"I think he's still here," she whispered, glancing around the parking lot.

"What for? The guy's made his point," Stan replied, looking at the damaged garage. "He'd have to know that the cops and firetrucks are on their way."

"But Hedley's text to Travis said something big was going down. Could be more than the lunchroom." Casey spotted movement by the high wooden fence. "There! He's by the west fence, behind a bush." All the angst, sorrow, and anger she'd been feeling since the riot rushed out of her. "We see you, Hedley!" Her voice reverberated throughout the yard. "Get your sorry ass out here!"

Stan placed his hand on her shoulder. "Not helping," he murmured, and moved toward the fence. "It's over, son. Police are on their way. There's nowhere to go."

Gas can in hand, Hedley dashed toward the parking lot, tossing something behind him. Seeing that he was wearing an MPT uniform infuriated Casey.

"Put the can down!" Stan shouted. "No one needs—"

An explosion at the fence ignited some of the boards. Hedley dashed toward the damaged garage. Stan ran after him. Casey followed, aware of approaching sirens.

"Hedley!" a voice shouted behind her.

Casey slowed down and looked over her shoulder, horrified to see the Friends.

"Get out of here!" she shouted.

Two patrol cars pulled up behind the kids. Travis raced past Casey. "Travis, get back here!"

Officers hurried out of the vehicle and ordered everyone to stop running. Del, Felicity, and Lawrence did so, but Travis kept going. Casey spotted Hedley climbing the chain link fence with impressive athletic skill.

"Suspect's climbing the fence!" she shouted to the cops.

"Everyone, stay back!" one of the officers shouted.

Stan joined Casey as Hedley reached the top. More patrol cars were pulling up to the fence just a few yards from him. Hedley hesitated, then dropped back down to the ground.

"Hedley!" Travis yelled

"Why are you here?" Hedley answered. "I thought you were on my side!"

"I am! But this is wrong, man."

Her heart pounding, Casey stepped closer to Stan as one of the officers ordered the Friends to leave. He then marched up to Travis and told him to step back. The cop, a beefy man with fierce determination etched on his face, stood in front of Travis, blocking his view of Hedley. Travis turned around and trudged back to the Friends. Another officer escorted all of them off the property.

"Put the jerry can down, son," the second officer called out. "No one has to get hurt."

"This is Gwyn Maddox's fault!" Hedley shouted. "He ruined everything!"

"How?" Stan asked.

"Ask the shithead yourself!"

Casey spotted a pair of cops scurrying toward the smoking tree. If she could keep Hedley distracted, maybe he wouldn't see what was coming.

"Why wear a driver's uniform, Hedley?" Casey asked.

"Can't you figure it out?" he shot back. "Thought you were smarter than that."

"Obviously, I'm not. So tell me."

"For Gwyn's benefit, of course. His suspicions would upset drivers enough to cause a lot of shit and cost him money. It worked too, from what I hear. Gwyn had to be shown how weak he really is."

Casey didn't know how to respond to that. Instead, she took a step closer , but the officer held his arm out in front of her.

"Why strike so early in the evening this time?" she asked Hedley. "You had to know you'd get caught."

"To show Gwyn that everything he values can be destroyed anytime, anywhere. It was fun seeing his stupid face when he watched his car burn."

"Gwyn isn't here," Casey shot back, "and why hurt my coworker? She never did anything to you."

"Casualty of war." Hedley shrugged. "Shit happens."

War? Casey sighed. Clearly, Charlie Applebee wasn't the only with mental health issues.

"Besides, Gwyn doesn't give a shit who's hurt as long as it's not him," Hedley went on.

"He cares more than people give him credit for," Stan said.

"Bullshit!" Hedley raised the gas can higher.

Casey shook her head. The guy would never accept any responsibility. Out the corner of her eye, she saw the cops step out from behind the smoking tree, their weapons drawn.

"Put the can down," the officer next to her ordered.

Hedley didn't acknowledge him but rather began pouring gasoline over himself.

From a distance, Casey heard a female scream.

"No!" Lawrence and Del yelled at the same time.

Why were the Friends still here? They shouldn't be watching this. None of them should be. Yet, Casey found herself unable to turn away, terrified she'd trigger the wrong response. She held her breath as a firetruck pulled into the lot. Cops crept closer to the fence. If Hedley turned around, he'd see them.

"Please." The officer near Casey edged toward Hedley. "Put the can down."

To her surprise he did so, but a moment later Hedley pulled a small object from his pocket. A lighter? Oh god.

"Hedley, stop!" Felicity shouted. "Don't do this!"

The Friends were now on the sidewalk, gripping the chain link fence. Felicity started to cry.

"Del!" Casey called out. "Take Felicity away from here!"

Del reached for her, but she shrugged him off.

"N-no!" Felicity began running down the sidewalk.

Firefighters joined the officers, who spoke too quietly to hear what was being said. They then eased toward Hedley until they were only a few yards away. Still, if Hedley flicked that lighter, he'd be in agony before anyone could extinguish the flames. Sweat trickled down Casey's sides.

"You folks need to go too," the officer told Casey and Stan.

The cops at the fence were pointing weapons at Hedley. If they were accurate shooters, they could hit him through the fence. But would the bullets trigger a conflagration? Casey prayed she wouldn't find out. She hugged herself to control the trembling.

"Casey," Stan said, "we'd better back."

She forced herself to move until Felicity bolted past her. How on earth had she managed to slip past everyone?

"Felicity!" Casey darted forward and grabbed her arm. "Stop!"

"Let me help!"

"Absolutely not." Casey maintained a firm grip while the girl squirmed and attempted to yank free. Del and Lawrence soon appeared and helped her restrain the sobbing Felicity.

"What the hell is going on here?" a familiar and unwelcome voice bellowed.

Gwyn Maddox stormed past Casey. Oh lord. Things had just gone from bad to worse. Stan and the cop intercepted Gwyn and spoke quietly. Gwyn nodded, then edged toward Hedley.

"I'm the one you're mad at, Mr. Hedley," he said. "Why take it out on yourself?"

"My life's over because of you!"

An officer ushered all of them further back while the fire-fighters drew nearer. Casey's heart pounded.

"You're a bright kid who's going to college," Gwyn said. "What exactly is over?"

"A university scholarship and my job for starters!" Hedley replied, "thanks to you telling my employer and UBC that I'm a criminal who can't be trusted."

What? Casey turned to Gwyn. How could he have been so mean? She noted the shock on Stan's face and the icy glare that would have given Gwyn a freezer burn if he'd seen it.

"You destroyed my future!" Hedley shouted at Gwyn. "I'm returning the favor."

"Spraying graffiti and starting fires are illegal actions," Gwyn shot back. "Mine were not."

Casey's shoulders tensed. How was that response supposed to defuse a life-threatening situation?

"What about ethics and morality? Human decency!" Hedley yelled. "Look at the shitty way you treat employees while you live in a mansion and drive expensive cars."

"That's not—"

"Gwyn!" Stan called out. "Back off!"

Gwyn scowled at Stan a few moments, then lowered his head.

"All right, you've made your point," Gwyn said to Hedley. "Maybe I can make some calls and fix this."

"Too late!"

The back of Casey's neck prickled. Hedley lifted his arm high in the air. The lighter hovered above his head. Hedley kept his attention on Gwyn, didn't see or apparently hear one of the cops scale the fence, jump down, and slink toward him.

Hedley glanced over his shoulder just as the officer leapt, and Casey gasped.

THIRTY-FIVE

"**A**re you ready?" Summer asked, her expression radiant. "It's almost time."

Casey smiled, "Just one more minute."

She took a calming breath like she used to in her yoga days. To be the center of attention felt overwhelming and kind of surreal, yet she'd never been happier. Wedding day. Finally. She wanted to absorb every moment, to create a lifetime of incredible memories.

"Kendal's mom did an awesome job with the decorations," Summer said.

"She sure did."

Casey strolled to the window and looked out at the enormous lawn below. To her right, white chairs decorated with bows were adjacent to a colorful garden. On the left, a canopy, tables, and chairs had been assembled for the buffet to come later. A dance floor would appear after dinner. By then it would be early evening. Kendal and her mom had arranged to have twinkling lights threaded throughout tree branches. It would be romantic and festive. Spectacular.

"How about you?" Casey turned to her. "Looking forward to spending the next two weeks with Lou's mom?"

"Yep. It'll be cool."

It was a great relief to see Summer genuinely happy. An emotional visit with Rhonda last week had sent all three of them into a tailspin for a couple of days. The surgery had taken place and Rhonda assured them that her prognosis was good, yet chemotherapy would soon begin.

Unwilling to have Rhonda completely miss out on this day, Casey had hired a videographer to record everything. Who knew when she'd be allowed to see it, but it would happen someday. She touched Rhonda's pearl necklace, the "something borrowed" that Rhonda had insisted she wear.

Kendal appeared, her long blond hair pulled up into an elaborate French twist braid. The backless turquoise dress looked stunning on her tanned body.

"Lou's taking his place in front of the minister," Kendal said. "We're ready to roll."

"Does he seem nervous?"

"He looks petrified that you'll change your mind." Kendal chuckled. "You need to marry the poor man. He's waited long enough."

"One sec!" Summer said. "I should use the bathroom."

"I probably should too," Kendal replied, turning to Casey. "How about you?"

"I'm fine, thanks."

"We'll just be a minute."

Casey turned back to the window. Stan and at least another thirty coworkers were here. But there were absences too. Marie was still recovering from her injuries. Gwyn Maddox had sent his regrets, stating that he was now on a leave of absence. Stan told her that Gwyn had decided not to sell the company, for now.

She and Lou had sent last-minute invitations to the Friends. Del, Felicity, and Lawrence accepted. Travis did not. The Friends thought he was too ashamed about helping Hedley.

Late at night, while trying to sleep, Casey often found herself reliving that terrible night two weeks ago. She also remembered the relief she'd felt when the cop prevented Hedley from setting himself on fire. He was scheduled to undergo a psychological evaluation. Maybe he already had. Sadly, the kid had damaged his future more than Gwyn ever could.

Kendal reappeared and grinned. "You look so gorgeous."

"Thank you."

She had found the dress last August. A sleek, ivory gown with two wide straps crisscrossing in the back.

Summer rejoined them, as did the third bridesmaid, Lou's sister. All four made their way downstairs.

At the bottom of the staircase, Kendal's mom, Deanne, beamed at Casey. "You're breathtaking."

Casey embraced her. "Thank you for everything. This means so much."

"I'm thrilled to do this for you, darling."

Once Deanne was escorted to her seat, the best men and bridesmaids took their places. Casey could almost feel their composure settling in. The music began to play. One by one, each bridesmaid moved with graceful assurance.

She thought of her deceased parents and wished they were here. Stepping outside into the sunlight, Casey inhaled the scent of freshly cut grass and roses. The moment she saw Lou's awestruck face, she knew that all was right with the world. She was exactly where she was supposed to be.

Nodding to friends and coworkers, she welcomed their warmth and love like a longed-for hug. Benny Lee stood by the aisle, a broad grin on a face that was still a little too pale. The tears in his eyes made her own eyes glisten. She reached out her hand. He grasped it, then gently kissed the back. Standing next to Benny, Stan winked at her.

Dimitri was also here, the cut to his forehead just a thin scar now. Wesley's beefy wrestler's arm was no longer in a sling, but it probably still bore a scar from Charlie Applebee's knife. Wesley nodded, which was about as warm and fuzzy as he was likely to get, and this was just fine.

Casey smiled, grateful that these wounded warriors were here. This was a perfect day for family and friends and celebration. For gratitude.

BOOKS BY DEBRA PURDY KONG

Alex Bellamy Mysteries
Taxed to Death (1995)
Fatal Encryption (2008)

Casey Holland Mysteries
The Opposite of Dark (2011)
Deadly Accusations (2012)
Beneath the Bleak New Moon (2013)
The Deep End (2014)
Knock Knock (2017)
The Blade Man (2020)

Evan Dunstan Novellas
Dead Man Floating (2015)
A Toxic Craft (2017)

ABOUT THE AUTHOR

Debra Purdy Kong's volunteer experiences, criminology diploma, and various jobs, inspired her to write mysteries set in BC's Lower Mainland. Her employment as a campus security patrol and communications officer provide the background for her Casey Holland transit security novels.

Debra has published short stories in a variety of genres as well as personal essays, and articles for publications such as *Chicken Soup for the Bride's Soul, B.C. Parent Magazine,* and *The Vancouver Sun.* She is a facilitator for the Creative Writing Program through Port Moody Recreation, and a long-time member of Crime Writers of Canada.

For more information about Debra and her books, visit her website at www.debrapurdykong.com
or contact her at dpurdykong@gmail.com